ALL THE LONELY PEOPLE
by Martin Edwards

'Pungent Mersey whiff . . . A nice starter'
The Times

'Tremendous atmospherics . . . all in all, a grand debut'
Frances Fyfield

'Promise-filled first . . . Detritus-littered trail leads
through film noir version of Liverpool's seedier streets.
Encore'
Guardian

'A remarkable achievement'
Liverpool Echo

'A well-placed mystery'
What's On

Also by Martin Edwards
and published by Bantam Books

All The Lonely People

Suspicious Minds

Martin Edwards

BANTAM BOOKS
TORONTO • NEW YORK • LONDON • SYDNEY • AUCKLAND

SUSPICIOUS MINDS
A BANTAM BOOK 0 553 40486 5

Originally published in Great Britain by Judy Piatkus
(Publishers) Ltd.

PRINTING HISTORY
Judy Piatkus (Publishers) edition published 1992
Bantam Books edition published 1993

This book is set in 11/12pt Linotron Times

Bantam Books are published by Transworld Publishers Ltd.,
61–63 Uxbridge Road, Ealing, London W5 5SA, in Australia by
Transworld Publishers (Australia) Pty. Ltd., 15–25 Helles Avenue,
Moorebank, NSW 2170, and in New Zealand by Transworld
Publishers (N.Z.) Ltd., 3 William Pickering Drive, Albany,
Auckland.

Printed and bound in Great Britain by
Cox & Wyman Ltd., Reading, Berks.

Dedicated to Helena

Author's Note

This is a work of fiction, not faction. I have borrowed – and adapted – geographical settings in Liverpool, Wirral and Cheshire from the real world, but all the characters, firms, businesses and incidents described are imaginary.

Chapter One

'Do you think I murdered Alison?' asked Stirrup.

Harry Devlin shaded his eyes against the glare of the mid-day sun. They had stepped out of the police station into a wall of heat and he needed a moment to catch his breath. As well as to judge how to answer a question better left unasked.

'What if I say yes?'

Stirrup stopped in his tracks.

'Remember, it's easier to get rid of a solicitor than a wife.'

Tiredness had rubbed the varnish off Stirrup's good humour, leaving his Brummie accent ugly and bare. Small wonder: the interrogation had stretched through four long hours into a test of patience and nerve.

Stirrup had phoned at seven that morning with the news that the police had called at his home again; they wanted to re-interview him about his wife's disappearance.

'Said I was willing as long as you could make it too. All right?'

'I'll meet you there. And remember, you haven't been arrested. You're not forced to say any more. They'll try to get under your skin, that's what they're paid for. So keep your temper under control.'

'No problem. They've nothing against me, Harry boy. Nothing at all.'

DI Bolus evidently thought otherwise. Fresh-faced and bespectacled, he resembled an inquisitive schoolboy more closely than Tomas de Torquemada. Yet his ingenuous manner camouflaged the persistence of a Toxteth kerb-crawler.

1

'People like your wife simply don't vanish into thin air,' he kept saying. Lines of puzzlement creased his brow. 'There must be an explanation. Don't you agree?'

Harry watched his client straining to keep himself under control. To his relief Stirrup stuck to the straight denial they had agreed on when first it became clear the police suspected that Alison was dead.

'I've no idea where she is.'

'Do you care?' Bolus sounded genuine in his anxiety to be reassured.

'I want her home again. And the sooner you get off my back and find her, the better.'

And so it continued, with Bolus determined not to let go without a struggle and Stirrup intent on giving nothing away. Eventually the time came for Harry to stand and say that his client, a free and respectable man with a business to run, had helped enough with inquiries for one day and that now they would be going. The moment of decision. And Bolus had dismissed them with a courteous nod of thanks. Stirrup wasn't to be charged today.

'Want a lift?' asked Harry as they reached his rust-scarred M.G.

Puffing and grunting, Stirrup squeezed into the passenger seat.

'What do you say, then, Harry boy? Do I look to you like a wife killer?'

Sweat shone on Stirrup's bald head and well-fed jowls. Harry wondered if it was a clue to fear lurking beneath the customary bravado. But the sun was harsh and they had spent half a day in a tiny airless room which had it been a cell would probably have been in breach of some convention on human rights.

Harry slung his jacket and tie in the back of the car. Inside, the shabby upholstery burned his palm. The steering wheel felt too hot to hold.

'Jack, take my advice. Guilt and innocence are for a jury to decide.'

'Are you saying it'll come to that?'

'Look, if Bolus had enough to pin something on you, you'd be changing your suit for something made of paper by now.

2

So relax. Or worry about something constructive, like staff pilfering or last month's sales figures.'

Stirrup gripped Harry's shoulder. 'Listen, you know me well enough. I didn't kill her, all right? She's as alive as you or me, take my word for it.'

'Unless I learn something to make me do otherwise, my job is exactly that. To take your word for it.'

Stirrup fell silent as the car moved off. Out of the corner of his eye Harry glanced at his client. On that bulky frame the Armani suit had no more elegance than a vacuum cleaner bag.

You know me well enough. Was that true? Harry had once been let into the secret that his client's full name was John Aloysius Kendrick Stirrup, but more meaningful confidences had been few and far between. His firm had handled Stirrup Wines' legal work for three or four years, buying sites for off-licences throughout Liverpool and here on the Wirral peninsula, appearing regularly in the magistrates' court to secure the right for each branch to sell alcohol to the public. So many of Crusoe and Devlin's other clients were rogues or traders (or both) in a small way of business. Representing a boom company was a lawyer's dream. Harry had wined and dined Stirrup, had in turn accepted the man's hospitality; it was as close as he ever came to attempting to market his practice. Yet they did not have enough in common to call themselves friends and for all their frequent contact Harry realised that he could not say he knew Jack Stirrup well.

'Straight on.'

'The sea front?'

'Why not, Harry boy?' Joviality again. 'Terrific day. Where better to spend it than at the seaside? The weather forecasters reckon it might touch ninety today.'

'If you'd told me earlier, I'd have brought my raincoat.'

Stirrup laughed. 'Know your trouble? You're a sceptic, Harry. You ought to have more faith.'

'For that, I'd need a change of job.'

'Not a bad idea. Earning a living out of legal loopholes is enough to turn any bugger sour. But save me from Strangeways first, all right?'

Soon they were driving along Mockbeggar Drive, looking out from Wirral's tip to Liverpool Bay and the Irish Sea. At

3

this distance, the cloudless sky and blue sea came straight out of a tourist's idyll. If you could forget about global warming and gaps within the ozone layer, they were sights to lift the heart and soothe the mind.

Yet Harry always had a feeling of melancholy when he returned to New Brighton. He couldn't help casting his mind back to Sunday afternoons he had spent here with Liz, his wife. Afternoons which now seemed to belong to another life. But more than that, the resort itself reeked of days beyond recall. Like a senile, smelly old woman who still believes herself to be sweet and sixteen.

Round every corner lurked a reminder of the past: in the theatres converted into bingo halls, in the shops boarded up because they could no longer pay their way. So much had gone over so many years. The Tower; the old pleasure grounds; the pier demolished to save it from sinking into the sea.

Here and there, signboards promised building work and regeneration. New litter bins had been put out and lamp-posts painted, but it would take much more to tempt the sun-seekers away from Torremolinos.

'Pull up over there. We'll call in at the Majestic. Never know your luck, we might bump into Bryan Grealish.'

'Isn't that something we'd both prefer to avoid?'

After parking they stood together on the broad prom-enade. In front of them squatted the red sandstone mass of Fort Perch Rock Battery, built to guard the Port of Liverpool from seaborne invaders who had never even bothered to arrive.

'Listen, Harry boy, someone's setting me up with the police. Someone with a grudge against me, yes? Grealish fits the bill.'

'So what are you after? Do you seriously expect him to break down in tears and confess?'

Stirrup pursed fleshy lips. 'I'll be honest with you – he's not my number one suspect. But seeing as we're here . . .'

'Okay, okay. But don't start World War Three over it, Jack. You've got enough problems as it is.'

'Don't I know it? But after that session with Bolus, I need a bit of sustenance. Talk about the third degree. Anybody would think I was a murderer.'

He bellowed with merriment, but Harry could still recall the earlier apprehension, understandable even in an entirely innocent man, yet out of character in Jack Stirrup.

Curiosity began to stir inside him. He recognised it as a weakness, like hunger pangs in a glutton. But Alison Stirrup's vanishing trick intrigued him, tempted him into wanting to understand.

'So where do you reckon she is, then?'

Stirrup screwed up his eyes as if to keep out the sun. 'Wish I knew.'

'Won't you hazard a guess?'

Stirrup spread his arms. 'What's the point? She might be anywhere. Women aren't logical, Harry, they're unpredictable, surely by now you've learned that?'

The hard way, Harry thought. He said nothing.

'I could never read Ali's mind. Never tried. In her way, she was deep. Course, she'd been to college, not like me. I'm a university of life man myself, as you well know. School of hard knocks.'

'Even so . . .'

'Even so my arse.' Stirrup wagged a thick finger under Harry's nose. 'For God's sake, you know her. Have you ever managed to figure her out?'

You know her. Again that false assumption. Harry had met Alison Stirrup several times. On each occasion she had been in the company of her husband – and in his shadow. She had seemed a slight, insubstantial figure, wraith-like in comparison. Harry pictured her in his mind. She was fifteen years Jack's junior and attractive enough, but somehow unremarkable. Harry struggled for more than a vague impression of short blonde hair and a quiet way of speaking. Out of the blue, he recollected once catching sight of her smothering a yawn as Stirrup recounted an anecdote which she must have heard a dozen times. An understandable reaction; Harry had attached no importance to it at the time. He had found her pleasant but reserved and had simply taken it for granted that she must enjoy the moneyed lifestyle which marriage had brought. With hindsight he wondered if her appearance of calm masked a deep discontent.

'She's your wife. You must have some idea about why she left so suddenly.'

Saying that prompted memories of his own. When Liz had left him, he had known precisely to whose arms she was running. And knowledge, however painful, was surely preferable to the prickling of uncertainty. For the first time that day it occurred to him to feel sorry for Stirrup.

'Can't fathom it. Didn't I tell the bobbies that till I was sick of the sound of my own voice?'

'Has Claire any ideas?'

'She's as baffled as me.' Invariably Stirrup's tone softened when his daughter came into the conversation. 'Alison and her were never close, of course. Couldn't expect it, after all. They didn't have much in common. Only me.'

'They quarrelled?'

'Don't get me wrong. Ali's no wicked step-mother. And Claire can be a she-devil – but she knew better than to try to throw her weight around too much, I wouldn't have stood for it. No, they never had much to say to each other, but there were no rows, no slanging matches. Perhaps it would've been better if there had been.'

'Was Claire upset when Alison went?'

'She hasn't said much. You know what teenage kids are. And she's been seeing this lad, not been at home as much lately. He's older than her, I don't approve. But when did young girls take any notice of their dads when they first start up with a boyfriend?'

They began walking. Past the Floral Pavilion and the ten-pin bowling alley, past hot dog stands and a place which sold bags of broken pink and white rock. Madame Rosika, the clairvoyant, was open for business. Harry wondered if she would dare predict if and when Jack Stirrup would be re-united with his missing wife.

'And you?' he asked gently. 'How are you coping without her?'

'All right.' Stirrup scratched his nose. 'Look, I won't pretend it was the ideal marriage. I never said otherwise to that bloody police inspector, did I? Ali and me, we had our differences. You think, going into it the second time around, you're older and wiser, you won't make the same mistakes again. But you do. You do.'

'So you still say you can't understand why she walked out without a word?'

The bonhomie faded again. 'Yes, I do say that. Whose side are you on?'

Harry didn't respond. It was his job to be on Stirrup's side and he had no grounds for believing his client guilty of murder. The case against him was flimsy and circumstantial. Yet Stirrup was telling less than the whole truth, of that Harry was certain. Instinct and experience insisted that something was being withheld. There was more to be known about the disappearance of Alison Stirrup.

And against his better professional judgment, Harry wanted to know it.

Chapter Two

The Majestic had been built in New Brighton's hey-day at the turn of the century, when packed ferries brought trippers over from Liverpool by the thousand. Minstrels had played on the beach, bathing machines and oyster stalls were everywhere. In Harry's lifetime, the hotel had been in visible decline, under-occupied and in need of more than a lick of paint. When you sat on the famous old verandah gazing out at the hot dog sellers on the promenade you felt like a representative of the Raj watching a civilisation on the brink of collapse.

Bryan Grealish had changed all that with the help of the fortune he'd made out of office catering, feeding the faces of middle-aged executives whose idea of a calorie-controlled diet was steak and french fries without the trimmings. The Majestic was still not the Savoy, but even on this week-day lunchtime, the place was packed.

After they had ordered, Stirrup fiddled absent-mindedly with his napkin.

'Business doesn't get easier, Harry boy. The company's grown, it's not like the old days. I'm ruled by cashflow and licensing laws. By accountants and solicitors. No offence – but life's too short. Sometimes I think about jacking the lot in and getting away from it all. The Caribbean, maybe. Or the States.'

He tore the napkin into small strips, screwing the paper into tight little balls. 'This thing with Ali, it's hit me harder than you think. I'm not saying we had the perfect marriage, but I wish to hell she hadn't just pissed off like that, without even saying goodbye.'

Stirrup had not talked like this earlier in the morning. At first, he'd parried Bolus's questions, bland as any politician. When the repetition began to irritate, his brow had darkened and his replies had become curt whilst Harry chewed his nails, afraid of a self-incriminating explosion. In the end Stirrup had survived; he would not break easily. Yet none of his denials had convinced Harry as much as the simple lament he had just uttered.

'Two scampis.' The waiter's Scouse accent contrasted with his Gallic air.

Stirrup smacked his lips and wielded his knife and fork like cudgels, his humour restored.

'*Bon appetit*, as they say in Bootle.'

As they ate, Harry summed up in his mind all that he knew about Alison Stirrup's disappearance. She had last been seen on a Friday in May. Stirrup had left her in bed at their home in Caldy; he had been due to attend a meeting with his legal and financial advisers to discuss the offer which Bryan Grealish had made to take over his business. Harry had been present at that meeting, together with his partner Jim Crusoe. At the time all their thoughts had concentrated on the subject for discussion. The auditors sealed the fate of the bid by describing it as one which Stirrup could not refuse. For a self-made man proudly independent of thought and deed, the urge to prove an accountant wrong was irresistible. Thumping his fist on the table, he had declared his intention to tell Grealish what he could do with his money.

No hint of anything wrong at home, nor of any inner preoccupation. That did not in itself count for much. Harry realised that most successful businessmen had the ability to divorce any domestic traumas from their company lives. But surely even someone more phlegmatic than Jack Stirrup would have been twitchy if he had spent the previous night burying his wife in a wood or under concrete?

Alison had been alive and kicking the previous evening; so much was certain, for her mother had called round unexpectedly. Harry knew Doreen Capstick slightly and had not been surprised to learn that the visit was unannounced. Unless she was a particularly close and loving daughter then Alison would have found that a little of Doreen went a long way. She might have made an excuse if given prior warning of an impending call. Mrs Capstick had been at the house between eight and nine. Her departure had been hastened by Stirrup's late arrival home; he left her in no doubt that after a long day closeted with his business advisers, he was more interested in a hot meal than in small talk with a woman whom he detested.

Stirrup had again been late back the following day. After deciding not to sell to Grealish, he had devoted the afternoon and early evening to desk work before being the last to leave the office at – he said – about half-past seven. Alison was not at home and had not left a note for him. He told the police he was surprised, because this was unusual, but not at first alarmed. Only when she had not returned home by midnight, Stirrup said, did he realise that something untoward might have happened. That was when he dialled 999.

The police were faced with a mystery. Stirrup was not the kind of man to take a close interest in his wife's wardrobe, but he did not think that Alison had taken any spare clothes with her. No significant withdrawals had been made from their joint bank account. Her Toyota two-seater was locked in the garage. And from that day to this, a six-week span, he had heard nothing from her. Nor had anyone else, so far as he or his mother-in-law were aware.

'I could murder a slab of that cake on the trolley.'

Stirrup's expression didn't suggest that he regarded his choice of words as unfortunate. Harry was still working his way through the pile of vegetables on his plate. He was saved from the need to reply by a mocking voice from over his shoulder.

'Well, look who we have here. The Majestic is honoured. The North's premier viticulturist and his tame Perry Mason.'

Bryan Grealish bore as much resemblance to the seaside hotelier of old as a *Miami Vice* cop to Father Brown. Today he wore a purple vest, white slacks and sandals. Tattooed snakes slithered down the thick muscular arms and his hair was tied back in a pony tail. He was breathing hard, as though fresh from a work-out in the Majestic's new gym.

Stirrup smiled back, as if paid a compliment. His business relied upon wines imported from the Continent's less prestigious vineyards; its success had been founded on keen pricing rather than wine snobbery. Over the years he had coped with endless gibes about the quality of his products.

'Bryan, good to see you. Decent meal and not a single bit of glass to be seen.'

The previous week guests attending a wedding reception at the Majestic had discovered small shards of crushed glass in their salad dressing. The bride's father had rung the Press in a fit of fury. Health scares sell newspapers and the resultant publicity had embarrassed Grealish into lavishing compensation upon the distressed and sacking two of the kitchen staff for good measure. But Egon Ronay was unlikely to recommend the Majestic this year.

Grealish flushed, his jaw lifting in annoyance. But his features quickly regrouped into their usual self-satisfied formation. False modesty was not one of his vices.

'To what do we owe this welcome visit, Jack? Changed your mind about selling out? Or were you simply after a filling lunch? I hear you're short of home cooking at the moment.'

Stirrup's tongue flicked at his lips. 'Word gets around.'

'Right. Sorry to hear Alison's moved to pastures new. I always felt she and I ought to get to know each other better.'

'Funny, I'd have thought she was too old for you. It's years since she wore a gymslip.'

Winking at Harry, Grealish said, 'Must keep a broad mind, don't you think, Mr Devlin? Good to see Jack's sense of humour is intact. Rumour has it, he's keeping you busy these days. Despite those slanderous stories doing the rounds.'

'You'd have made a good lawyer yourself,' said Harry easily. 'Shame to waste all that bullshit.'

'What stories?' demanded Stirrup.

'I dunno.' Grealish's innocent expression was as phoney as a pimp's tax return. 'People say you've been going in for midnight gardening, though Christ knows what you'd be digging up so late at night. Or burying.'

'Are you calling me a murderer?'

With an economy of effort surprising in a man so big, Stirrup reached for the sweet trolley, picked off a slice of Black Forest Gâteau and shoved it, circus-clown fashion, into Grealish's face with a force which sent the hotelier staggering backwards onto the floor.

A woman at an adjoining table screamed. Two waiters came running up to help their boss back to his feet. A gallows grin had spread across Stirrup's face. He took a fifty-pound note from his wallet and tossed it at Grealish.

'That should cover any damage to your vanity as well as the nosh. And next time, take more care who you fart around with.'

A fair-haired girl in a halter-neck bikini came on to the verandah. Her tanned body was a woman's but her spoiled pout belonged in a kindergarten. Catching sight of Grealish wiping the creamy mess off his face, she put her hands on her hips, not saying a word. In twenty years, Harry wondered, would she be a nagging wife with a husband harbouring secret thoughts of murder?

Grealish mustered a humourless grin. 'Pleasure calls, gentlemen. No hard feelings, Jack, but you need to watch that temper of yours. It'll put you inside one of these fine days.'

He slipped his arm around the girl's bare brown shoulders as they walked away. It was less a gesture of affection than of ownership.

In the M.G. five minutes later Stirrup said, 'Makes your flesh creep, doesn't he? Feller of his age shouldn't be messing around with kids like that. She can't be any older than Claire.'

Harry wasn't sure his client was well equipped to make moral judgments. Better change the subject.

'So do you think he's the one stirring it with the police?'

Stirrup grinned with a child's delight. 'Not really, he was just trying to take the piss out of me. That'll learn him. See his face covered in cake?'

Trying to conceal his impatience Harry said, 'Who else might have a grudge against you?'

Stirrup laughed: a raucous noise, like bricks falling off a wagon. 'You kidding? The list's a mile long. My bloody mother-in-law's always hated me. And how about Trevor Morgan?'

'Heard anything of him lately?'

'Far as I know, he's still on the dole. Like most of the people I've fired over the years.'

'I'll ask around if you want, see if I can find out who's been making waves.'

13

'Thanks,' Stirrup grunted. 'And since you're too delicate to enquire, I'll tell you. No, I didn't murder Alison.'

Harry didn't find it hard to restrain his delight at the unsolicited denial; he had the lawyer's dread of a client who answers questions which have not been asked.

He switched on the radio for the local news. A council row about over-spending. A strike on the docks. Harry yawned: political peace and industrial harmony would have been more of a scoop. Then came an item which seized Stirrup's attention, had him straining his seat belt, trying to follow the story through fuzzy reception.

'*Police are searching for a man who raped a fourteen year old girl at Eastham Country Park yesterday evening. Detectives have declined to give further information but it's believed they are linking the incident with a rape committed by a masked man last month on the Wirral Way and several other recent attacks on teenage girls with fair hair. The man has been dubbed 'The Beast' because the masks he wears have animals' faces. The police have warned of the need for extra vigilance until he is caught.*'

'That bastard,' said Stirrup. 'When they get hold of him they ought to cut his balls off. Then lock him up and throw away the key.'

'He'll be some pathetic sod. Most sex offenders are.'

Stirrup's snort expressed disgust for namby-pamby tolerance. 'Easy for you to say, I've got a teenage girl to think about. One of her mates from school was raped by that pervert only a few weeks ago.'

Harry could understand a father's angry apprehension, although The Beast's victims were all supposed to have had blonde hair whereas Claire was dark. But to expect Stirrup to take comfort from the past consistency of a sick mind was asking too much. On the radio, news gave way to sport and talk of nothing more criminal than England's batting in the last Test Match.

They reached the sprawling outskirts of Birkenhead, passing the strange oasis of Port Sunlight, a garden village in the midst of a slough of urban despond, built by a soap millionaire to house his workers. On the opposite side of the dual carriageway the head office of Stirrup Wines stood in functional, flat-roofed contrast to Lord Leverhulme's prettified estate. Jack Stirrup's major contribution to the local landscape had been to put up a flagpole in the visitors' car park.

'Ta for the lift. And the help this morning. You must come over to my place. Never mind the Majestic, sample Claire's cooking. Tell you the truth, I'd eat her stuff rather than Ali's any day. But don't tell that bloody Bolus. He'll be thinking I did away with her 'cause I couldn't stomach her grub.'

'I'll be in touch.'

They shook hands. 'How about dinner tonight? You'd be very welcome. My girl can rustle something up, no problem. What do you say?'

Harry had other plans for the evening. But Stirrup was insistent and made him promise to phone later once he had checked whether he could unscramble a previous, unspecified commitment.

'Half eight do you? I'll call Claire soon as you let me know. I won't be away from here much before seven. With no right hand man and half a day wasted in the nick, there's plenty to do.'

Harry nodded a farewell, his mind already turning to what lay ahead for him that night. He did not intend it to be a meal with a suspected murderer.

Chapter Three

Queen Victoria was still not amused. Her black statue frowned down at Harry from beneath its green cupola as he walked across Derby Square. He winked at the monarch on his way to the Law Courts, a gesture misinterpreted by a woman strolling in the opposite direction. She hurried off, as if convinced that she was about to become The Beast's latest victim, causing Harry a qualm of guilt. But as he pushed through the revolving doors of the court building, he couldn't help whistling a Beatles song from the days before the Cavern became a car park: 'Love Me Do.'

Once on the first floor he followed the corridor which led to the rooms reserved for lawyers. Pleasure flooded through him as he turned the last corner and saw Valerie Kaiwar, deep in conversation with Quentin Pike.

'At least justice has been done,' she was saying.

'In that case, appeal at once,' said Harry lightly. 'Hello, Quentin, saved another criminal from punishment?'

'Thanks to Miss Kaiwar here. A most capable piece of advocacy, in my opinion.' Pike beamed. He looked more like Billy Bunter with every year that passed, but remained one of the city's shrewdest solicitors. Harry was conscious of being scrutinised by porcine, bespectacled eyes.

'Congratulations,' said Harry. 'But don't let that fool you, Valerie. He'll haggle over your next brief fee just as if your man had been sent to the gallows.'

'I was representing a woman, actually,' said Valerie Kaiwar. Her tone was not sarcastic: simply flat, as if the strain of pleading on her client's behalf had drained the strength from her frail body. 'Accused of sticking a pair of kitchen scissors into her boyfriend's stomach. The fact that he'd beaten her black and blue for years, put her in hospital twice, didn't enter into it as far as the police were concerned.'

'Typical chauvinism,' said Harry. But as soon as he spoke, he knew he had struck the wrong note. Val was still keyed up, not in the mood for swapping poor jokes.

Pike sensed it too. 'I'll be off, then. Many thanks once again, Miss Kaiwar. A splendid performance.'

With a wave of his podgy hand he was gone. Harry turned to the woman. The severe black and white of her professional uniform complemented her honey-coloured skin. Something about her smooth high-boned cheeks made him want to touch them. But now wasn't the time or place. Instead he asked her about the day's events in court.

'Probation,' she said, brushing a wisp of black hair off her face. 'A good result in the circumstances. Though I'd bet a pound to a penny that before the year's out she's living with the brute again. Some women never learn.'

Harry thought briefly of his dead wife, of how he had yearned for Liz even after years of drifting apart from her, even after learning of her infidelity, sometimes even now, almost eighteen months after her violent death. Some men, too, never learned.

But he simply said, 'Going back to chambers? I'll come with you, carry your papers.'

They walked together through the commercial centre of Liverpool without speaking. He could tell she was re-living the battle she had fought and won, getting the tension of the case out of her system in readiness for tomorrow's brush against the cobwebs of justice. For his part, Harry thought of telling her about his morning with Stirrup, confiding his uncertainty about Alison's fate. But it would keep until the evening. He had in mind a meal at the flat and the previous day had bought a vegetarian cook book especially to cater to her tastes. He was normally a microwave man, and he preferred red meat to lentils any day, but the plan was to wash everything down with plenty of wine and see how things developed from there.

Now and then passers-by gave them a second, curious glance. In the dying years of the century, some people still seemed to think it strange to see a white man in the company of a dark-skinned woman. And Valerie and he were an odd couple in more ways than one. She was small, delicate and smart, with a burning determination implicit in every step she took along the street. Harry was solidly built and shambling in his gait. No onlooker would doubt for an instant which of the two of them knew the way ahead.

At a news-stand he picked up the early evening edition of one of the local papers and glanced at the front page. BEAST STRIKES AGAIN shrieked the headline. By his side, Valerie made a hissing noise through her teeth.

'What kind of society is it where the women aren't safe to walk through a park in daylight?'

'How would you feel,' he asked gently, 'about defending the culprit when he's finally caught?'

He heard a sharp intake of breath, as if she were about to explode with rage at the very idea. But no words came. He could tell that she was confronting the prospect: how one day her unshakable faith in the sanctity of the defence lawyer's role might commit her to pleading on behalf of a man who had repeatedly violated young women.

Valerie's chambers were in Balliol Court, off Rumford Street. A brass plate by the door listed the dozen members of Mr Arnold Lloyd-Makinson's set. Her name was the most recent addition. Inside, the mustard-tiled walls reminded Harry of public conveniences built pre-war. The lift had a metal cage and looked as if its next journey might be its last. He and Valerie had a tacit agreement that they would walk up the stairs.

A sad-faced woman sat in reception, reading a pamphlet about the law on divorce. Valerie led Harry into the senior clerk's room, where the business of chambers was done. David Base stood by his desk, cradling a receiver against his neck and simultaneously tossing a peppermint up and down with his free hand whilst he assured an anxious solicitor that the papers being chased would be ready tomorrow. To back up his promise, a young girl at the opposite desk pounded an aged Remington with more gusto than skill.

Valerie gave David the thumbs-up sign and gestured to Harry to deposit the papers he was carrying on the floor by the

19

main desk. The clerk hung up and flipped the sweet into his mouth with a casual flourish.

'Not an easy man to please, Mr Fingall. So – another success, Miss Kaiwar?'

She smiled, the first unstrained expression Harry had seen from her that afternoon. 'The legal aid fund had value for money, I think. And haven't I warned you those wretched peppermints will rot your teeth? Anything new come in?'

'A County Court claim in Runcorn.' David Base was still in his twenties, but his manner was as discreet as that of a veteran civil servant. Nevertheless, his thoughtful face yielded a hint of sympathy. 'A matter concerning a soiled carpet.'

'Marshall Hall never had to put up with this.'

'The case has more twists than a Berber,' the clerk assured her solemnly. 'And you never know, it might lead on to greater things.'

'A dispute over an Axminster, you mean?'

The three of them laughed. Harry regarded most barristers' clerks as the professional equivalent of used car salesmen, flogging the services of clapped-out Rumpoles with mendacious protestations of faith in their performance. But he felt in David Base's debt.

A few weeks earlier, Crusoe and Devlin had sent a brief on a Crown Court trial to one of the middle-ranking barristers in chambers, only to be told at the last minute that the chosen advocate was unavailable because one of his cases had over-run. David had offered as a substitute a young woman new in chambers called Valerie Kaiwar. Accustomed to last minute let-downs, Harry had feared the worst. Usually some wet-behind-the-ears kid would foul up a winnable case, earning experience at the luckless client's expense. To Harry's amazement, Valerie not only mastered the papers overnight, but also achieved an acquittal, to the chagrin of the prosecutor presenting the case against the light-fingered accused.

Afterwards, Harry had chatted with her over coffee. She talked animatedly, using her hands to emphasise the points she made. Justice, integrity and principles were words she often used, though sometimes with a cutting irony. Her pride in her performance and her instinctive sympathy for the underdog were worthy enough. But what entranced Harry was the passion invested in everything she did or said, from her mimicry of her opponent's lacklustre closing speech to the way her eyes shone with pleasure when he complimented her on a job well done. Unlike the second-rate advocates whom he encountered day after day, trudging round the courts like sleepwalkers, she was not simply in it for money or security, but because what mattered most to her was fighting for a cause.

At first sight they had nothing in common. She came from a wealthy background; her old man was a Ugandan Asian who had been kicked out by Idi Amin only to settle in the North West of England and make a fortune by building up a chain of cut-price supermarkets. She had read law at Somerville and learned the art of public speaking by arguing for radical motions before chinless sceptics at the Oxford Union. Harry had been born in Liverpool's bandit country, within spitting distance of Scotland Road. He'd lost his parents in his teens and Liz through murder after a short failed marriage. Yet at least he and Valerie shared a questioning mind. To say nothing of an addiction to *film noir*.

One thing led to another. Dinner at the Ensenada, an afternoon spent wandering around the Maritime Museum. Neither of them wanted to push the relationship too fast, too soon. They had kissed long and hard a couple of nights back after watching the original version of *D.O.A.* at a city film club, but that was all. So far.

'Hello, Valerie. Triumphed again?'

Julian Hamer had emerged from his room. Harry could forgive the barrister's Charles Dance looks and Charterhouse and Cambridge charm, because Hamer never posed or patronised. With his easy manner and sharp mind he was a difficult man to dislike. But not impossible, for he fancied Valerie. Harry felt sure of that: something in the way Hamer spoke to her stretched beyond an established man's courtesy to a colleague a dozen years younger.

'Another fine result, Mr Hamer,' confirmed David Base.

'Did she make old Kermincham wake up, Harry? Poor old devil, he's been on the bench so long I'm surprised he hasn't got piles. Tell us about it, Valerie.'

The warmth of her smile made Harry itch with irritation.

'Some other time, perhaps. Right now I have a case to get up.'

Hamer nodded. He seemed tired for once: lines of fatigue edged the corners of his eyes. Starting to look his age, Harry thought with a stab of malice. In days gone by – and especially in the midst of tedious trials – he'd wondered idly about Hamer's sexual preferences. For someone so smooth to escape marriage for so long must say as much about his instincts as his luck. But now Harry was gloomily convinced that his rival was a bachelor gay only in the most traditional sense.

'First things first. See you later then.'

'Sure.'

Did they exchange a glance of complicity? Whenever he saw Valerie in Hamer's presence Harry had the sense of a secret shared, from which he was excluded. He told himself not to be paranoid.

Valerie set off down the passageway. Feeling awkward, Harry followed. He wanted to talk to her alone, but realised that now was not a good time. Perhaps tonight would be better, when she had shaken off the courtroom blues.

She occupied a corner of the building more akin to a cupboard than a room. The shelf running along the rear wall overhung the chair behind her desk. A taller woman would have cracked her head if she rose to her feet without ducking.

He cleared his throat, embarrassed by his own nervousness. 'I was wondering – would you like to come round to the flat tonight?'

She considered him from under long black lashes.

'I can't make it tonight, Harry. Sorry. But – I've got things to do. You know how it is.'

Although spoken kindly, the words slapped him. He realised how much he'd been counting on her saying yes. He told himself he didn't own her, and there would be other nights, but he felt a boy's frustration at the denial of a longed-for treat.

'Okay.'

Something in his tone prompted her to stretch a hand across the desk and touch his fingers. 'Maybe tomorrow, how about that?'

He tried to look don't-careish. 'Shall I give you a call?'

'Please.'

There was a short pause. He wasn't certain whether she intended to say anything else. Finally he stood up. 'All right then, Val. I'll leave you to your carpet.'

'Thanks so much for coming back with me.'

'The pleasure was mine.'

On the way out, he stopped again at David's desk and asked if he could use the phone.

'Feel free.' The clerk flicked a peppermint into the air with elaborate top-spin and caught it nonchalantly between two fingers. 'If only England's wicket-keeper could do the same, eh? Heard the news about the Test team, by any chance?'

Harry shook his head. 'When England play the West Indies, ignorance is bliss.'

He dialled Stirrup's direct line. Propped next to the handset was a framed photograph of a pretty blonde girl. David's fiancée, Valerie had explained the other day. Harry thought again about The Beast, who threatened the safety of so many girls like her. When would the man be caught?

'Jack? I've checked and the diary's clear. If the offer's still open, I'd be glad to see you this evening after all.'

Stirrup was hearty. 'I'll ring young Claire, tell her to put the oven on, roll out the red carpet. You've not seen the new place yet, have you? Just make sure the charging meter's switched off before you arrive, all right?'

'I'll see you at half-eight.'

He put down the receiver. 'Good win for Valerie today,' he said to the clerk. Something prompted him to add, 'Especially picking up the brief at the last minute.'

David Base glanced up from his paperwork. 'Today's case? The stabbing? No, you must be thinking of something else. Windaybanks instructed her a long time ago. Mr Pike admires Miss Kaiwar as much as you do.'

'My mistake.'

But as Harry went down the stairs he knew he had not misunderstood. Yesterday, when turning down his offer of a visit to the Everyman, Valerie had said she'd been landed with a new brief for a case today. She'd even thrown in a moan about Quentin Pike's lack of consideration; she would have to sacrifice her evening to mug up all the facts. He felt sickened by the silly little lie. Sicker still that he could guess the reason for it.

Chapter Four

Driving through the boulevards of West Kirby on the way to Jack Stirrup's home, Harry wondered if Valerie was at that very moment with Julian Hamer. *See you later*. Hamer's casual farewell to her must have been literally meant. Since Liz's death, Harry had lived without jealousy and it was a shock to recognise envy nibbling like a rat at his guts.

Maybe he was doing Valerie an injustice. Starting out on her career, she was bound to be busy some nights. And if she were seeing Hamer, what of it? As professional colleagues they might have a dozen good reasons to socialise from time to time. But that argument held no more water than a recidivist's alibi.

Harry bit his lip. No point in agonising – life was too short. Better by far to do something positive to occupy his mind. Such as puzzling over Alison Stirrup's disappearance.

Stirrup lived in affluent Caldy, at the end of a lane which petered out into an unmade track leading to the crest of a sandstone hill overlooking the Dee. Harry approached the house by way of a drive which wound through beech and lime trees, finally revealing after the last bend a large redbrick building with a much-gabled roof and a mass of small, irregularly placed mullioned windows. Prospect House dated back to the eighteenth century and according to Jim Crusoe, who had handled the conveyancing, so did the plumbing. Outside the front door, a tarpaulined builder's lorry and a skip full of rubble signified that the repair programme still had a long way to go.

As Harry locked his car Stirrup appeared at the front door, two glasses of beer in his hands. His short-sleeved designer leisure shirt did not flatter his paunch.

'Glad you could make it. Here, quench your thirst. Care for a quick trip round the estate?'

He led Harry along a path of crazy paving which rambled around the side of the house. The overgrown gardens extended for acre after acre. Rhododendron bushes loomed on either side, blocking out the low evening sun. Brambles poked at the two men with tendrils like the fingers of menacing strangers. They walked past an empty greenhouse with cracked and cobwebbed panes and a tumbledown stable block. Even the estate agents' particulars had described the place as a challenge.

Harry guessed that the most diplomatic course was to admire the view. Doing so was no hardship: a heat haze shimmered over the river, making the grey-green Welsh hills beyond seem remote and mysterious. Stirrup enthused about the sunsets in this part of the world, then apologised for the state of the grounds.

'Can't find a gardener, believe it or not. You'd think people would be glad of a job. Anyway, Rome wasn't built in a day. Thought I'd concentrate on the house first. Christ, I knew it was a big job when I started, but if I'd realised . . .'

He launched into a jeremiad about the tribulations of modernising an old property. The expense, the defects not revealed even by an expensive survey, the delays, the inadequacies of tradesmen. Harry speculated that Alison might simply have grown tired of the inconvenience of living in an approximation to a builder's yard.

When they went inside, the progress made became apparent. The entrance hall boasted polished walnut wainscoting, a low ceiling with exposed beams and half-timbering in the old Cheshire style. All it lacked was a lifesize portrait of the lord of the manor.

'Woodworm treatment alone cost me a bloody fortune,' grumbled Stirrup, although there was a note of pride in his voice.

Harry was making all the right noises when a door banged and a girl appeared. She glanced theatrically at her watch.

'You'd better be sitting down in the next two minutes.'

'Hello, Claire,' said Harry. 'Sorry we're late, your dad's been showing me round outside.'

Stirrup's daughter was the child of his first marriage. Her mother had died in a car crash when the girl was still at infants' school. Her figure had filled out since Harry had last seen her. A tight jersey and narrow-waisted jeans did nothing to disguise curves which, for a fifteen year old, were generous. A year or two ago she had been a quiet daddy's girl, a flat-chested, androgynous kid with the abstracted appearance of someone who has spent too long listening to a personal stereo. Round-framed spectacles had been abandoned in favour of contact lenses and she had grown her black hair to shoulder length. Her nose was too big, and her jaw too long, for her to claim prettiness, but she was now unmistakably a young woman. She even had the sulky look which in Harry's teenage memories was inseparably associated with girls who had just become aware of their power to appeal to men.

'You remember Mr Devlin?' asked Stirrup, all paternal good humour.

'Yeah.' She turned her back on them. 'I'm putting the stuff out on the table this minute, okay?'

Stirrup winked at Harry, who had never fathomed why so many parents regard their offsprings' rudeness as a source of amusement. They went into the dining room, a large oak-panelled place. The round table was set for two.

'Claire ate earlier on,' explained Stirrup. 'Busy young lady, you know, she wanted the rest of the evening to herself.'

As the girl served them with melon, Harry recalled that her father had told him that she had her heart set on a career in catering. He asked if that was still the case and she nodded curtly before withdrawing, leaving Harry to reflect that he found it no easier to converse with fifteen-year-old girls than he had done when he was the same age.

Over the meal – beef cooked in wine, simple but excellent – Stirrup talked about his company, interrupting himself only to shove forkfuls of food into his mouth. Loudly he bemoaned the iniquities of the tax system, the greed of customers and the unreliability of suppliers. And above all, the difficulty of finding competent staff.

'What's the latest on Trevor?' asked Harry, pouring the last of the wine.

'Morgan? Christ knows. No one's asked me for a reference. Last time I asked around, he was drinking more than ever. The man's a fool to himself.'

Harry put the wine bottle down guiltily. 'Pity,' he said. 'You and he were close at one time.'

'Close?' Stirrup leaned over the table and snapped his fingers. 'We were like that, Trevor Morgan and me, ever since the days when I had one off-licence and a scratty little wine bar in Wrexham called The Stirrup Cup. Claire was just a toddler then, it was in the days when Margaret was still alive. He and I have been together ever since. If he could have kept his hands off the female staff, he'd be with me now. But he went too far.'

'How did Cathy take his sacking?'

'No idea. Never seen her from that day to this. Tell you the truth, I could never stick the woman. Hard-nosed bitch. She gave Trev a hard time, no wonder he played away from home. Ali got on with her all right, reckoned she was cultured. But once I'd given Cathy's old man the push, that was the end of it. The girls could scarcely keep on socialising.'

Claire came in, bearing mints and cups of coffee. Harry congratulated her on the meal and received a shrug in response. Stirrup said genially, 'She still fancies going to catering college. Sometimes I worry I've bred a female Bryan Grealish, God help us. I keep telling her to go to university, take a degree in law. Make yourself a fortune like that feller Devlin, I keep on saying.'

As he bellowed with laughter, his daughter looked briefly at the heavens and went out again.

'I didn't go to university,' said Harry mildly. The Polytechnic had been good enough for him. Studying in his spare time while he took a succession of casual jobs to keep his head above water. After the death of his parents, money had always been tight.

'What? Well, you know what I mean. No way will a solicitor ever starve. Not while . . .'

He was interrupted by the roar of a motorbike engine coming close to the house before cutting out. A look of anger darkened his face for a moment, then was gone. Harry heard footsteps: Claire hurrying to the back door.

Lowering his voice, Stirrup said, 'That'll be lover boy. Sly little creep.'

'Claire's young man?'

Stirrup made a noise, part belch, part expression of disgust. 'Not so young. Twenty years old, would you believe? Claire's only a kid yet. Oh, yes, I know she's got a figure. And she can cope with any lad who tries to go too far. She's got a yellow belt in karate, would you believe. All right, things are different from when you and me were young. All the same, I don't like it. A cradle snatcher, that's what he is.'

Harry didn't think a five-year age gap put the lad in Bryan Grealish's class as a cradle snatcher. Nor was he thrilled to be bracketed with Stirrup in age.

'Don't get me wrong, Harry boy. I'm no Mister Bloody Barrett of Wimpole Street. I know a thing or two about the younger generation, how they behave. Forbidden fruit and all that. My girl's no angel, she's flesh and blood. I haven't asked her not to keep seeing him. That's the mistake my first wife's old man made with me. Margaret and me, we simply ran off and got married. No, matter of fact, I encourage her to bring him into the house. Let her see him in surroundings she knows, not some back street pub or disco. That way she'll realise soonest he isn't for her.'

'What does the lad do?'

'Not a bloody hand's turn! That is, he's a student. Studying law, would you believe? At the Poly though, not a proper university.'

Words failed Harry this time, but his host was unaware of it. Stirrup wiped his mouth with the back of his hand and stood up, gazing through the dining room window. After a moment he strode from the room. Harry could hear him shouting to Claire, urging her to invite her friend inside. The reply sounded mutinous, but within a couple of minutes Stirrup was back, wearing the complacent expression of a man who has scored a point.

Claire followed, her face red with embarrassment or rage or both. A pace behind came a young man in leather biking gear. Thick black hair fell forward over his pallid face. He had a sullen mouth which might have been purpose-made for registering a sneer. A gold ear-ring glinted from one lobe.

'You want to be a lawyer, don't you . . .' Stirrup ostentatiously reached into his memory for the young man's first name '. . . Peter? Well, this is my company's solicitor. Mr Harry Devlin – meet Peter Kipper.'

'Kuiper,' snapped Claire. She pronounced it 'caper'.

Stirrup smiled and Harry guessed the mistake had been deliberate. Stretching out a hand, he said, 'Pleased to meet you.'

Peter Kuiper curled his lip as if an attempt were being made to contaminate him with a social disease.

'I don't intend to practise law. There's too much routine in legal work to satisfy me. It's just a qualification, a mental discipline, as far as I'm concerned.'

He had a faint South African accent and Harry could picture him giving the kaffirs a hard time.

'You'll change your tune when the taxpayer stops paying your board and lodging,' said Stirrup with breezy confidence.

Kuiper bestowed a look of pity upon the girl. Her face crimsoned again and she said, 'Peter's got too much imagination to be a wage slave.'

Harry decided to mediate. 'I can do without the competition anyway,' he said affably. 'So what are your plans, Peter?'

Permitting himself a smile of superiority, Kuiper said, 'To make money. In an interesting way.'

'Do me a favour, then. When you discover the secret, let me in on it.'

Claire didn't bother to hide her boredom with the conversation. 'Peter can't stay long.' She shot a resentful glance at her father and waved a hand towards the dining room table. 'And I suppose I'll have all the meal to clear up. So if you don't mind . . .'

'You can use the living room,' said Stirrup, exuding magnanimity.

'It's okay, I'm going soon,' said Kuiper. 'Just called to say hello. Got plenty of things to do.'

Distress blotched the girl's face. 'But you said . . .'

'Only a flying visit, I told you. I'll give you a call.'

As the young man left the room, Stirrup said with a glance at his watch. 'Nice to see you again, er – Peter. Better look

30

sharp, though. You've only a couple of hours or so left today to make any headway towards your first million.'

Kuiper responded with a just-you-wait scowl and was gone, Claire hard on his heels. Harry and Stirrup could hear the two of them talking in the hallway. Their voices were low, urgent.

Stirrup broke the silence as soon as he realised that he could not hear what was being said without overt eavesdropping. 'See what I mean? The surly young bastard's not fit to lick her boots.'

Harry was not convinced that Claire and Kuiper were unsuited to each other, so he simply shook his head in a gesture that might have meant anything.

Stirrup sighed. 'It's not easy for the girl, you know. I can't be mother as well as father to her. I work long hours, you know that. There ought to be an older woman about the place.'

The front door banged. They could hear Claire going into the kitchen; her footfalls had a defeated sound. Harry seized the opportunity to turn the conversation in the direction which interested him most.

'Maybe Alison will be back home soon.'

'You think so? I don't know, Harry boy, I just don't know.'

'A woman doesn't walk out on all this' – Harry's wave of the hand encompassed the magnificence of the room – 'without a good reason. Any idea what it might be?'

'If I only knew. Any road, least said, soonest mended. Come on, have a look round the rest of the house?'

Stirrup led the way with the pride of a mother showing off a new-born child. The billiard room, the study, the conservatory. It was like seeing a Cluedo gameboard brought to life. 'Not bad, eh?'

They climbed turning stairs to a galleried landing half the floor area of Harry's flat. Doors led off to bedrooms. 'Mine,' said Stirrup, pointing to one of them. 'Alison's. Claire's. Couple more for the guests, plus an attic upstairs.'

So the husband and wife occupied separate rooms? Even as Harry mulled that one over, his client sought to forestall curiosity.

'Always each had our own room, Ali and me, right from when we were first married. The coppers raised their eyebrows when they came round the first time, but I told them, don't read anything into it. Things were all right between her and me. But you don't spend a fortune on a place like this and then stint yourself for space. Besides, I'm a bit of a snorer and Alison sleeps light. But we had plenty of nights together with no time for either snoring or sleeping, let me tell you.'

Harry ignored Stirrup's do-you-want-to-make-anything-else-of-it gaze. Like so many clients, he was protesting too much.

He strolled into Alison's bedroom. His first impression was that everything was blue. The carpet, the curtains, the elaborate patchwork quilts hanging from the wall. No fluffy feminine touches for Alison Stirrup. The room matched her appearance and her personality – or at least, as much or as little of her personality as she had cared to reveal. Immaculate, attractive, but cool and remote as Lapland.

He bent to examine the contents of the bookcase. Other people's taste in literature always intrigued him. Alison, it seemed, enjoyed the Victorians. *Cranford, North and South, Villette* and *Silas Marner* stood side by side with Winifred Gérin's life of Elizabeth Gaskell. And they were sandwiched by a clutch of books on patchwork techniques.

'Ali always had her nose in a book. Either that or she was busy with her needlework.' Stirrup jerked a thumb at one of the wall hangings, a five feet wide hexagon composed of innumerable blue and green triangles. 'Not bad if you like that sort of thing. I used to say, turn your hobby into a business, make a few bob out of it.'

Harry wondered what Alison had ever seen in her husband. Not a shared love of cultural or artistic pursuits, that was for sure. Money must be the answer. It usually was, whatever the question. But if she was still alive, what was she using for money now?

As they went downstairs Stirrup said, 'Fancy a game of snooker before you go?'

Harry realised, for the first time, the man's sense of isolation. If he was as bemused by Alison's vanishing as he claimed, life must at the moment seem an unexplained mystery.

'One game, then.'

They played on a full-sized Thurston table, talking spasmodically about this and that. Stirrup drank liqueurs steadily, but they neither affected his calculation of angles nor prompted him to volunteer anything more about Alison. Harry matched his opponent shot for shot and with only a few balls left on the table, Stirrup needed snookers to win. But Harry let his mind wander. What was Valerie up to? When he missed an easy pot, Stirrup didn't try to hide a grin. He seized his chance and finally sank the black to win the game.

'You let it slip,' he said. 'I'd not have made that mistake in your shoes.'

Harry nodded rueful agreement.

'Know the secret, Harry boy? I'll tell you. It's simple. And it's the same in love or war, business or snooker.' In high good humour he slapped his solicitor matily on the back. 'You need the killer instinct.'

Chapter Five

'Hanging would be too good for him,' said Bernard Gladwin.

Harry's mind was on whether Stirrup had killed his wife and disposed of the body. Where might the corpse be hidden, if he had? Surely not at Prospect House – Stirrup wouldn't be so naive as to court almost inevitable detection. The police had already with his permission taken a cursory look round the building and grounds. Finding nothing. So far they had stopped short of digging up the overgrown garden, although Harry guessed that if Alison did not reappear soon, Bolus would insist on a much more thorough search.

A touch of steel across his neck brought Harry back to the here and now. His barber was talking about The Beast, not Jack Stirrup, and had momentarily paused for breath. To give Harry the chance to confirm him in his prejudices.

The razor's reflection gleamed in the wall mirror. Harry gazed back at it, not letting his expression give a clue to his thoughts.

'What punishment do you suggest? The guillotine?'

Bernard grunted. 'I'd be willing to do the job myself if no else had the bottle.'

He emphasised the point with a flourish of his shaving arm, causing Harry to flinch in anticipation of a severed jugular.

Bernard was a burly, red-faced man who cut hair with the same ruthless simplicity with which he expressed his views on law and order. And yet Harry had never surrendered to logic and taken his custom elsewhere. He found something compelling in Bernard's unashamed awfulness. Coming here was a bad habit, like eating chocolate fudge cake or watching a TV soap.

'The bloody streets aren't safe to walk these days. I blame the government. To say nothing of the bloody social workers.'

Harry forbore to point out that none of The Beast's victims had been accosted in the street. Fine distinctions would be as wasted on Bernard as would piped music or comfy chairs in this place of his.

Bernard's wasn't a hairdressing studio or a unisex salon. It was a barber's and proud of it. There was even a red and white striped wooden pole outside the door. Sitting on a ledge beside a card display of unbreakable combs and a tub of styptic pencils was a scruffy box of condoms, its contents no doubt long past their useful life. A pin-up calendar provided the only touch of glamour; June's lovely lady rejoiced in the name of Inge. Occasionally, Harry noticed in the mirror, Bernard would glance at Inge, as if to refresh his memory about the exact dimensions of her ballooning breasts.

'The bloody police aren't much better. Months this pervert's been on the loose, and has anyone been arrested? Have they buggery!'

'Difficult case,' said Harry to plug a gap in the conversation while Bernard tried to take a lump out of his left ear.

'What is it – six attacks now, seven? All in public places. Surely to God they ought to have an idea who's responsible.'

'There's no pattern. He strikes at different times of the day. And all over Wirral, isn't that right?'

Bernard nodded. 'Birkenhead Park, Eastham Ferry, the Wirral Way, Raby Mere. You name it.'

'Hard to catch up with someone like that.'

'Bloody disgrace.' Bernard held up a hand mirror. 'How's that? Bit more off the sides? Anyhow, see that identikit picture in the *Echo*? Could have been anyone. Might be you. Might even be me.'

He bared large yellow teeth in an angry grimace and finished snipping. 'All right? Want anything on it, keep it together?' Without waiting for a reply, he squirted a dented metal canister of something ozone-unfriendly at Harry's head, then stepped back to admire his handiwork.

Waiting while Bernard brushed bits of hair off his shoulders, Harry turned his mind to The Beast. Beyond reading the reports in the Press, he had not given the assaults much thought. What intrigued him were the quirks and oddities of human life and death. A plot, a puzzle, a hint of mystery, whether on film, in a novel or in the real world, all could fire his imagination. But the recent spate of attacks across the water had seemed commonplace in a dangerous age. Harry had assumed that the perpetrator would soon be caught. Their paths were only likely to cross if The Beast wanted Crusoe and Devlin to act as his solicitors.

Bernard was right, though. Upwards of half a dozen attacks in public parks and other open spaces since spring and the police seemed no nearer to arresting The Beast than to nailing Jack the Ripper. Meanwhile he was becoming more violent. At first he had been content to flash at a couple of pre-pubertal girls. Then he had touched one. Next he turned to rape. Each attack seemed more brutal than the one before. Now the police were warning that the man might kill. And in the past few weeks the Press had made a running story out of two common themes linking the attacks. The Beast always wore a rubber mask with the snarling faces of an animal – a dog, a leopard, a wolf – of the kind currently popular and sold in shops up and down the country. And each young victim's hair was blonde.

'Know what I'd do if I got hold of him?' asked Bernard.

Harry handed over his money with a hasty word of thanks. 'I can guess,' he said. He was about to leave when the door opened and through it a familiar figure hobbled on arthritic legs clad in cavalry twill trousers which had seen better days.

'Hello Jonah. About time you had those shaggy locks trimmed.'

'Very funny.'

The newcomer had a cover of grey hair as thin as a spider's web. He was a stocky man, sixty if a day, and Harry found it impossible to imagine his leathery face ever having yielded a carefree smile. Despite the heat, over a white shirt with fraying cuffs he was wearing an old maroon cardigan.

'Sure you're warm enough?' asked Harry. Like everyone else, he'd never been able to resist teasing Jonah Deegan.

'Nothing better to do with your time than crack silly jokes?'

'As it happens, I'm glad I've seen you. There's something you can do for me.'

Although he must have scented business, Jonah's watery eyes didn't flicker. He said to Gladwin, 'With you in a minute, Bernard. Just let me have a word with Clarence Darrow here.'

They stepped to one side and the barber made a token effort at sweeping the floor whilst trying to eavesdrop.

'What can I do for you?'

'Still got contacts over the water?'

Jonah had been in the Merseyside police from leaving school until retirement. He'd been a good detective by all accounts, though the sights and sounds of the city's twilight world had soured his view of the human race. Long since divorced, he lived in a flat near the Anglican cathedral with an endless supply of foul-smelling cigarettes for company. Nowadays he worked for himself, mostly chasing – or limping after – the occasional debt. And what he lacked in social graces he made up for with cussed persistence.

'I'd like you to find the answer to a question for me.'

'Ask away.'

Harry explained about the police interrogation of Jack Stirrup. 'Someone's stirring them up. Must be. Missing persons usually rate low on the priority list.'

Jonah nodded. 'And you want to know who's stirring? I've heard of this Bolus. He's just a whippersnapper. Doubt if he's thirty. I'll have a word round.'

'Thanks.'

'It'll cost, mind.'

'Jack Stirrup can afford it.'

'The price went up when you made the crack about this cardigan.'

'You're a hard man, Jonah. Give me a ring at the office when you have any news.'

Outside the sky was cloudfree. Mid-afternoon on the hottest day of the year so far and Liverpudlians were relishing it, equally careless of sunstroke and skin cancer. In Church Street, opportunistic vendors bellowed the price of dark glasses whose provenance and effectiveness were both in doubt. Shirt-sleeved old men sat on benches, picking their noses and eyeing the women who passed them by.

Harry looked at the women too. Overweight middle-aged ladies panting as they lugged heavily-laden shopping baskets towards the bus stop. Mothers in sleeveless dresses, dragging fractious children away from ice-cream barrows. And teen-agers in tight tee-shirts and shorts, displaying figures good, bad and indifferent. One red-head had emblazoned on her ample chest *I'm not fat – just pregnant*.

Several girls had fair hair and Harry wondered how many of them feared that one day soon they might become a name in the paper when The Beast struck again. As surely he would. The thought angered Harry. Why should they not be safe? Why should their sex and their age and the colour of their hair make them vulnerable to a man for whom they were not living individuals but simply lumps of female flesh? His head said that Bernard's lynch-mob justice never worked. His heart was not so sure.

All was quiet back at the office. He was greeted by Fran-cesca, the temp who was deputising whilst his secretary and her family sunned themselves on the Algarve. A slender girl whose perm resembled an exotic form of marine life, Fran-cesca had a Shakespearean indifference towards consistency in spelling. The shortness of her skirts and the smoothness of her bare legs were scant compensation for her inability to type accurately at speed.

'Too hot to be inside working on a day like this!'

Ten times at least that week she had greeted him with the same remark. Harry responded with a weary smile and asked if there were any messages.

'On your desk, together with your post.'

Down the corridor, a door swung open and a big bearded man emerged. Jim Crusoe, his partner, back after a morning spent with an old lady in Formby who wanted to add an umpteenth codicil to her will. Rumour claimed she had ambitions for a place in *The Guinness Book of Records*. More testamentary dispositions than she had personal effects.

'Good lunch? Christ, old son, call that a haircut? You haven't been to Sweeney Todd's again? He could make a Rasta look like Dennis the Menace.'

'Does wonders for my street cred down at the magistrates'.'

'Don't bank on it. Anyway, what's the latest on Jack Stirrup?'

Harry described his visit to Prospect House. 'He's holding back on me, Jim. I'm certain of that, but nothing else.'

'You think Alison's dead?'

'Wish I knew.'

'You know your trouble.'

'No, but I'm sure you're going to tell me.'

'You're too interested in the truth to be a defence lawyer. If I'd killed someone, I'd want a brief who wasn't too fussy about right. A Ruby Fingall. No wonder he's cornered the market in big league villainy.'

'Stirrup's not short of a few bob.'

'But he's an amateur in crime, isn't he? No track record. Piling the booze high and flogging it cheap is no training for a career in homicide.' Jim put a huge hand to his mouth in mock embarrassment. 'Sorry. You're going to remind me about the golden thread. Our client's guilty until proved innocent and all that leader column garbage.'

'So you think he killed her?'

Jim Crusoe looked him in the eye. 'Let's just say I've seen him lose his rag a time or two and I wouldn't like to be in his way when it happens. And I went over to Prospect House during the sale negotiations. The grounds are a jungle. You could hide half the bodies from West Kirby cemetery there.'

'Careful, I may start thinking you're the one who got the police to swarm over there.'

'Not me, old son. I'd hate to be proved right and see Jack behind bars. Believe me, we need his fees.'

They parted and Harry had done an hour's much-needed desk work when the phone rang and Jonah Deegan spoke his name.

'Got something? That was quick.'

'I can still pull a few strings.' Jonah could make even a boast sound like a lament.

'And?'

'Name Doreen Capstick mean anything to you?'

'Stirrup's mother-in-law.'

'Right. She's the one who's agitating. Ringing the station by the hour complaining about the lack of progress in finding her daughter. She's convinced the marriage was on the rocks and that Stirrup topped the girl rather than see her run back to mummy.'

Even from his brief acquaintance with Alison, Harry doubted whether she would have been eager to take refuge with her loud and tiresome mother except as a last resort.

'Anything else?'

'It's a genuine mystery.' Jonah didn't give the impression of being intrigued. 'No evidence to pin anything on your bloke. And no explanation of the woman's disappearance. The betting is, she had another man on the quiet. But if so, it was very, very quiet.'

'Thanks, Jonah. Send me your bill.'

'I posted it five minutes ago.'

While Harry mulled over the news, Francesca came in and left her day's work for him to check, together with a handful of phone messages. He rifled through the papers, cringing at the ragged margins and mistakes in the correspondence, signing all the letters which were not so ineptly presented as to make re-typing essential. This week's investment in correction fluid alone could send the firm into the red.

Two of the telephone calls made him pause. Valerie had rung – it must be her from the return call number, though Francesca's spelling of Kaiwar was imaginative and wildly inaccurate. SORRY CAN'T MAKE IT TONIGHT CALL TOMORROW AND FIX SOMETHING UP was the message, printed out in a child-like, unformed hand. Harry swore, crumpled the piece of paper into a ball and hurled it into the litter basket.

And Stirrup had been on as well. The message was stark. RING BACK ASAP. Such a command from a blue-chip client was not to be ignored, but Harry allowed himself a few moments of speculation before picking up the phone. Were the police pressing harder? He found himself hoping desperately that there was good news at last, that the woman had by some miracle re-appeared.

As soon as Stirrup's voice came on to the other end of the line, Harry realised the social mood of the previous evening had evaporated.

'I want you to do something for me and do it fast.'

Words to make any solicitor quail. Harry said cautiously, 'What's the problem, Jack?'

'That bitch! That bloody bitch!' The disembodied voice was choking with anger. 'Capstick, I mean. Would you believe it?

She's written to Claire – Claire of all people – suggesting that I killed the kid's step-mother.'

Harry gazed heavenwards in despair. 'I think,' he said carefully, 'that I'd better take a look at that letter.'

'You'll do more than bloody look at it. I've been libelled. In a letter to my own bloody daughter, I've been called a murderer. The bitch, how dare she? I want you to issue a writ at once. Take her for every penny she's got.' Stirrup took a deep breath. 'I want to destroy her.'

Chapter Six

Acting for Stirrup in a libel action against Doreen Capstick held as much appeal for Harry as backing one pit bull terrier to savage another. True, the case would be a money-spinner for Crusoe and Devlin. But whatever Jack Stirrup and Doreen Capstick might think, the last thing they needed was to become embroiled in acrimonious litigation. Instead of spoiling for a fight with each other, they should be making common cause in the search for Alison.

Starting an argument about it would simply cause Stirrup to become more entrenched. When he managed to get a word in, Harry opted for an oblique approach.

'Leave it with me. Let me fix up a conference with a barrister.'

'Why do we need to see a bloody barrister?'

'This is a High Court case you're talking about,' Harry explained. 'Not like applying to the magistrates for a liquor licence. The professional rules don't allow a solicitor to handle the case even if he has the specialist knowledge. Which I don't. So if you have to use Counsel, you might as well take his advice sooner rather than later.' He thought of an argument which might appeal to a businessman suspicious of lawyers' excuses. 'Don't give him the chance to say in twelve months' time he would have handled the case differently if he'd been brought in on day one.'

Grumbling, Stirrup agreed. 'Where do we go from here, then?'

'I'll organise a conference as soon as I can. Do you want a local man or someone from London?'

'I don't want to hang around. Find the smartest man in the city who can see us fast.'

As he put down the receiver, Harry wondered whom to instruct on Stirrup's behalf. Only a handful of Liverpool barristers had a sizeable libel practice. And of them perhaps the most experienced was someone whom he felt instinctively reluctant to brief. Julian Hamer.

Forget the pride and the prejudice, he told himself. Any work which he had sent Hamer in the past had been handled efficiently and with speed. Julian was good in conference, and that was important: Stirrup would want to satisfy himself from the outset that he had the best counsel whom money could buy. And with any luck Hamer's advice would be to keep the case out of court. That way, both Stirrup and his foolish mother-in-law might still be saved from themselves.

Nevertheless, Harry could not help experiencing a surge of irritation when he spoke to David Base on the phone. The clerk assured him that, by good fortune, a trial of Julian's had collapsed only a couple of hours earlier. So an urgent conference would be possible the following day. Never mind the law of libel, thought Harry, sod's law invariably prevailed. Had he been desperate to have Hamer act, and no one else, the barrister would have been fully booked for months ahead.

'Four o'clock?' he suggested gloomily.

'Ideal,' said David Base, his glad-to-please tone simply rubbing salt in the wound. 'I'll mark it in the diary. You'll have the papers sent round tomorrow morning?'

'Will do.'

A few minutes later came a knock at his door. Francesca appeared, bearing a slim brown envelope.

'Just arrived. Special delivery, by motor-bike courier,' she announced. The faraway look in her eyes suggested the courier had taken her fancy.

'Re-typed those letters yet?' asked Harry. The girl was a convenient target for his ill humour.

Her eyes widened. 'You didn't say you wanted them all done for tonight's post.'

He gave up. 'Doesn't matter.'

'They'll be ready in the morning.' She spoke tolerantly, like a mother promising an importunate child jam tomorrow.

44

He managed a wan smile and opened the envelope as she left the room. The sender was Stirrup; the dashing courier had made good time in bringing the allegedly libellous letter over from Wirral.

Six sheets of paper were covered in green ink. Doreen Capstick wrote in a flowing hand which lent itself to much use of italics and underlinings. Ostensibly, she was writing to invite Claire to spend the summer holidays with her. It was important, Doreen said, for Claire to feel that she had a *bolthole*. After her step-mother's tragic disappearance, a young girl would scarcely be *human* if she did not feel a little *frightened*, particularly when her father was such a *hottempered* individual. Doreen did not omit to mention that Alison had in the past referred to a *violent* streak in her husband's personality. It would be *terrible*, and Doreen could *never* forgive herself if brave Claire were to fall victim to her father's wrath. It was heart-breaking to lose one's only child – for Doreen confessed she had no doubt that Alison was now dead and buried somewhere; she would never be seen again – but it would be *horrific* if another life were to be sacrificed as well.

And so on. No outright accusation of murder, but an innuendo as plain as blood upon snow. Harry had little doubt that the letter was defamatory in law. What puzzled him was Doreen Capstick's motive for writing it. There was no reason to think that she and Claire were close. After all, they only had Alison in common; Doreen doted on her and the girl disliked her. Nor was there any trace of genuine affection beneath the prolix expressions of concern. The invitation to stay was an excuse for making a string of hints about Stirrup's guilt, hints so thinly veiled as to be indecently exposed.

Francesca came in without knocking. 'Mind signing my time sheet, Harry?'

She thrust into his hand a pre-printed form headed THE AU REVOIR EMPLOYMENT AGENCY. Harry winced at the number of hours recorded for so little end result, but signed all the same.

'Thanks. Going to the party tonight?'

'What party?'

Francesca raised her eyebrows in a parody of astonishment. 'How could you forget? The agency's cocktail party, of course. Don't tell me you weren't invited, 'cause I saw the card on your window sill only the other day.'

Harry glanced involuntarily at the ledge behind him. It was bare. Vaguely, he remembered chucking the invitation into the wastepaper basket. Golf days, luncheon seminars and cocktail parties . . . all were part and parcel of a solicitor's life and all left him cold. As a means of drumming up business, he rated them on a par with chasing ambulances. But perhaps this shindig should be an exception to his rule of non-attendance, in view of what he had learned today. For the proprietor of the Au Revoir was Mrs Doreen Capstick.

'Slipped my mind for a moment. Six o'clock, isn't it?'

'Half past.'

'Will you be there?'

Francesca made a face. 'Yeah, handing out the drinks and sausages on sticks, worse luck. Doreen made me and some of the other girls on her books an offer we couldn't refuse. A publicity gimmick, that's what it is.' A thoughtful look passed over her face. Harry could see her mind working; she was wondering if there was any personal motive behind his question, if he was looking for an opportunity to chat her up outside work.

'I have to be away by ten,' she said in the end. 'My boyfriend's coming to pick me up.'

Thus did she administer the brush-off. Harry, whose enthusiasm for false eyelashes and dirty fingernails was limited, could restrain his disappointment.

Amiably, he said, 'See you later at the Traders', then.'

'G'night.'

After she had gone, he dictated into his tape recorder the instructions to Julian Hamer. He prepared the brief with the ease of long practice, his thoughts elsewhere. What did he hope to gain by turning up at this party? If he did not already have a business acquaintance with Doreen, he would never have contemplated confronting Stirrup's mother-in-law. But he felt he should try to persuade the two of them to abandon hostilities. If he succeeded, he would have sacrificed a fat fee, but it would be worth it. Life was too short for members of a family in crisis to go to war with each other.

He finished work for the day and strolled in the evening sunshine through the gardens of Liverpool Parish Church towards the Traders' Club. The discreet decor of that nine-teenth century monument to the city's mercantile greatness was today disfigured by the gaudy green and red posters which festooned the entrance hall. Each of them bore a picture of an impossibly attractive woman working with demonic zeal at a word processor. Each was captioned THE AU REVOIR STAFF AGENCY – SO CALLED BECAUSE YOU'LL NEVER WANT TO SAY GOODBYE TO OUR GIRLS. Harry winced. The minute Lucy returned from her holiday, he would be only too happy to bid Francesca farewell.

'You're early,' breathed a voice in his ear.

Think of the devil. Francesca had changed into a green skirt and red blouse and doused herself in enough perfume to mask the smell of a glue factory. She pinned a green and red name badge to his lapel and handed him a green and red complimentary biro, which looked as if it might last a week before leaking its contents into his jacket pocket.

'First to arrive,' she said, picking up a tray of wine from a nearby table. 'Fancy a drink?'

'Thought you'd never ask. Where's the boss?'

Francesca waved a hand vaguely. 'All over the place. Bellowing orders. Panicking about whether anyone's going to turn up.'

He scanned the room. Half a dozen girls loitered in corners, chatting and filching crisps and peanuts intended for the guests. A door at the back opened and Doreen Capstick swept in. Her tight pink summer dress – no green and red uniform for her – displayed a deep and impressive cleavage down which Harry couldn't help staring. Their eyes met and her scarlet lips relaxed into a welcoming smile. All nervous energy, she bustled towards him, arms outstretched.

'Lovely to see you!' She presented a powdered cheek for Harry to kiss. 'It's been a long time. How are you, my dear? Fran's working for you at the moment, isn't she? Marvellous. One of our very best girls, you know.'

Christ, thought Harry.

'Busy as ever?'

'Can't complain,' he said. 'Matter of fact, your son-in-law is keeping me fully occupied at present.'

The smile died and the fulsome note left her voice. 'Jack Stirrup? Of course. I'd forgotten you act for him.'

'You'll be getting a direct reminder soon. Jack saw your letter to Claire. As you obviously intended. The letter's libellous, Doreen, you must know that. You're as good as accusing him of having killed Alison.'

A dangerous light sparkled in her blue eyes. 'Are you saying he's innocent?'

'Of course. There's not a shred of evidence to justify your pointing the finger at him.'

'The police don't agree.'

'They interviewed him again yesterday. After you'd been agitating. And they released him without charge.'

'My daughter has vanished,' said Doreen Capstick, her voice hard with anger. 'It's not in her nature. She's always been quiet, not a tearaway, like me in my younger days. There can only be one explanation.'

'Parents don't know everything about their children. There might be plenty of reasons why she wanted a break. For example, another man.'

A bitter laugh. 'I may not know everything, but you don't know anything about Alison. She simply wasn't like that. I took care bringing her up. She never messed around with boys as a kid. Jack Stirrup was one of the first men she ever went out with. That was why he managed to take her in. With a bit more experience she'd have recognised him for what he was. A self-centred, arrogant, male chauvinist pig. I warned her, but she wouldn't listen. And I was proved right. He never made her happy.'

Harry sighed. 'You simply can't say that.'

'I can and I do! I could tell she was miserable. Right from the start. I didn't pry. Alison was very self-contained, a very private person. And she was loyal to a fault, wouldn't say anything against the man. But a mother isn't easily fooled.'

'So what does writing to the girl achieve? From all accounts, she isn't your number one fan.'

'I'll be honest with you. I rang the police yesterday afternoon. They told me they hadn't arrested Stirrup. He's clever, all right. But he's got a temper – sooner or later it'll snap. To get at the truth I have to needle him, bring him out into the open. I knew that little slut would show him the letter and that he'd be angry enough to do something about it. So go ahead,

Harry. Issue a writ, see how much I care. I'd love all this to come out in court.'

She folded her arms and challenged him with her stare. Harry thought of Alison Stirrup, slight, pale and not in the least over-bearing. If she had nothing in common with her husband, her resemblance to her mother was only skin deep. They shared little more than blonde hair and blue eyes. Harry felt a sudden rush of sympathy for a woman to whom he had scarcely given a thought prior to her disappearance. She was one of life's outsiders.

'Maybe she was so unhappy she decided she had to get up and go without a word – not even to you.'

'Ridiculous! She's my daughter, remember. Besides, weeks have passed now. She would have got in touch. She wouldn't have let me worry myself sick like this.'

'I know you're worried. Don't blame you for that. Any mother would be. Surely you and Jack could get together? Talk things through. You might be able to find some common ground. He's just as distraught as you are, there's . . .'

'Talk things through?'

Doreen's scorn was histrionic. Out of the corner of his eye Harry could see Francesca and her cronies watching them with undisguised interest, wondering what was being said, barely giving a second glance to the handful of men in business suits who had drifted into the room during the last few minutes and were now standing around with puzzled faces, waiting for attention.

'How do you talk things through with the man who has murdered your only child?' Doreen hissed. 'No, it's impossible. Alison is dead, I've simply got to reconcile myself to that, terrible as it is. She wouldn't have left so suddenly, saying not a word to anyone, taking nothing with her. He's killed her and hidden the body, there's no other explanation. And I'm not going to rest until he's made to pay for his crime.'

Tears began to fill her eyes. Gulping for breath, she said, 'Now, if you'll excuse me, other guests are arriving. My solicitors are Windaybanks. Correspond with them if you feel so inclined.'

She stalked off, head held proudly in the air. Harry groaned inwardly. Her emotion might be actressy but her logic was hard to fault. Why should Alison have walked out on her marriage without even seeking to cash in on a divorce? It didn't make sense. Unlike the suggestion that she was dead. And if she was dead, was it suicide, accident or murder?

'Hello again.' It was Francesca, speaking huskily in his ear. He turned and noticed that she was a little unsteady on her feet. Perhaps that tray of wine had proved too tempting.

'Guess what?' she asked. 'My boyfriend isn't picking me up this evening after all.'

She gave Harry what was, he guessed, intended to be a meaningful look, but the effect was spoiled by the tipsy vagueness in her eyes and the way she slurred her words.

'Men are bastards,' he said. 'Ask your boss if you don't believe me. Anyway, I must be off now. Otherwise I'd offer you a lift home myself. Have a good evening, anyway. See you tomorrow.'

Before she could reply, he had left the room. Her clumsy overture had reminded him that he had forgotten to make arrangements to see Valerie. He hurried to the payphone in the lobby and dialled her number.

Nothing but the ringing tone. He hung on for five full minutes until the impatient coughing of an elderly man whose frown would have intimidated Churchill forced him to admit defeat. Where was Valerie? He told himself not to speculate. All he could hope was that, like himself, she would be spending the night alone.

Chapter Seven

'Julian Hamer?' At the other end of the telephone line, Stirrup spoke the barrister's name slowly. Measuring it, testing it for weight. 'Good, is he?'

'Recommended,' said Harry tightly. As the sun streamed in through the small window of his office, his mind was clouded by a sudden vision of a well-manicured white hand caressing a honey-coloured cheek. He'd not been able to smother his fear that Hamer had spent last night with Valerie.

'Fine. I'm bringing Claire along this afternoon. She can tell the barrister how the letter upset her.'

'No need for that, Jack.'

'Who's paying for this meeting, this – what d'you call it? – conference? She's coming and that's final. The experience will do her good. Give her an idea of life in the legal profession. She'd make a first-rate lawyer, Harry boy. God knows, she can be argumentative enough.'

'Sure you want to go through with this? Suing Doreen isn't going to get Alison back.'

'What else can I do? Specially now you've told me she's the one telling the police I've done away with her precious only daughter. Strikes me, everyone's so busy calling me a murderer, nobody's bothering to find where Alison's run off to.'

You didn't seem so bothered yourself, at first, Harry thought. Aloud, he said, 'Easier said than done.'

'I've been thinking. What if I hired someone to try and track her down?'

'You mean a private detective?'

'Right. The police are no use. They wouldn't be bloody bothered if Doreen hadn't made herself such a pain in the

51

arse. Now they're more interested in harassing me than finding Ali.'

'The Salvation Army sometimes . . .'

'No, I want my own man. Someone who only answers to me. Any ideas?'

'There's a feller I use sometimes. Ex-police. He's the one who found out Doreen was stirring it with the police. Miserable as sin, mind you.'

'I want a private eye, not a bloody court jester. Get him to call me.'

After putting the phone down, Harry considered Jack's initiative. Even now he seemed more concerned to get Bolus and Doreen off his back than to re-build his marriage. Hiring someone to trace Alison looked like the act of an innocent man. Or might it be a double bluff, a calculated gamble taken on the assumption that the detective would not chance upon the truth?

He had a case before the Dale Street bench that morning. A plea of guilty to handling a dodgy video recorder. Harry was in the corridor outside the courtrooms, half-listening to his client's implausible story about buying the VCR in a pub from a man whom he had never met before or since, when he spotted in the crowd a familiar head of tousled black hair, bobbing towards the exit.

'Back in a minute.'

Harry was lost in the crush of people before his receiver of stolen goods could reply. Battling his way through, he managed to stretch out an arm and tap his quarry on the shoulder.

Trevor Morgan turned and stared. His eyes seemed to take a minute to focus. Even in his prime, he'd been no Adonis. He had a rugby player's solid build and his years in the Aberavon front row had left him with a nose so mis-shapen it was a wonder he could breathe. He used to claim he'd broken it as often as the Seventh Commandment. But by any standards, this morning he was looking rough. On his left cheek a scratch was barely covered by a cheap sticking plaster that had traces of dirt around its edges. The whiff of stale beer on his breath was enough to make anyone take the pledge.

'Harry. All right?' The words were slurred. No stranger himself to hangovers, Harry realised he was in the presence of a classic of its kind.

'Okay. I won't ask if you are.'

'Thanks, pal.' Morgan pushed a hand through his hair, screwing up his eyes as if in pain. 'Jesus, I need sleep. Not this bloody farce.'

'What are you doing here?'

'Bit of trouble with the law. Disorderly conduct on Lime Street station last night, so they tell me. Argument with a porter. Can't remember the details, think I got into this drinking contest in The Legs of Man and simply wanted to sleep it off on one of his bloody platforms. Not much to ask, wouldn't you think?'

'Are you working yet?'

'That a joke? Who wants to employ a guy of forty-five who's been turfed on to the street without even a reference? I wouldn't be here now if not for Jack Stirrup.'

'You didn't give him any choice.'

Trevor Morgan's career as Operations Director for Stirrup Wines had been punctuated by episodes of sexual misconduct with members of staff. In better times his macho manner and Welshman's way with words had been a passport to endless affairs with women who worked in the branches. Stories were legion of off-licences throughout the North West displaying the CLOSED EARLY DUE TO STAFF SHORTAGES sign when Trevor and the manageress could be found in bed together in her flat upstairs. If only he'd been content with that, Stirrup would have kept turning a blind eye.

But easy affairs hadn't been enough. From time to time Trevor Morgan's fancy was taken by a new assistant or manageress who remained immune to his charms. Stories reached Stirrup that if cajolery failed, Trevor would threaten the lady with the consequences if she did not come across. Stock deficits might be discovered, disciplinary warning notices issued. The company lost three or four female members of staff suddenly and inexplicably. Before long Stirrup had been forced to admit to Harry that there was no smoke without fire.

Stirrup's solution was to take Trevor on one side and tell him to reserve his attentions for those who welcomed a fling with the boss's right hand man. For a time all was quiet until an incident in the stock room of a branch in West Wirral.

What actually happened, no one would ever know. A young assistant claimed that Trevor had tried to rape her. He said she'd welcomed his advances. The police were called, although in the end charges weren't pressed. The Equal Opportunities Commission started breathing fire and brimstone and the girl claimed a small fortune in compensation from the company. For once Stirrup accepted Harry's advice that discretion in the law was the better part of valour and settled out of court. The only outlet for his temper was to sack Trevor Morgan.

Morgan said now, 'He didn't have to take that little bitch's word rather than mine.'

'Christ, Trevor! Let's not go over old ground. After all, he was willing to pay you off.'

Realising how hard Morgan would find it to get another job, Harry had persuaded his client to offer six months' pay in a severance deal. But Trevor had prepared for his dismissal interview with the aid of a bottle of whisky and when Stirrup had told him of the loss of his job, he'd grabbed his boss by the tie. Within seconds they were wrestling. A couple of Stirrup's teeth had been loosened; Morgan finished up with a smashed cheek-bone. After that the opportunity for constructive industrial relations had been lost. The money hadn't been paid and as far as Harry knew the men had not been in contact since.

Trevor Morgan was about to respond fiercely, but something restrained him. He looked first at Harry, then at the floor.

After a moment he said, 'Wish I'd taken the money now.'

'Things must be difficult for you.'

'You're not wrong.'

'How's Cathy taken it?'

Morgan avoided Harry's gaze. 'You know what bloody women are like.'

Harry wasn't sure he did. More particularly, he didn't know what Cathy Morgan was like. He'd only met her once, at a dinner party thrown by the Stirrups before their move to Prospect House. Strong, steely-eyed and sarcastic, she delighted in cutting her husband down to size in front of others. Harry had assumed it was her revenge for numberless infidelities, a kind of marital quid pro quo.

54

'Want me to have a word with Jack?'

'No point.'

'Take a look in the mirror, Trevor. You can't carry on like this. You'll kill yourself.'

'No great loss, Harry.'

'For God's sake, you need to pull yourself together. Give Ossie Fowler a ring. He's a solicitor in the Albert Dock, if anyone can squeeze blood out of a stone, he can. Get him to write to Jack. I'd have to advise on the whys and wherefores, maybe some deal could be struck. It's what Jack really wants, as well as you. But once he's taken a decision, he'll not change it without a little pressure.'

Trevor Morgan rubbed his stubbly chin. 'I won't go to him cap in hand. I'll have to think about it. You . . .'

'Mr Devlin, you're wanted.'

The voice was low and insistent. Harry felt a bony hand grip his shoulder. He turned to look into the eyes of Ronald Sou, his court clerk.

'Your case is on. The bench is ready.'

'Okay, Ronald. Thanks.' Harry nodded at Morgan. 'Must go. Accept the advice, won't you? Free, gratis and for nothing – and I haven't even asked you to sign a legal aid form.'

He hurried into court and atoned for his lateness with a plea in mitigation (a sick wife and a brood of young kids, always handy) which probably shaved his larcenous client's fine in half. When it was over he dropped his briefcase back at the office before dodging through the traffic on the Strand on his way towards the river.

He felt a rare sense of self-satisfaction as he approached the front of the dock complex. Making his way from the Pump House to the waterfront, pint of beer in hand, was a stooped but sturdy figure. Even from a rear view, the cardigan was unmistakable.

'Wondered if I might find you here,' Harry said as he caught the man up.

Jonah Deegan didn't reveal any surprise at being thus accosted. He sipped his beer and looked at the ships moored at the quayside.

'Brought my cheque?'

'Not even received your bill yet. Teach you to rely on second class post.'

Jonah contrived a grumbling noise while sipping at his pint. 'I don't come here every day, you know.'

'Never said you did, Jonah. But I know how you like looking at the old ships.'

Jonah nodded and jerked a thumb towards a brigantine on the Canning Half Tide Dock. A horde of small boys was swarming over it, whooping with glee.

'Don't make 'em like that any more. Though it's a sad end. Proud vessel that sailed the seas. Become a bloody tourist attraction for kids who've never seen anything rougher than the Mersey from the side of a ferryboat.'

'Did you prefer this place when it was derelict for all those years?'

Jonah did not reply. After a while he said, 'So you fancy yourself as a detective, eh? Tracking me down here. What d'you want?'

Harry explained about the disappearance of Alison Stirrup. Jonah showed not a semblance of interest. Most of the time he kept his eyes on the ships.

'Not my usual kind of thing,' he said when Harry had run out of breath.

'Don't play hard to get. The money's good.'

'So you're not my client?'

'Very witty. Of course, you're acting for Stirrup. I'm just the messenger.'

Jonah drained his glass. 'Needed that. Get us another, will you? Have one yourself if you want.'

He made no offer to pay but Harry went to The Pump House anyway. When he returned with two full glasses, Jonah wandered over to the walkway leading to the riverside.

'Used to come here as a kid, you know. To watch the ships. More of 'em in those days, of course. I used to think they were all off to America. Reckoned the States were just the other side of the horizon.'

He took his beer without comment. 'Did he kill her, d'you think?'

'Stirrup?'

'Who else? Does he want to look like an anxious husband? Hiring me when the trail's gone cold?'

'What more can he do? You work on the assumption he's innocent till proved guilty.'

'Said like a true lawyer.' A lifetime's cynicism packed into five words.

'So you're turning the job down?'

'Never said that. I'll look for her.' The old man shrugged his shoulders. 'Besides, you said yourself, Stirrup is loaded. I don't mind taking a few quid off him.'

'Now who's talking like a lawyer?'

Chapter Eight

Harry arrived at Balliol Chambers on the stroke of four to find Stirrup and Claire already in the waiting room. His client sprang to his feet, breezy and confident, a typical litigant at square one, as yet unconcerned by the law's uncertainties and delays. The girl looked preoccupied and didn't respond to Harry's hello.

'All set, Harry? Ready when you are. The – what d'you call him? – clerk was here a minute ago. He said this Mr Hamer would like a word with you first.'

Julian's door was ajar. As Harry walked in, the barrister came from behind his desk to shake hands.

'Good to see you.' His smiled lacked humour. 'Especially as you seem to have a client with money to burn.'

'If only there were more of them.'

'Yes, yes. But this letter – really, he's a fool if he doesn't simply write it off to experience. You weren't born yesterday. You know that as well as I do.'

Hamer's testiness surprised Harry. Usually he was as urbane as a hereditary peer. Today shadows lurked under his eyes, as if he were short of sleep. What were you up to last night? Harry hoped he didn't know the answer.

'How will he take being advised to forget the whole thing?'

'Badly, Julian. He's after blood.'

'For Heaven's sake! He's more than likely killed his wife and got away with it. Does he want to bump off his mother-in-law too? And his daughter's here, I'm told. Really, Harry, you should have spared me the child.'

'Waste of time, I agree. But Jack insisted. He has ideas about her studying for the Bar.'

At least she's got the basic attribute, a touch of the prima donna, he might have added. But didn't.

'Very well. Wheel them in.'

As Harry made the introductions, he saw Stirrup absorb with approval the mahogany furnishings, the instructions to Counsel tied with pink ribbon which were piled high everywhere, the bookcases filled with calfskin-bound law reports and a complete set of *Halsbury's Statutes*. Claire confined her greeting to an adolescent mumble.

Denise, David Base's deputy clerk, came in bearing a tray of tea in a silver pot and dainty china cups. Stirrup beamed. Value for money, his expression said, civilised behaviour in the finest tradition of the English legal system. Julian rather spoiled the moment by letting his cup slip from his hand, spilling its contents on to the carpet. A moment of clumsiness out of keeping with his customary elegance of word and deed. But Denise mopped up and order was restored.

When at last Hamer spoke he had switched to his courtroom manner. Each syllable had a resonance that even Harry found compelling.

'I must congratulate you, Mr Stirrup.' A sentence of imprisonment might have been pronounced with less gravity.

'I don't follow.'

Hamer indicated the slim bundle of papers which Harry had sent round to him. His expression of judicial solemnity matched his tone. 'I have read the letter. In my view, it contains a plain libel. I take it for granted that in your daughter's eyes your reputation is excellent and this Mrs –' he cleared his throat before enunciating the name with as much distaste as an old maid might describe a crude bodily function – 'Capstick, has certainly done her best to tarnish it. Yet it takes a man of some courage to pursue an action of this kind in your – ah, present circumstances. A man, as well, with a deep pocket, for in the case of a libel published to a single party, your daughter here, your damages will be small and the cost great. Not merely cost in terms of legal fees, although those will be heavy – even, I should emphasise, if your claim ultimately succeeds. But there are other costs in litigation and . . .'

'What other costs?'

'Time is money where a businessman is concerned and this case will take up a good deal of your time. Moreover, in a matter such as this, where principle is at stake, I presume you will not be satisfied with a mere apology. You therefore have to expect that Mrs Capstick will be advised to throw as much mud as possible at you in the hope – a feeble one, I trust – that some will stick. Naturally that will be distressing and might harm your business. The police, who have according to my instructions already been involved in this matter, may be urged to press their enquiries further. You must be ready to face prolonged interrogation from them as a result. Many of your acquaintances and business colleagues may tell themselves that no smoke exists without fire. And then, there is your daughter to consider.'

Hamer paused. He spoke of Claire as if she were not present. Which in a sense, thought Harry, seeing her stare absently at the ceiling, was right.

'She may well be subject to cross-examination and the experience is likely to prove traumatic. I am delighted, therefore, that you asked her to accompany you today.'

Hypocrite, thought Harry.

'It is only right to warn you,' the barrister continued, 'that it may be several years before the action comes to trial, but it is best for her to be prepared from the outset for the ordeal that lies ahead.'

Little creases of anxiety had begun to criss-cross Stirrup's forehead. Claire was still miles away, plainly indifferent to the prospect of becoming embraced by the tentacles of the legal process. Harry suspected she was daydreaming about being in Peter Kuiper's arms instead. He settled more comfortably in his armchair. Julian was doing well, even if the picture he was painting of the legal process had a touch of the Salvador Dali about it.

'You – er – mentioned an apology.'

'Yes, Mr Stirrup. To seek a retraction is the usual first step in litigation of this kind.'

'A climb-down?'

'Yes, that is a fair description. In practice, few of these cases reach the courts. Usually, the factors which I have mentioned deter those involved from taking matters so far and the point at issue is settled in correspondence.'

'Well, shouldn't we be asking for the woman to apologise?'

Hamer appeared to give the question serious thought. 'It would be the orthodox initial move, certainly. But there would be scant likelihood of compensation being paid. We would ask for damages, of course, but you can expect the response to be negative.'

'I'm not in this for the money, you know.'

'Indeed, and as I have explained, you can expect to incur a financial loss as the outcome of a full trial.'

Stirrup glanced at Harry, who had already taken the precaution of arranging his features into the worried expression to which they were well suited.

'What d'you think?'

An inviting full toss, easily struck to the boundary.

'It would be wrong for me to encourage you into a law suit if you could find an easier solution.'

Stirrup hesitated. The working of his mind was almost visible.

'You know,' he said, 'it's all very well you legal fellers talking about litigation and rubbing your hands with glee over the fees. No offence, Mr Hamer, it's just that I don't like to beat about the bush. That bitch Doreen Capstick has gone too far and she deserves to be made to pay. But I'm not a vindictive man. And I certainly don't want Claire here to be hassled because of a bitter old hag's stupidity.'

While Harry tried to imagine how carefully preserved Doreen Capstick would take to being described as a bitter old hag, Stirrup folded his arms in a gesture of finality.

'I'd settle for an apology.'

Julian Hamer's nod was approving yet ambiguous. Harry didn't doubt that Stirrup would take it as acknowledgement of his magnanimity, rather than as a sign of Julian's own sense of satisfaction at achieving the lawyer's ideal – to put words into a client's mouth without making him aware of it.

'Very good, Mr Stirrup. If you wish, I shall be pleased to discuss with your solicitor the wording of a suitable letter.'

Hamer rose and extended his hand, his manner courteous yet unmistakably dismissive. He was evidently unwilling to prolong the conference a moment longer than was necessary. Quite right, thought Harry. In five minutes Stirrup might change his mind again.

As Stirrup moved towards the door, he said to Harry, 'You'll be in touch, then?'

'Sure. Talk to you soon. Goodbye, Claire.'

The girl muttered something unintelligible and followed her father out of the room. She avoided looking at anyone. As the door closed behind them, Stirrup could be heard chastising her for her lack of manners.

Harry winked at the barrister. 'Well done.'

Julian Hamer sighed. His voice returned to its natural, low pitch. 'Thank you. Forget about ninety-nine per cent perspiration, one per cent inspiration. I sometimes think the legal genius is all about understanding people, not rules in books. I did rather hope that our friend might be susceptible to a little ham acting.'

'Doreen won't rush to apologise. I met her last night. There's no doubt she's got it in for Jack.'

'Quite. Even so, a suitably worded letter will probably do the trick. Firm, but not too heavy. Allow both the combatants to feel that they have made their point, that's the secret. I'll draw something up this evening and have it delivered to your office tomorrow.'

'Fine.'

'As a matter of interest,' said Hamer, 'what's your own view of this whole sorry episode? Did Mr Stirrup murder his wife?'

'He's not been charged. The police have no evidence to link him with her disappearance.'

'Tactfully put,' said the barrister. 'So you think he's guilty?'

'Did I say that?'

'Well, let's agree that if he is a killer, he's either lucky or clever.'

'Makes a change for any client of mine to qualify for either description. Thanks again, Julian. I'll see myself out.'

He went back to David Base's desk. The clerk was sucking a peppermint as usual and pensively doodling hangmen on the back of a county court summons. Harry coughed to attract his attention, making him jump.

'Is Valerie about?'

'Oh – I think she's in her room. Is the con. over?'

'Yes, the client and his daughter left a couple of minutes ago.'

'So when are we off to the High Court?'

'Never, I hope.'

He wandered into Valerie's poky little room. It was knee deep in learned treatises on the law relating to boundary disputes. She was studying a plan of a housing estate, her brow furrowed.

'Sorry you couldn't make it last night.'

'Me too. Something came up at the last minute.'

He could not ask her straight out: Were you with Hamer? He wanted to get a better idea of how she thought about her colleague, but she would never give away in conversation anything more than she wished.

'Jack Stirrup and I have been seeing Julian.'

'Yes, David told me Stirrup's mother-in-law is accusing him of murder. Did it go well?'

'Fine. Julian's excellent in conference.'

Harry scanned her face for a reaction, but she simply nodded and said, 'Yes. He is.'

In the short silence that followed he caught her glancing at the papers on her desk. 'I won't keep you any longer. Would you . . .'

'Yes?'

'I just wondered if you were free . . . say on Saturday?'

He'd never been good at this sort of thing. Now was the time for her to say that she was involved with Julian Hamer and thanks all the same, but she really didn't think that . . .

To his surprise, she smiled.

Chapter Nine

'Long time no see.'

Brenda Rixton beamed as Harry walked down the corridor towards his flat. She lived next door and she was standing in front of the outside store cupboard, putting away her vacuum cleaner.

Harry said hi and rifled through his limited stock of neighbourly small talk for a follow-up remark. Something pleasant so she would not feel hurt, something bland so there was no risk that either of them would be embarrassed. Their affair hadn't lasted long, but he'd never felt comfortable about ending it and although she had accepted rejection without making a scene, the very decency of her behaviour added to his sense of guilt.

She saved him the trouble by saying amiably, 'Busy as ever, I suppose. Been into the office this morning?'

'At least the telephone doesn't keep ringing on a Saturday.' He gestured at the cupboard. 'Having a last tidy round? When do you move out?'

'Monday, God willing. Though how all the packing will get done in time, I simply don't know.'

'I hope Colin's going to give you a hand.'

She smiled. 'Yes, he's very good about things like that. Extremely methodical.'

Harry could believe it. Colin Redpath was a pleasant enough man but he had an accountant's fondness for order and his conversation was crammed with sentiments like 'A place for everything and everything in its place'. How would Brenda take to married life with someone like that?

Very well, he realised as he murmured some platitude in reply. She would be well looked after. No money worries, no creeping doubts. Protected by the safety blanket of a shared faith from the casual cruelties of the everyday world. A little boredom was a small price to pay. He ought to envy her. And perhaps, at times, he did.

'And the new house?'

'It's fine. Lots to be done naturally, but Colin's getting various tradesmen round in the next few weeks. And he'll be coming over for a couple of hours himself each evening. He's keen on do-it-yourself.'

Although Harry found the appeal of D-I-Y unfathomable, he could well believe that Colin would dutifully return each night to his own semi in Sefton until the wedding night gave him the right to enter Brenda's bedroom. Rather than pursue that line of conversation, he considered Brenda herself. The hairdresser's art concealed the grey in her blonde hair. For a woman who had celebrated her forty-fifth birthday only a few weeks before, she had kept her figure well. He knew her body to be soft and warm. Colin might be dull, but he was luckier than he yet realised.

'I'll miss you, Brenda.'

'I doubt it.'

Another smile. Gentle, but not easily deceived. She didn't speak with bitterness, but with realism. For the hundredth time he wondered why she had got involved with the Fellowship of Believers, an evangelical crowd who specialised in poster slogans saying things like SEVEN DAYS WITHOUT PRAYER MAKES ONE WEAK. Colin led a bible class in a meeting room above a burger bar in Sir Thomas Street; that was where she had met him. During the weeks when she and Harry had been sleeping together, she had never mentioned religion once. Not long after their low-key parting, however, he'd met her in the lift and she'd told him about becoming a born-again Christian. Something had been absent from her life and faith, she had found, could fill the void. Harry hadn't understood, but he saw that she was brighter than before, more confident. Having something – and, before long, some-one – to believe in had strengthened her.

He tried without success to imagine having the assurance of salvation. A few years ago he'd have mocked the smugness of a Colin Redpath. Still today he could not bring himself to envy it. It was escapism, like identifying with a story about James Bond. All the same, every now and then, he wondered what it would be like to share such a faith.

'I think a friend of yours is here.'

Glancing over his shoulder, Harry saw Valerie walking down the corridor. No dreary barrister's garb today, but a blue mini dress which displayed more brown skin than it concealed. With a slight sense of shame Harry realised that he wouldn't find it difficult to put Brenda out of his mind.

'Found you at last! Quite a warren, this place.'

'Brenda Rixton, this is Valerie Kaiwar. Valerie's a barrister.'

Harry watched the two women weigh each other up under cover of exchanging inanities about the hot weather and how long it would be before the heavens opened up. Harry was glad when Brenda said that she would have to tear herself away, as she was going to watch Colin umpire in a cricket match this afternoon. She made it sound like a treat rather than a chore.

'Your old flame?' asked Valerie when they were inside Harry's living room.

Harry had told her a little about his affair with Brenda. He'd wanted to build the trust between them. No secrets. And she'd mentioned a few young men she'd been involved with, at university and during the Bar finals course. Nothing serious by the sound of it. But she'd said not a word about Julian Hamer.

'Wasted on Colin,' said Harry. 'Though he's a decent enough feller.'

'Sometimes women have to take what they can get.'

'Men, too.'

She raised her eyebrows but instead of pursuing the point walked over to the window and gazed up the Mersey.

'You're lucky to have this place, Harry. So peaceful.'

'You should hear the gales howl down the river on dark February nights.'

'Sounds exciting.'

'Sounds bloody noisy. Anyway, never mind that. Did you enjoy seeing your parents?'

It wasn't an idle enquiry. She'd told him she would be staying overnight at the family home. Although he hated himself for doubting, he wanted to be reassured she'd been telling the truth.

'So-so. My father's got things on his mind. The business is ruling his life at the moment.'

'In a company like Saviour Money? Surely he's reached the stage where he can delegate.'

Harry never looked at the City pages in the Press; they might have been written in Sanskrit for all he knew or cared about stocks and shares. But everyone reckoned that the old Liverpool supermarket business which had been on the brink if insolvency when Bharat Kaiwar bought it was now one of the most profitable in the North.

'It's not an ordinary kind of problem.' She hesitated. 'Look. I'll tell you about it. But this is strictly between you and me. All right?'

'Sure.' His reply was matter of fact, but he couldn't help feeling flattered by her willingness to confide in him.

She picked up from a chair a battered green and white Penguin edition of *Tragedy At Law* which Harry had been reading the previous night. She flicked idly through the pages, as if reluctant to embark on her promised disclosure.

'Mystery stories appeal to you, don't they? But crime has changed since books like this were written. It's less ingenious, more frightening.'

'Cyril Hare might not have agreed. And he was a barrister too.'

'Really?' She scrutinised the book again for a moment then tossed it aside. 'Anyway, I was about to tell you. Daddy's worried sick. He's being blackmailed.'

'What?'

'Or rather, Saviour Money is. It comes to much the same thing.'

'I don't understand.'

'Someone is trying to hold the business to ransom. Threatening to poison products on the shelves unless they are paid a hundred thousand pounds.'

Harry whistled. 'Do the police know?'

'Yes, of course. Daddy didn't take kindly to the first threats. Made by phone to one of the stores, as you might

68

expect. Apparently it's not uncommon in the food and drink business these days. Cranks mostly. The police are informed routinely. Nine times out of ten, nothing more is ever heard.'

'And this time?'

'First the caller asked for a payment of twenty five thousand. No response was made. Then another warning call was received by the shop in Birkenhead. The manager was told to check the yoghurt. He soon found a couple of strawberry surprise pots had been tampered with. Lab tests were carried out. The yoghurt contained finely ground glass. Possibly not enough to kill, but anyone who ate it would have suffered serious injury.'

'The wrong kind of surprise.'

'Yes. Within twenty-four hours he'd rung again. The price had gone up fourfold, he said. That was yesterday morning.'

'Presumably your father has store detectives out in force in the shops?'

'Yes, but it's like searching for a twig in a forest. I gather the usual modus operandi in this sort of case is that the poisoner tampers at home with goods which he may have bought quite legitimately in the shop. Then he brings them back into the stores and puts them back on the shelves when no one is looking. Done well, it's almost impossible to spot.'

'Is your father going to pay?'

'I don't know. He wouldn't tell even me. I assume the plan will be to play along with the crooks and try to pick them up when they come to collect the money, but of course they'll be alert for that. They're bound to insist on hand-over arrangements which give them maximum safety. Daddy's in despair. He's caught between the devil and deep blue sea.'

She stared moodily out of the window. The picture Valerie had previously painted of her father was of a shy man who worked round the clock and shunned the limelight. He regarded the Saviour Money chain, she'd once said only half-jokingly, as his second child, the son he'd never had. Harry imagined that Kaiwar would feel any attempt to ruin the business he had spent twenty years building up almost as keenly as an attack on Valerie herself.

He went to stand by her side and put his arm on her shoulder.

'What would you like to do this afternoon? Something to take your mind off your father's woes would be a good idea.'

'What do you recommend?'

He was acutely aware of her perfume, a subtle and delicious fragrance, and of the closeness of her. This is an important moment, he thought. I mustn't blow it by being too eager. But nor must I miss the chance.

'Well . . .'

The telephone rang, shredding the silence like a knife through satin.

Shit, thought Harry. One of my regulars, got himself locked up after supping too much at lunchtime. Ignore it.

The phone kept ringing.

'Aren't you going to answer?'

'I wasn't intending to.'

'You should,' Valerie said. 'It might be something important.'

'A wrong number, depend upon it.'

But he found himself walking across the room and snatching up the receiver as if it were the hand of a naughty child.

'Yes?'

'Harry? I need to see you right away.'

Jack Stirrup's never-take-no-for-an-answer Brummie tone prompted Harry into mutiny.

'Sorry, Jack, it'll have to wait. If . . .'

'Listen, this is a matter of life and death.'

Something in Stirrup's inflection stopped Harry from putting down the phone.

'Tell me.'

'It's Claire. She's disappeared.'

Chapter Ten

'Call the police,' said Harry for the twentieth time. 'It's the only way.'

'What kind of advice is that?' Stirrup banged his fist on the pine table. 'So they can lock me up?'

Frustration enveloped Harry like a pre-war London fog. How easy it would be to lose sight of what mattered, when all that was clear was Stirrup's stubbornness. He fought an urge to take hold of the man and try to knock some sense into him. Brawling with a client was bad for business. And it would not bring Claire back home.

'Don't be paranoid. They're not going to lock you up because your daughter has disappeared.

'Paranoid, you say?' Stirrup laughed scornfully. 'You'd be bloody paranoid if you were in my shoes. Fat lot of help you are. My own bloody solicitor advising me to turn myself in. You'll really make it to Lord Chief Justice, you will, with a legal brain like that.'

They were in the kitchen at Prospect House. The room was smart and clean, elegant and lifeless as a picture in an ideal home magazine. The silence was broken only by the sullen burbling of the coffee machine in the corner.

'Jack, there's no question of your turning yourself in. Be realistic, you have no choice but to report Claire as missing. How long has she been gone now? Four hours? Five? Every minute you delay could make matters worse.'

'Worse?' Again the harsh laugh. 'And will they be better if I'm charged with killing her as well as bloody Alison?'

'Nobody's going to charge you. No way. Any fool could tell you'd never harm a hair on her head.'

71

'No more I would.'

Stirrup shut his eyes. He looked like a sick sleeping old man who had no wish to wake again. Harry wanted to sympathise, to assure him that everything would turn out right in the end. But it was a promise no-one could make.

After receiving his client's telephone message, Harry had driven straight over from Liverpool. To abandon Valerie as soon as she had arrived dismayed and embarrassed him. If only they had left the flat before the call came. At least she understood at once that he could not let his client down. His apologies she waved away with a philosophical smile.

'There'll be other times.'

The promise cheered him on the journey, but he forgot everything when he arrived at the house. Stirrup was pacing up and down outside the front door, kicking at the gravel. As he explained what had happened he wheezed as if on the verge of a coronary.

Claire had left the house at nine-thirty, saying that she was going down into West Kirby to change her library books. She often did that on a Saturday morning, according to her father, catching the bus which stopped on the main road, a short walk away, at twenty to ten. She had mentioned that she would make lunch for twelve because Peter Kuiper was coming round to see her later that afternoon and she had wanted to blow-dry her hair before he arrived.

Noon came and went and Stirrup began to worry. At half past, he got out the car and drove slowly down the road to West Kirby to see if he could spot her if she had decided to stroll back on foot. No sign at the library. People he spoke to couldn't recall having seen a girl matching her description.

Increasingly frantic, he tried one shop after another. Nothing. Walking the length of the promenade, he scanned every inch of yellow sand but saw no Claire. Convinced that he must have missed her in coming down the hill from Caldy, he raced back along the winding road to Prospect House. It remained as he had left it, locked and undisturbed. At that point, in desperation, he rang Harry.

'Any problems with her lately, Jack? Was she worried, depressed, sulky? Had you quarrelled?'

'Course not. All right, she acted a bit off colour Thursday afternoon and evening. Time of the month, for all I know. Or maybe she was mooning over that feller at – whatsit? – Balliol Chambers. Anyway, she went out to see some schoolfriend that evening and yesterday she was as right as rain. That young turd Kuiper came to see her, but he didn't stop more than a couple of hours. She and I watched the late night movie on the box. Then she kissed me as usual and went up to bed.'

'And this morning?'

'No different. She pulled my leg as I was reading the paper. You know, I still read the *Mirror*, though it's a Labour rag. Force of habit, my old man used to take it when I was a kid. Claire said when she came into money, she'd insist on having quality newspapers. Nothing but the best for her. And that was it. Next thing I knew, she was sauntering down the drive without a care in the world. Matter of fact . . .'

'Yes?'

Stirrup frowned. 'No, it's gone. Something odd struck me for a moment, but I've lost it.'

'Have you rung her friends? She may have bumped into one of them unexpectedly in the town. They could have wandered off together without giving their parents a second thought.'

'Claire wouldn't do that. She's an only child. I know it sounds corny, but there's a special bond between us.'

It did sound corny, but Harry merely said, 'Have you checked?'

'She hasn't many friends,' said Stirrup reluctantly. 'At least, not what I'd call real friends. But yes, I rang a couple of people. Karen Lawler's folks. Pam Macdougall's. They'd not seen her. All they said was – phone the police.'

'What about this meeting with Peter Kuiper? If . . .'

The roar of a motor-bike interrupted Harry, seizing the attention of both of them. It grew louder before suddenly cutting out. The two men exchanged a glance.

'That's him!' Stirrup jumped to his feet. 'By God, if he's done anything to her . . .'

'Jack.' Harry rose and laid a restraining hand on his client's arm. 'One step at a time. There's nothing to suggest the lad has any connection with Claire's disappearance. Before you inflict any grievous bodily, shouldn't we establish a few facts?'

'Let go of me.' Stirrup shrugged himself free. But he had become sulky rather than violent.

73

Harry followed him outside. Kuiper had stopped his bike next to the old stable block. The young man looked over his shoulder at them.

'You!' shouted Stirrup. 'Come here!'

Kuiper approached, wary as if confronting a rottweiler. He had forgotten to affect a swagger and his expression betrayed puzzlement at the older man's naked hostility.

'Yes?'

'I want to talk to you.'

'All right. Here I am.' Cocky again. 'Talk away.'

'Where is she?'

'What are you on about?'

'Don't give me that, smart-arse. Claire. My daughter. The girl whose boots you're not fit to lick.'

'I never thought of licking her *boots*.' With a scarcely suppressed snigger, Kuiper laid heavy emphasis on the final word.

'You dirty little shit!' Stirrup lunged forward with unexpected speed and yanked Kuiper's arm behind his back, forcing a yelp of startled protest mixed with pain.

'Jack! Leave him.'

Harry grasped his client by the shoulder and Stirrup let Kuiper go, though not without one last wrench of his captive's arm to send him spinning to the ground.

'Whose side are you on?'

'Be quiet, Jack.' Breathing hard, Harry stood astride the fallen youth. 'Now listen to me, Peter. Claire has been missing for hours. Jack is worried sick. Do you know where she is?'

Kuiper blinked. 'Missing?'

The lad sounded mystified. Harry's heart sank. Until that moment he had hoped that a childish elopement of some kind would explain Claire's sudden departure. If the boyfriend was equally in the dark, the puzzle became more sinister.

In his frustration, he yanked Kuiper back to his feet. Not gently.

'Why did you come here this afternoon?'

'To see Claire, of course. We'd fixed to meet. Look, what's going on?'

'You heard. She's nowhere to be found. Said she was going out to the library, but never came back.'

74

'Shit.' Dismay spread across Kuiper's face. If he was faking it, Harry thought, he deserved to tread the boards at the Playhouse.

Harry turned to Stirrup. 'He's telling the truth.'

Stirrup glowered. 'Is he? I don't know. Claire was never a moment's bother till he turned up.'

'She's not a child,' said Kuiper. 'Even if you'd like her to stay that way. She's a person in her own right. Intelligent. Ambitious. And far more . . .'

'Shut it, both of you,' said Harry. 'This is getting us nowhere. Time's ticking by and none of us has any idea where Claire may be. Jack, I don't mind what you say. I'm going to phone the police myself.'

Stirrup started towards him. 'I told you . . .'

'What matters most, Jack? Of course there'll be tough questioning. But you can take it, when Claire's safety may be at stake. Can't you?'

'She's all I care about. You know that.'

'Yes,' said Harry. 'Shall we go inside and make that call?'

The two of them walked towards the house. As they reached the kitchen door they heard the motor-bike engine flare into life again. Stirrup spun round and ran to where Kuiper had been. Long before he reached the stable block, however, the bike had gone and with it the young man. Stirrup shook his fist at the emptiness. An absurd gesture of defiance and yet, Harry thought, strangely moving. He felt a surge of pity for his client and went to join him.

'He was lying,' said Stirrup. 'He must have Claire tucked away somewhere.'

'Do you really believe that?'

Stirrup turned a ravaged face towards Harry. 'What else can I believe?'

Harry didn't answer. Kuiper had expected to find Claire here, of that he was certain. If not, why turn up? Screaming in on a motor-cycle was hardly furtive. His shock when told she had vanished had surely not been feigned. But why ride off again if he was as anxious as Stirrup for the girl to be found?

For a second time they crunched along the pathway to the house. Stirrup was silent, plainly turning ideas over in his mind. Eventually he spoke in a raw, cracked voice.

'Doesn't look good, does it? First Alison goes, now Claire. What will Inspector Bolus make of it, do you think? After all, I can't prove either of them left of their own free will.' He gestured towards the untended grounds. 'Where do you think they will start digging? Here or under the beech trees?'

As they reached the kitchen, Harry said, 'A fifteen-year-old girl is a different proposition from a woman twice that age.'

'Spit it out.' Stirrup took a deep breath and said, 'You must be thinking what I'm thinking. What if that bastard has got hold of her?'

'Peter didn't . . .'

'No. You know who I mean. If you're right and Kuiper really had nothing to do with it, there's only one explanation, isn't there?'

Harry stared at Stirrup.

'The Beast.'

'Christ, Jack. Let's not start thinking on those lines. Make your call.'

As Stirrup began to dial, however, Harry reflected that their secret fear was indeed the same. It was easy to take refuge in the knowledge that Claire's hair was dark and that the monster supposedly craved blondes. But can a monster always be relied upon for logic and consistency?

Suddenly Stirrup slammed down the receiver. He swore as if stung by a wasp.

'What is it, Jack?'

Stirrup pointed to the internal door. From a metal hook hung a gaudily coloured PVC cook's apron and a shopping bag in a Liberty print.

'I remember now. When Claire set off this morning, I thought there was something strange. She wasn't carrying her bag with the library books. And look, it's still there.'

He strode over to the bag and ripped it from the hook. Three hardbacks in protective covers spilled out onto the floor. Stirrup picked up one of the books, called *To Be The Best*, flipped it open and shoved it under Harry's nose.

'See the return date? Today. She lied to me. The little witch – she never meant to go to the library at all.'

Chapter Eleven

'Still no news about Claire?' asked Valerie.

Harry shook his head. 'Close on thirty-six hours now and none of us has any idea where she is.'

They were studying the dinner menu at the Ensenada. It was their first time together since Stirrup's anguished summons had interrupted their Saturday afternoon. Harry hoped a meal in his favourite Liverpool restaurant might make amends; he refused to think of its effect on his bank balance. At the door Pino Carrea, the amiable and loquacious proprietor, had greeted them as if favoured by a visit from royalty. Pino had kissed Valerie's hand and extolled the virtues of the Chateaubriand. But then an actress currently starring at the Everyman had arrived in the company of a gentleman other than her husband and, with a flurry of apologies, Pino had turned to welcome the newcomers and glean as much gossip as possible.

'What do the police think?'

'Bolus obviously reckons Jack's eliminating his family one by one.'

'And you?'

'No way he'd ever harm that girl.'

Claire had vanished into thin air. A search of her room at Prospect House had revealed no hint of the assignation from which she had failed to return. Assuming there had been an assignation. But why else would she deceive her father about the purpose of her visit to West Kirby? The police had rapidly obtained confirmation from a bus driver that he had picked Claire up at the nearby stop on Saturday morning. He remembered her getting off the bus on the edge of town.

Thereafter the trail petered out. No sightings either in West Kirby or elsewhere.

Harry had spent most of the day with Stirrup and the police. Not once had Bolus even raised his voice. But his questions had become scalpel-sharp.

'For your wife to go missing, that's unfortunate,' suggested the policeman late in the afternoon. 'But for your daughter to disappear as well . . .'

For Stirrup that had been the last straw. He'd leapt to his feet, the veins in his head bulging.

'You stupid bastard! While we're here wasting time, my daughter . . .'

Only the combined efforts of Harry and a burly constable restrained him. Bolus never flinched, assessing his suspect's demeanour with unruffled calm. After his outburst, Stirrup had sat down again, head in hands. Not weeping, but not far from it, Harry judged. And Bolus had been content not to push any further. At least for the time being.

All the obvious leads were being followed. Detectives were interviewing Claire's schoolfriends, her teachers and people she knew locally. As yet they had turned up nothing helpful. Bolus wanted urgently to see Peter Kuiper. The student was not to be found at his digs and no-one there could say where or with whom he might be.

'Is it possible,' suggested Valerie gently, 'that you may have been wrong about the boyfriend?'

'Okay, he may have something to hide – Claire's under-age, after all. Yet I'm equally sure he expected to find her at home.'

'What about Jack Stirrup? Perhaps Claire discovered he'd done away with Alison? She might have tried to blackmail him. There may have been a struggle. A violent blow. A more or less accidental death.'

'Nothing's impossible,' said Harry slowly.

'But?'

'Okay, there were occasional hesitancies. Contradictions. Useful for a prosecuting counsel, perhaps – but nothing to convince me Stirrup killed his own daughter. He loves the girl. Even if he did murder her in a moment of madness, he wouldn't be able to hide his guilt.'

'Then if he's innocent . . .' She broke off to demand: 'What are you looking at?'

'See over there,' whispered Harry. 'The feller who has just come in with the young blonde.'

'Don't tell me he caught your eye, rather than her.'

'Jealous? I can't believe it. Anyway, the answer is yes. You know who he is?'

'As a matter of fact, I do. Bryan Grealish and I go back some way.'

'Seriously?'

'Now who's jealous?'

Pino had entrusted the actress and her escort to a minion and was now lavishing hospitality on Grealish and the girl. Bearded, pot-bellied and barely five feet tall, the restaurateur resembled a pint-sized Pavarotti; Harry always half-expected him to burst suddenly into song. For once Pino seemed unconcerned that a male diner was tieless; perhaps he realised that by Grealish's standards of sartorial elegance, a plain open-necked shirt and grey slacks were much the same as formal dress.

The businessman took the welcome as his due, like a film star being flattered at an Oscar ceremony. Harry recalled the blonde from his visit to the Majestic; the low cut and brief length of her expensive white cocktail dress meant that she was almost as skimpily clad by night as by day.

'How do you come to know him? Is he a client?'

'No, I met him through Daddy. They've had business dealings for years. Bryan bought a lot of shares in Saviour Money and he was elected to the board a month or so ago.'

'Small world. I ran into him myself the other day. He also happens to be an old rival of Jack Stirrup. What do you make of him?'

'I can resist the bedroom eyes. He's one of those men who thinks he's committing a social gaffe if he doesn't put his hand on your bum. Though I'm a little old for his tastes, it's ages since I was sweet sixteen.'

Harry muttered, 'That's all we need. They're being shown over here.'

Pino was conducting the newcomers to an adjacent table. Harry saw Grealish recognise first him and then Valerie, and watched the man's eyebrows rise.

'We meet again. Evening, Mr Devlin. And Valerie, how are you?'

Grealish clasped her hand and lifted it to his lips whilst the blonde at his side gave Harry a surly nod.

'I'm fine, Bryan. I understand you know Harry?'

'Right. He and a client granted us the honour of their custom one lunch-time last week. Though I had no idea that the two of you were friends. I always understood that barristers and solicitors moved in separate social circles. Like gentry and tradesmen.'

'I'm willing to slum it once in a while. What about you – deserting the Majestic for the Ensenada?'

Grealish flashed his teeth in a wolf's grin as he and his girlfriend took their seats. Leaning over to continue the conversation he said, 'Need to check out the culinary competition on this side of the river every once in a while. And how is Jack Stirrup, Mr Devlin? Still short of a wife?'

'Not only a wife,' said Harry.

'Don't follow.'

'His daughter went missing yesterday.'

'You mean Claire?'

The question was so unexpected that it took Harry a couple of seconds to realise that it had been uttered by the blonde girl. He switched his gaze to her. Beneath the heavy layers of mascara, worry had cast a shadow.

He said, 'Sorry, I don't think we've been introduced.'

'My fault,' said Grealish, oozing lazy charm. 'Darling, meet Miss Valerie Kaiwar, barrister of this city. Her father and I do a little business together. And this is Harry Devlin, a local solicitor. Val, Harry, say hello to Stephanie Elwiss. A very good friend of mine.'

'You know Claire?' asked Harry.

The blonde fiddled with her napkin, a nervous gesture. Perhaps she regretted her intervention. 'Well, yeah, actually I do.'

'How's that, may I ask?'

She glanced at Grealish before replying. 'Through – through school, actually.'

'You used to go to the same school?'

Grealish threw back his head and roared with laughter. 'See, lover, you're able to fool even a man-about-town like Mr Devlin. Now do you believe you're grown up?'

To Harry, he said, 'Matter of fact, Steph's still supposed to be *at* school. Christ knows why. Life's got more to offer her than swotting for exams and wasting her time with a bunch of pimply students.'

When Harry thought about it, he could believe that she was no more than, say, sixteen. She looked sophisticated in the evening dress, but when she opened her mouth a child spoke.

'Are you a friend of Claire's?'

'I wouldn't say that, exactly.'

'What, then?'

'Well, we have friends in common. What's happened to her?'

'Wish I knew.'

Harry explained the previous day's events. No point in hushing them up now that the police were involved. Any chance that he might be able to pick up some clue to Claire's whereabouts was worth taking.

Stephanie's eyes widened. 'That's terrible.'

'Is the girl with her step-mum?' suggested Grealish.

Harry stared at him and only narrowly avoided saying, 'Now, why didn't I think of that?' On reflection, the answer was clear and twofold. First, he suspected that Alison was dead. Second, Claire and Alison were supposed to be on frosty terms. And yet the first premise might prove false and the second an exaggeration. Claire was, after all, much nearer to Alison in age than her father. Was it possible that the two of them might have more in common than people had realised?

'Unlikely, I think. But even if you're right, that still leaves the question – where is Alison?'

Grealish spread his arms. 'Don't ask me.'

Harry became aware of someone hovering above his elbow.

'Ready to order, sir?'

Harry dealt with the waiter and then turned back to the blonde girl. Out of the corner of his eye he saw Valerie shifting impatiently in her seat.

'Sorry, love,' he whispered. 'Won't be a minute.' To Stephanie he said, 'The police are sure to be in touch with you soon. Any idea where Claire might be?'

'None. None at all. You don't think . . .'

'What?'

'That she might have been murdered by – you know – The Beast?'

'For Chrissake,' said Grealish. 'What sort of conversation is this for a Sunday evening? The girl's done a runner, I expect. Lots of kids do. Who wouldn't with old Jack as a father? Don't worry yourself about this Beast, Steph. He hasn't murdered anyone yet. That's not how he gets his fun.'

Again his bared his teeth in a crafty grin. And for a moment Harry found himself comparing the face of Bryan Grealish to a vulpine mask, like something worn by The Beast himself.

Chapter Twelve

'Now will you accept he's a murderer?'

Not even a fuzzy telephone line could disguise Doreen Capstick's told-you-so triumph.

'Doreen, for God's sake! The man's daughter is missing.'

'Exactly. And why? I'll tell you. Because she's met the same terrible fate as Alison.'

Harry closed his eyes and reminded himself to be patient. 'So you're not letting us have the apology we asked for?'

'You must be joking! Your letter's in the wastepaper basket. Sue and be damned, that's what I say to your precious Mr Stirrup.'

'In that case, to borrow your slogan, au revoir.'

At the same time that Harry put down the receiver, Jim stuck his head round the door.

'Fancy a chicken salad at the Traders?'

After the Ensenada, club food had no more appeal than a school dinner, but Harry was glad to escape the phone. The morning's many interruptions had not helped him forget the unsatisfactory finale to the previous evening. He and Valerie had dined well and not been troubled by further conversation with Grealish. Harry's hopes had been high when he'd driven them to her flat in Crosby, but she hadn't invited him in. The turn-down had been gentle: she'd said she had a busy day ahead and wanted an early night, and he believed her. He didn't want to push his luck, so he had kissed her once then hurried away. But the sense of so-near-yet-so-far was impossible to shake off.

Waiting for Jim in reception, Harry felt a tap on his shoulder. He could somehow tell it was a gesture of reproach.

'On your way out? I've come specially to see you.'

Jonah Deegan's tone implied that he was the victim of a conspiracy. Harry uttered a silent prayer for strength.

'Any news?'

'Be reasonable. It's early days yet.' Jonah wrinkled his brow. 'And a difficult case. No two ways about it.'

'Heard about Claire?'

'Read about it in the paper. That's why I'm here. What happened?'

Jim came into reception. 'Hello, Jonah. Found the Maltese Falcon yet? Busy now, Harry?'

'I'll catch you up at the club. Mine's a pint of best.'

'Thought the chicken salad sounded too clean living to be true. See you around, Columbo.'

As the door closed behind the big man, Harry turned back to Jonah and gave him a brief account of the events of the past couple of days. 'So step-mother and step-daughter are both nowhere to be found,' he concluded. 'Coincidence? Hard to believe. But not impossible. Do you have any ideas?'

Deegan scratched his nose. 'I saw them both on Friday. Stirrup at his office, the girl at the house. Spoiled little madam, I thought. She didn't want to talk. But he seemed devoted enough. To her, not his old lady.'

'Could it be Stirrup murdered Alison – and Claire did a runner for some unconnected reason?'

'Possible.' Jonah contemplated the floor. His gloom was enough to wipe the smile off a Cheshire Cat. Perhaps he was remembering all the evil deeds he had encountered during his years with the police. Or perhaps his arthritis was troubling him. 'He might have disposed of them both and spirited away the corpses. But how the hell he'd do it, I don't know. The human body isn't easy to hide.'

'So what next?'

'I keep looking for Mrs Stirrup. I had a quick scout round her room at the house, it gave me one or two ideas. Long shots, mind. And I still need to talk to some friends of hers.

Stirrup's not paying me to search for the kid. The police can do that better anyway.'

'Do you think Alison's dead?'

'Maybe. Not suicide. Accident's possible. Amnesia too, come to that. But she might just have decided to pack in her old life and start again.'

'Abandoning her mother and her claim to a slice of Stirrup's worldly goods?'

'Hard to credit, I agree. Abandoning her mother's easier to understand, by all I've been told. Matter of fact, I'm seeing the Capstick woman this afternoon.'

'Good luck.'

'I'll need it, by the sound of things. I gather she's a tartar. Any road, don't let Stirrup confess to double murder till you've got some cash on account of my fees.'

'What happened to the poor but honest gumshoe, turning down the client's tainted money?'

'He didn't have Liverpool Corporation on his back, demanding a councillor's ransom in bloody poll tax.'

After Jonah had shambled out, the rumbling of his stomach reminded Harry that he was hungry. He sprinted over to the Traders', barely casting a glance at the bikini-clad girls sunning themselves in the Parish Church gardens. At the members' bar, the pint of best awaited him together with Jim, who was already in conversation.

His companion was a snappily dressed young man in dark glasses, who had put his portable phone on the counter as if he expected an urgent call at any moment. The Thatcher era might have drawn to a close, but Oswald Fowler remained a yuppie to his fingertips.

'Harry, mate,' he drawled. 'I've been meaning to give you a ring. You sent me a client. Trevor Morgan.'

'Don't tell me, you needed air freshener to kill the booze fumes after he'd gone.'

A smile flitted across Fowler's face.

'Your client's obviously driven mine to drink.'

'Between you and me, Jack may be willing to cough up a few quid if pushed. Without prejudice, of course.'

'I'd have to take instructions.' The tone was non-committal but Fowler could not quite hide the dollar signs in his eyes. A quick settlement was good for cash flow and he had long mastered the knack of matching the effective conduct of his clients' litigation with his own self-interest.

'Jack always wanted to see Trevor right financially. Until now, the problem's simply been one of pride. Neither of them wanted to make the first move. But Trevor needs the money.'

Fowler nodded. 'I had to take the case on legal aid.' He made it sound like a donation to charity. 'Morgan's life is in a mess. No job, no cash, no wife.'

'Has Cathy walked out on him now?'

'Earlier this year. His dismissal was the last straw, by the sound of things. The main danger is that any compensation he gets will be eaten up in alimony if and when she starts proceedings.'

Harry kept a discreet silence. If anyone could advise Trevor on how best to keep a windfall from Stirrup Wines out of any matrimonial negotiations, it was Ossie Fowler.

'He's at the end of his tether,' continued Fowler as he sipped the last of his G and T, his tone as indifferent as that of a Met. Office man forecasting typhoons in the tropics. 'Desperate. I did wonder if he might top himself. Though I imagine he's never sober enough to knot a noose to swing in. However, we aren't our clients' keepers. Thank God! Anyway, I must dash. Got to arrest a ship this afternoon.'

'Hope it gives up without a struggle.'

'You recommended Morgan to see Ossie?' asked Jim as they found themselves a table. 'Why exactly are we advising someone to sue our best client?'

'Trust me.'

'Last man I heard say that is serving three years in Walton for forging a security document.'

Over lunch Harry outlined the conversation he had had with Morgan in the magistrates' court. The big man gave every appearance of concentrating on his food and when the story was told, said simply, 'Soft bugger.'

'Me or Trevor?'

'Both of you. Him for messing up his life, you for getting involved. Anyway, mine not to reason why. Question is, will Jack Stirrup settle?'

'I can persuade him. Trevor hasn't much of a case, but it's worth paying a few bob to avoid all the hassle. Deep down it's what Jack wants to do.'

'Mind-reading now, are you? Take care. The thoughts of some of our clients would make Hannibal Lecter queasy. Anyway, how long will it take Trevor to drink the cash away?'

'That's his business. But if Cathy's left him he ought to be celebrating, not drowning his sorrows.'

'Never met her.'

'She used to give him a hard time, by all accounts. Jack couldn't stand her and I gather the feeling was mutual.'

'Some people might say that was a point in her favour. And she'll have had plenty to put up with.'

'Suppose you're right. Perhaps fighting with Trevor made her feel better about his infidelities.'

Jim grunted. An undemonstrative but uxorious man, he had little patience with marriages that did not work. He called the waitress over to order desserts which undid the good of a healthy main course and turned the conversation to the forthcoming Test Match.

When they arrived back in the office only a couple of minutes after the end of the official staff lunch hour Suzanne, cradling a telephone under her chin, waved to attract Harry's attention. Her lips were pursed in disapproval and she glanced unsubtly at the clock on the wall opposite the switchboard.

'There you are at last. Detective Inspector Bolus from Merseyside Police is holding for you.'

'I'll take it in my room.'

A call direct from the chief rather than a uniformed indian? Must be important. Harry broke into a run down the corridor. When he picked up the phone Bolus's voice sounded grim.

'Mr Devlin? I have some urgent news for you. Your client wants you here.'

'What's the problem?'

'It's about his daughter. She's been found.'

Harry almost fooled himself into a reaction of relief. But a moment's thought made him realise that good news would not be broken like this.

'Where?' he asked cautiously.

'In one of the caves at New Brighton.'

Bolus paused. Not for dramatic effect, Harry sensed, but from weariness. The weariness of a man, still young, who has seen too much violence, too much misery.

'We don't have the post mortem results yet. But there's no real doubt. She was raped first, then strangled.'

Chapter Thirteen

'Are you saying I killed my own daughter?'

Jack Stirrup sounded like a man in the midst of a combat course. Identifying Claire's corpse had been a physical as well as emotional ordeal. Anger burned in his eyes as he jabbed his forefinger at Bolus, who stood on the other side of the table in the small room at the back of the police station.

For a moment no one spoke. In one corner a fan whirred, seeming unnaturally loud in its vain effort to dispel the heat of the day. Dark patches of sweat were visible on Stirrup's once-white shirt, beginning to spread from underneath his arms down each side of his body.

With a slight movement of his shoulders to emphasise his disclaimer Bolus said, 'We have to check everything.'

Harry said, 'It's okay, Jack. Tell the man what he wants to know.'

Stirrup scowled. For an instant Harry thought his client was about to make a futile lunge at his inquisitor. But then he bit his lip and started to describe again the sequence of events on Saturday morning and afternoon.

Harry knew further enquiries would be made about the times when the bus driver had dropped Claire off and when, later, Stirrup had searched West Kirby for sight or sound of her. Bolus needed to calculate whether it was possible for the father to have picked up the daughter in town – she would trust no one more, after all – taken her to New Brighton on a pretext, and there violated and murdered her. Detectives could afford neither to overlook anything nor to have any illusions about a human being's capacity for evil.

All this Harry understood. Police routine did not make him fear for his client. Studying Stirrup, seeing the agony carved in the lines round his mouth and eyes, listening to him and hearing the harsh distress of every word he had uttered this afternoon, no-one could believe him guilty of this crime.

'Thank you,' said Bolus. He thought for a moment and rubbed his chin. 'I realise this is difficult for you, Mr Stirrup, but I'd be grateful if you'd tell me more about your daughter. What sort of girl she was.'

'What do you mean?'

'It may help me to find the man who did this if I can understand her. What made her tick.'

'I don't know what you're on about. Fucking hell, there's a killer out there!' Stirrup flailed an arm towards the narrow window at the rear of the room. 'Why aren't you out there too, hunting for him?'

'I appreciate your concern, Mr Stirrup. That goes without saying. And many of my officers are engaged on the enquiry at this very moment. No time has been lost since the boys who found your daughter called us. All the same, we need to learn as much as possible about her. The way she behaved. Her friends, her interests. Anything at all.'

Stirrup glanced at Harry, who nodded.

'All right, have it your way.'

Leaning forward in the cheap orange plastic chair, Stirrup began to talk.

Harry watched Bolus listening. The policeman was young for his rank. Well-spoken, no doubt a graduate on a fast track for promotion. More than likely better educated than either Harry or his client. Today, enmeshed in a murder enquiry, he looked older, no longer like a boy doing a man's work. Thin, with carefully combed hair and blue eyes glinting behind steel-rimmed spectacles, he had a habit of quirking his lips every now and then to indicate disbelief. How long before this joyless job soured him as it had soured Jonah Deegan years ago?

'Course I idolised her,' Stirrup was saying. 'She was my only kid. And after her mother died we became closer than ever. Had to. As a way to survive. All right, maybe I spoiled her. But I was out seven days a week, building the business up so she would never go short. There were girls I had in. Live-in au pairs, that sort of thing. None of them much good. Things weren't easy. I was glad when I met Ali. Thought it would give Claire a bit of home life. A bit of stability.'

'And did it?'

Belligerently, as if accused of child neglect, Stirrup said, 'She had a step-mother at last, didn't she? Another woman she could talk to. All right, the two of them weren't cut out of the same cloth. But Claire never lacked for anything, let me tell you. Any present she wanted she could have. Alison used to say I doted on her. Well, what if I did? She hadn't had it easy. She deserved the best.'

And expected it too, thought Harry.

'What about boyfriends?'

'There weren't any. Not until lover boy showed up. Kuiper.'

'How did they meet?'

'At a place in New Brighton. The Wreckers, I think.'

'That's no youth club, Mr Stirrup. Your daughter was only fifteen. Why did you let her go to such a dive?'

Guilt slid across Stirrup's face, making his cheeks glisten. He rubbed them with the flat of his hand.

'Didn't know, did I? She said she was going out ten-pin bowling with some of the girls from school. When she came in I gave her down the banks and she promised never to do it again. Too late. She'd met the bugger by then.'

'What else do you know about him?'

'Precious little, and even that's too much. He's a student, isn't he? A layabout.'

'Did you try to break it up?'

'I'm not that daft. No, I let her bring him to the house. Not in her room, mind. They'd go for walks round the grounds, that sort of thing. I hoped it was a phase. A crush. You know what teenage girls are like. Easily impressed.'

'Anything else you can tell us about him?'

'Look, do you think Kuiper – did this to her?'

'I'm not saying that, Mr Stirrup. But Peter Kuiper still hasn't returned to his digs. We don't know why. So we need to see him, if only to eliminate him from our enquiries.'

'By Christ, if he –'

Harry judged it was time to intervene. 'What about The Beast, Inspector?'

'What about him, Mr Devlin?'

'This is a sex killing of a teenage girl. You've a man on the loose who has been terrorising young women for months. Surely that's no coincidence.'

'I don't need you to teach me my job,' Bolus said. It was the first time he had been betrayed into even a hint of temper or impatience. 'And you can rest assured that we are already taking steps to – what's the phrase in that old film? – round up the usual suspects. Even so, we need to investigate whether there may have been a more personal link between the murderer and your client's daughter.'

'Are you bothered because Claire didn't have blonde hair?' Harry persisted. He wanted to provoke Bolus into showing more of his hand. 'Worried simply that this crime doesn't fit the nice little offender profile your people have built up?'

'No,' said the detective. 'We think Claire knew her killer.'

'What makes you say that?' demanded Stirrup.

Bolus took off his glasses and slowly polished them with a bit of cloth he had pulled from his pocket. Taking time to think. Weighing up, Harry felt sure, the relative tactical advantages of frankness and concealment.

'It's like this,' Bolus said eventually. 'You'll remember, Mr Stirrup, that when we took a look at your daughter's bedroom on Saturday we removed with your consent a number of personal items?'

'Odds and ends, that's all.'

'One of them was your daughter's personal organiser.'

Harry remembered. Expensive in black leather, with Claire's initials in gold on the front. A present from last Christmas, Stirrup had said.

'You're barking up the wrong tree, Bolus. There wasn't anything in the diary part for Saturday. I looked. She wasn't much of a one for writing up a diary.'

'Yes, Mr Stirrup. But a page of brief notes in the memo section caught our attention. A list of items. Things you might expect to appeal to a young girl. Like a bottle of perfume by Christian Dior. A gold ankle chain. All of them crossed out – except for the last.'

'I don't follow you,' said Stirrup.

'What was last on the list, Inspector?' Harry asked.

'A dozen red roses.'

Stirrup said, 'So bloody what?'

Bolus brushed an errant strand of hair from his eyes. Harry felt himself tensing, awaiting the revelation.

'When your daughter's body was found,' the detective said, 'scattered over it were a dozen red roses.'

Chapter Fourteen

'Imagine how the kids who found her must have felt,' said Jack Stirrup. He was gazing blindly out towards the Irish Sea and Harry guessed he was seeing Claire's face in his mind. 'Two young scallywags larking about. I bet their parents had something to say to them. Everyone knows those caves are dangerous.'

At last his control broke and his heavy body began to shake with the strain of suppressed emotion. Harry slipped an arm round his shoulder in mute support. He and Jack Stirrup would never be close friends, but Harry had not forgotten how it felt to have someone ripped out of his life by brutal murder.

'The bastard, the bastard, the bastard.' Stirrup spoke softly; he might have been uttering a prayer. Harry could sense the tension in the man as he made an effort to steady himself and took a lungful of air before speaking again.

'Whoever did that to her, I'll find him. You wait and see. I'll find him, no matter how long it takes. And when I do, I'll kill him.'

Harry moved his arm away. 'Leave it to the police.'

Even as he uttered the words, he had a clammy feeling of hypocrisy. After Liz's death, he had experienced the same primitive urge for revenge. Nor did he regard that urge as unhealthy. To react less fiercely to the murder of the person whom one loved most in the world would surely be unnatural. And in the end, he hadn't carried out his own threat. At least, not directly.

They were sitting on a bench overlooking the front at New Brighton. In different circumstances, it would be pleasant to be here instead of cooped up in the office at the end of another glorious afternoon. But this was one day when no sun could warm them.

Behind them, out of sight but at the forefront of their minds, bramble-covered cliffs marked the original line of the coast. At one time, waves had lapped where they were now sitting. A few hundred yards away, opposite the swimming pool, outcrops of brightly coloured sandstone stood out against the greenery. The Noses. Yes, Harry remembered, that was the silly name given to them. The Red Noses and the Yellow Noses. Caves ran beneath the rocks, caves where once, according to local legend, smugglers had hidden their contraband. In days gone by, wreckers had plied their trade here. Forget *Frenchman's Creek* and all that Cornish crap, Harry could remember once telling Liz, after a glance at some local history book had aroused his interest in New Brighton's discreditable past. This is where the action used to be.

And so it was again today. Stirrup had insisted on coming here, as soon as Bolus had finished with him. He wanted to see where his daughter had been found and, unable to dissuade him with anything short of physical restraint, Harry had agreed to drive him here. The police were still on the scene, combing it for forensic clues. They had succeeded where Harry had failed in preventing the bereaved father from entering the cave. At last, Stirrup yielded to the inevitable and agreed to leave the investigators to their work. Yet he refused to go far, and from their bench they could hear the sound of crackling walkie-talkies wafting through the air.

'Look at them,' Stirrup said after a short while. He jerked his thumb in the direction of the crowd of sightseers which had gathered by the edge of the cordon which the police had thrown round the caves. 'Carrion crows. Feeding off the dead.'

It was good that he had chosen anger, thought Harry. A positive response. The alternative would be to surrender to the senselessness of it all. Let him start to work the rage out of his system now, with violent, cathartic words. But not deeds.

'They'll be telling their mates about it in the pub tonight,' muttered Stirrup. 'Trying to picture it. The body in that cold hole in the rocks. My daughter. My bloody daughter.'

Two ten-year-old boys had found Claire. The caves were supposed to be sealed and inaccessible to the public, but the kids had found an entrance to an old passageway at the bottom of the garden of Hasbrook Heights, a small guest house standing under the shelter of the cliffs. They had found a gap in the perimeter fence which was, Bolus said, visible from a nearby path. Any local person might be aware of how to gain access to that particular cave. It even had a nickname in the neighbourhood. The Mouse's Hole.

And so the boys had trespassed through flower beds, broken into the cave through a trapdoor of rotting wood set in the lawn, squeezed down a narrow chimney-like shaft and discovered something that would haunt the rest of their lives. Propped against the sandstone wall, the earthly remains of Claire Stirrup.

'Suppose I should be glad those kids found her when they did,' said Stirrup after a long silence. 'At least the waiting's over. Soon as she disappeared, I knew it meant trouble. And I knew I hadn't killed her, despite what the police thought.'

'You were never a serious suspect.'

'Are you kidding? There's nothing those bleeding idiots wouldn't accuse me of. Look at the way they've hounded me over Ali.'

Harry said gently. 'It's time you told me the truth. What happened the last time you saw Alison?'

Stirrup chewed his lip, evidently thinking hard. Harry felt a spurt of excitement. The man was checking off pros and cons, asking himself whether to reveal whatever he had been hiding from everyone for the past few weeks. For a second, Harry realised that he had now put the question he had long disciplined himself not to ask. What if the answer compromised him? What if Stirrup finally unburdened himself and confessed to committing murder?

The dilemma was stillborn. Stirrup stood up, lifting his chin and rocking back on his heels before he spoke again.

'Nothing happened, I told you. We had a few words, about nothing in particular. The mess in the house, I think. The builders' lack of progress. That's all.'

'So you don't know why she left?'

Stirrup looked straight at him and shook his head. 'And I don't know where she is, either.'

97

Harry was first to break eye contact. He inclined his head and looked back towards the knot of sensation-seekers. A haze of despondency blurred his vision. Stirrup had opted to keep his own counsel. From their long acquaintance, Harry was sure of it. Like most battle-scarred businessmen, Stirrup could lie without shame. And instinctively Harry sensed that he was lying now.

'I want the full story, Jack.'

'I've told you the full story.'

'I don't think so.'

Stirrup reddened. 'Prove it. Lawyers always go on about proof, don't they? Well, prove that I'm not telling the truth.'

For a long time neither of them said anything. Harry contemplated the scorched grass beneath his feet: the drought had led to a hosepipe ban in Merseyside and lawns and parks were suffering because of it. Bare patches were showing through too in Harry's relationship with his client.

'Another thing,' he said. 'When Bolus asked if you know of anyone who bore you a grudge, why did you say no?'

'What are you getting at?'

'Come on, Jack. Let's not kid ourselves. You have enemies.'

'Like who?'

'Trevor Morgan, for one.'

'Trev? Do me a favour. He knew I had no choice but to give him the elbow.'

'And Grealish too.'

Stirrup snorted with contempt. 'He's nothing.'

'You aren't popular with either of them.'

'For fuck's sake, Harry, will you listen to yourself? Business is tough, or haven't you noticed? You get knocks all the time. Trevor Morgan and Bryan Grealish have nothing to do with – with what happened to Claire. Even Bolus could tell you that.'

'You didn't give him the chance, because you never mentioned them.'

'Listen.' Stirrup leaned towards Harry so that their foreheads almost touched. 'All I want is for that lad to be found. Nothing else matters. I don't want Bolus fishing after any more red bloody herrings. He's wasted enough time accusing me of doing away with Ali.'

'The lad? You mean Kuiper?'

'Who else?'

'What makes you so sure he killed Claire?'

Stirrup glanced briefly skywards. 'Come on, Harry boy. Use your nut. At first, when they told me the news, I was like you. I thought it might be the madman. The Beast. But the roses now . . .' He made a choking sound, perhaps picturing the scene in the dank cave almost below their feet. 'The roses, they must mean something.'

'What?'

'She knew the man who killed her, of course. It wasn't The fucking Beast after all. Not Morgan, or Grealish either. They might be pricks, but they wouldn't kill Claire just to settle a score with me. I don't believe it. So who's left? It must be Kuiper.'

'Or what about some other boyfriend, someone you know nothing about?'

'No chance. You saw the way she behaved when that lad was around. She idolised him, she . . .'

Again he was on the verge of tears. After bowing his head for a moment while composing himself, he lifted it again and looked Harry straight in the eye.

'She must have had a purpose,' he said, 'going out to catch that bus into West Kirby without her library books.'

'Unless she simply forgot them. It has been known for kids to forget things.'

'I don't believe it,' Stirrup said doggedly. 'She'd fixed to meet Kuiper and he'd promised to bring her some roses. He brought her here on his bike. They had a row. I can guess what about, can't you? The randy little shit. And – well, you know the rest.'

Harry said nothing. The idea was plausible, he had to admit. And yet, if Stirrup was right, why had the student returned to Prospect House on the Saturday afternoon?

'All I want is five minutes with him,' Stirrup said. 'Five minutes, that's all I ask. I'll get the truth, even if it kills me.'

Chapter Fifteen

'He says it's a matter of life and death.' Suzanne yawned as she spoke. Crusoe and Devlin's clientèle had an infinite capacity for exaggeration. The switchboard girl never disguised her resentment of callers who interrupted her enjoyment of sex-and-shopping fiction with their petty worries about moving house or breaking parole.

Earlier in the afternoon Harry had instructed her to divert all calls to Francesca while he tried to make inroads on the work which he had abandoned the previous day after receiving Bolus's summons. Yet, like a gambler unable to resist one last bet, he reminded himself of the one-in-a-hundred chance that the caller's crisis might be genuine.

'Who is it?'

'Name of Peter Kuiper. He's ringing from a phone box.'

During the twenty four hours since the discovery of Claire Stirrup's body Harry had kept asking himself where the student was hiding. And why. Now his mouth went dry. A long-locked door might at last be about to open. What would it reveal?

'Put him through . . . Peter?'

'Mr Devlin, I need to talk to you urgently.'

The student's voice was barely recognisable. Gone were the sneer and the hint of swaggering smart-alec remarks to come. What remained was the sound of a young man, frightened and vulnerable.

'Where are you, Peter?'

'Never mind that.' Vulnerable, but nonetheless wary. 'I want your advice. Can you help me?'

'Is it about Claire?'

'It's true, isn't it? She's dead, murdered. I read the story in the paper last night. I couldn't believe it. Went out and got myself pissed to take my mind off things. She was so – so . . . Shit! I don't know how to tell you what's going through my mind.'

'Calm down, Peter. Take it slowly. One thing at a time. Why do you need me?'

'I might be in trouble with the police. It hasn't happened yet. May not happen at all.'

'Connected with Claire?'

'In a way.'

Was he worrying about an under-age sex charge? When that had been an unspoken possibility, he had seemed supremely unconcerned. Now his girlfriend had been killed and so had the chance of any prosecution. So what was he afraid of?

'Tell me.'

'We – no, you don't need to know that. Besides, you still haven't answered your question. Will you act for me?'

'I must know more before I can give you a straight answer, Peter. Surely you realise that? Advising you could put me in a conflict of loyalties – between you and Jack Stirrup.'

'I don't know any other solicitors,' said Kuiper. 'That's a laugh, isn't it, for someone studying law? True, though. Besides, you know the background. And I think I can trust you not to tell anyone where I am or what I've been doing. There's a place I go to in New Brighton. Will you meet me there tonight?'

'Let's get one thing clear before we go any further. Unless you're completely up front with me, there's nothing I can do for you.'

To Harry's anguish, the pips started to go.

'I haven't any more money. Your girl took an age to put me through.'

'Give me a number where I can phone you back. Come on, Peter, there isn't much time.'

'No. I must think it over. I see that now. You're Stirrup's lawyer after all, you're in his pocket.'

The line died before Harry could utter another word. He slammed the receiver down and let out a loud groan of despair. Francesca, passing by, poked her head round the door.

'You all right? I've got some Alka-Seltzer if that's any use.'

'No, thanks. Honestly.'

'Suit yourself.' She assumed a martyred expression and disappeared in the direction of the loo, banging the door behind her with the finality of one who has mistyped her last letter of the day.

When she was out of earshot Harry swore quietly, aware that he was no wiser than before Kuiper's call. He stared disconsolately at the pile of unfinished paperwork languishing in front of him. The heat had drained him of energy and the evening ahead promised nothing.

Valerie was out of town on a trial and when Harry had phoned Balliol Chambers, David Base said he thought the case would run on until tomorrow afternoon.

'Can I take a message?'

Unreasonably, Harry found the clerk's willingness to please grating and he had snapped, 'No message,' before banging the phone down.

His small office felt like the inside of an oven, yet if he opened the window traffic noise and roadworks make coherent thought impossible. Time for a positive decision. He would abandon the job for the rest of the day and go and get drunk instead.

On his way to The Dock Brief, he picked up an evening paper. BEAST LINK IN SCHOOLGIRL MURDER? demanded a headline. He leaned against a makeshift timber wall surrounding a redevelopment site and scanned the story.

From the front page a photograph of Claire looked out at him. A head and shoulders portrait of her in school uniform. Her expression matched the Mona Lisa's for complacency. As if she were pandering to an adult's whim in having her picture taken. She'd been at least as arrogant as her boyfriend, Harry reflected. He wasn't sentimental about speaking ill of the dead. Yet nothing she might have done justified the squeezing away of her life, the consigning of her body to that dark dismal cavern-tomb.

The journalist, Ken Cafferty, had improved bare facts with a skilful blend of innuendo and speculation. The old identikit picture of The Beast appeared next to the story. A non-descript face, stripped of all individuality. What had Bernard Gladwin said? *Might be you. Might even be me.* The picture had been composed, Harry suspected, ninety per cent from guesswork and ten per cent from the fleeting impression of a victim who might have felt she had some sense of the features beneath the animal mask.

Only on a close, lawyer's re-reading of the story could Harry tell that the police were not officially connecting Claire's death with the earlier attacks of The Beast. They were simply declining to rule The Beast out as a possible culprit. Cafferty made no mention of The Beast's supposed predilection for blondes: it didn't fit with the story. Nor did the red roses, of which he must be unaware. Bolus had made it clear to both Harry and Stirrup that no-one else should be told about the strange garland which the killer had left on the girl's corpse.

What did the roses signify? Nothing Harry knew about Claire suggested that anyone had a rational motive for murdering her. No grudge against her father, however bitterly held, could explain the savagery of her death. If Kuiper was innocent of the crime, as Harry still believed, the only credible alternative theory was that she had fallen prey to a maniac.

But there remained the question of the library books. Why had she lied about them?

He tucked the paper under his arm and strode to The Dock Brief. The pub was crowded but the hum of conversation disturbed him less than the knowledge that he was impotent to make good Jack Stirrup's loss. Midway through his fourth pint, his reasoning was fuzzier than before and his dismay at Claire's death had still not been submerged by the booze. As he gazed into the cloudy depths of the drink, he felt a hand grasp his arm.

'We meet again.'

Trevor Morgan. Glancing over his shoulder, Harry found Morgan's second-hand grin and unfocussed eyes as depressing as the beer fumes which enveloped him like poison gas.

'Pull up a stool.' At least Trevor was probably too far gone to spot the lack of enthusiasm in his words. 'How are you doing?'

'Never better, Harry. Never better. A pint glass in my hand and no one to hassle me. What more could any man ask, tell me that?'

'Sorry to hear about Catherine.'

In his present state, Morgan was unlikely to recall that at their last meeting he had pretended his wife was still living with him. Having a word now might minimise future embarrassment if they met again. Nothing unusual in a spouse's desertion these days. But the one left behind still often felt a sense of shame and of failure as well as the pain of isolation. Harry knew that from personal experience.

'What? Ah!' Morgan's free hand made a lavish easy-come, easy-go gesture. 'Women. You're better off without them. Don't you think so, boy?'

Harry thought about Liz, about Brenda, about Valerie.

'Maybe.'

'No maybes about it.' Morgan poked Harry in the ribs with his forefinger. 'They're bad news. Only good for one thing, if you ask me, and most of 'em aren't so bloody keen on that. A feller can only put up with so much. Some things he shouldn't have to take.'

'Yeah, yeah.' Morgan's voice was beginning to rise and Harry wanted to pacify him, not debate the numberless shortcomings of the other sex.

'Anyway, let's not talk about the bitches. Agreed?'

'Agreed.'

''Nother pint? I owe you one after you sent me to that feller Fowler. Good man, that. Good man.'

The prospect of a night-long drinking session with Trevor Morgan was sobering Harry fast. He checked his watch, then pushed his glass to one side.

'No more, thanks. I'll have to be on my way now. But let me buy you one before I go.'

Morgan's face darkened. Mention of Fowler had led his rambling thoughts down a new track. 'No way. You'd be paying with that bastard Stirrup's money. I know you're in hock to him up to your eyeballs.'

'He's only a client, Trevor.'

'Only a bastard.' Morgan stared moodily at his glass. 'Ought to be taught a lesson.'

There was no arguing with him. Harry prepared to mutter an apology and make his getaway.

'A lesson,' repeated Morgan stubbornly. 'Bloody murderer. I say, bloody murderer.'

His voice was rising again. Harry saw that, even in The Dock Brief's early evening hubbub, one or two people were turning round. Not in a spirit of censure. The regulars enjoyed watching a good fight every now and then.

'Cut it out, Trevor.'

He laid a restraining hand on Morgan's upper arm. With a bellow of rage the Welshman threw it off.

'Let go of me! You're no better than he is. The bloody murderer!'

'Take it easy. You don't know what you're saying.'

'Oh, don't I? And who do you think you are to tell me that, Mister Smart-Arse Solicitor? Who do you think you are? Sucking up to that bloody murderer. All right. This is what I think of you!'

Harry saw the swing of the arm holding the empty glass at the last possible moment. He ducked instinctively and the wild flailing movement swept over the top of his head. Someone screamed as the glass caught a man passing by on the side of the head. The man staggered and yelled at the same time. Harry lost his balance and felt, rather than saw, an answering blow shave his chin as one of the victim's friends aimed wildly at Trevor.

Within seconds the place was in pandemonium. Women were screeching, men were shouting, glass was breaking. Harry rolled over and saw Trevor hit the ground with a skull-cracking thud. His assailant, a young man in a leather jacket, was on him at once, firing indiscriminate punches to head and chest before a shirt-sleeved barman managed to pull him off. The man whom Trevor had hit was sitting in a pool of beer and debris, rubbing his temple and blinking back tears of pain. Trevor lay still. He certainly wasn't dead, but it would be a while before he rhapsodised again on the joys of single life. Blood oozed from a diagonal cut on the side of his forehead.

'Get the police,' someone said.

'And an ambulance, by the looks of things.'

Harry rubbed his eyes. The decent thing to do was to hang on, to see that the incident was explained to the police's satisfaction and that Trevor was shipped off to Casualty with minimum delay. But Harry's capacity for doing the decent thing was finite and he had been involved with enough police questioning for one day.

Time to go. In the confusion no one seemed to notice him clamber to his feet and totter towards the door. Outside the evening was still bright and warm. People wandered up and down the street, oblivious of the shenanigans inside the pub. He sucked in a lungful of the warm evening air before heading back to Empire Dock.

And as he walked, Trevor Morgan's drunken words kept reverberating in his mind.

Bloody murderer. Bloody murderer.

Chapter Sixteen

All the way home, Harry strove to dismiss Morgan's words as the babbling of an alcoholic who couldn't tell fact from fantasy. Whether Morgan was making a stupid, drunken accusation that Jack Stirrup had killed his own daughter or simply guessing that Jack had done away with Alison, it was inconceivable that he had evidence to back up either claim.

Yet as he took a TV dinner out of the microwave, Harry recalled Stirrup's evasiveness during their conversation the previous afternoon at New Brighton and all his old anxieties about his client surfaced again. Chewing a pizza, he sifted in his mind through the debris of Stirrup's life, hoping in vain to turn up something that would put an end to doubt.

Could Kuiper help? Whilst he ate, Harry wondered about the young man's telephone call. Possibly Claire had told her boyfriend something about either her father or her stepmother that would help to solve the mystery.

He glanced at his watch. Half-eight. Kuiper had suggested a rendevous in New Brighton. According to Stirrup, Claire had first met her boyfriend at the Wreckers, a pub-disco on a promontory overlooking the Mersey. Might he be there tonight?

A long shot, but tonight Harry felt that any shot was better than none. Pushing aside his half-finished pizza, he decided he would go to the Wreckers and see if he could find the young man. At least so doing would give him an illusion of doing something positive, not only on his client's behalf, but also to identify the murderer of that spoilt fifteen-year-old girl. Unlikeable she may have been, but she had not deserved to die.

109

The drive through the Queensway Tunnel was swift. Up above, unseen and unheard, the river flowed, dividing Liverpool and Wirral. Harry let his mind roam again around the events of the past few days, trying to find a pattern to them. Trouble was, he couldn't be sure there even was a pattern. Perhaps he was wrong in trying to make all the hints and allegations add up when all the time they might be random elements, like bits of a brain-teaser in a magazine spattered with printers' errors.

The Wreckers, a concrete and glass excrescence which might have been named after the architects responsible for its design, made the average amusement arcade look like St George's Hall. Outside the main door a group of leather-jacketed youths congregated, laughing and swearing. Every time a girl walked past them on her way into that place they treated her to a serenade of whistles and cat-calls. The girls pretended not to notice but the giggling remarks they exchanged with each other suggested this was all part of a ritual they would be lost without.

A dozen motor-bikes were parked round the corner. Harry did not know either the registration number or make of Kuiper's bike, but he spotted one which looked familiar and which had a thin layer of mud smeared over its number plate. He decided to take a look inside.

Stepping into the Wreckers, he felt like a maiden aunt blundering into a wife-swapping party. The room heaved with bodies pressed close together. No-one looked over twenty. Rap music droned from overhead speakers. If this was the pub, Harry wondered, why bother with the disco? He pushed past cuddling couples half his age and finally made it to the bar.

Drawing breath, he glanced round. Almost immediately he caught sight of his quarry. Kuiper was standing with his back to the bar, talking to a small fair-haired girl in a red and white striped tee-shirt. He was wearing his James Dean face and seemed to have his listener spellbound. Harry inched forward to get a better view of her and saw the smooth features of a girl no older than Claire. Kuiper obviously liked them young.

With difficulty and many apologies, Harry moved through the scrum of lads at the bar until he was close enough to touch

Peter Kuiper. The student had slipped his hand inside the back of the girl's tee-shirt and didn't appear to be meeting any resistance. It hadn't taken him long to get over the loss of one girlfriend and find another, Harry thought.

'Peter,' he shouted. 'I made it after all.'

Alarm brought a strange light to the young man's eyes as he turned round. His cheeks were flushed; the lager he was drinking was not his first of the night. He glanced over Harry's shoulder, as if he expected a posse of policemen to be fetching up the rear.

'What do you want?'

'To talk. You want that too. Well, here I am.'

Kuiper jammed his eyelids shut, as if to help him think. Then he made up his mind. He bent down to the girl and spoke into her ear. Dismay drained the colour from her face. He patted her head as if she were a pet spaniel and nodded at Harry.

'Okay. Let's talk.'

'Not here,' Harry bellowed. 'Outside. Where we can hear ourselves think.'

'I don't want to be conspicuous. The filth are looking for me.'

'Come on.'

Harry seized the collar of the student's jacket and frog-marched him to the door. Once they were standing outside and Harry had released his grip, Kuiper ostentatiously dusted himself down. The exertion seemed to have sobered him.

'That's a common assault, you ought to know that.'

'Peter, don't provoke me any more. You rang me this afternoon wanting my advice. The first piece of it is – stop acting like a child. This isn't a game. Claire's dead. If you didn't kill her, you're behaving like a fool. As well as distracting the police from tracking down the real murderer.'

'What makes you so sure I didn't strangle her?' Impossible for Kuiper to keep a sneer off his lips for more than a few minutes at a time.

'Did you?'

The intensity of Harry's tone and expression seemed to register. Kuiper shifted from one foot to the other.

'No. Believe me, I'd never have harmed her.'

111

'For what it's worth, I do believe you. Thousands wouldn't. Certainly not Jack Stirrup. He's baying for your hide.'

'The stupid old sod.'

'His daughter's dead – he wants a scapegoat. So grow up, and answer a few questions. Where have you been since Saturday afternoon?'

'Here and there. Out in the open, mostly. No problem in this weather. Last night I was out of my head after hearing about Claire on the tranny. Slept it off on Moreton shore.'

'Why do a flit?'

'I didn't want to get involved with the filth. Simple as that.'

'Why not?'

'I just didn't, okay? Anyway, it's not for you to cross-examine me. You could do with minding your own business.'

'Peter,' said Harry softly, 'that's not possible. What you do is my business, so far as it affects my client. Jack Stirrup's daughter has been raped and strangled, don't forget that.'

'Am I likely to? She was my girlfriend.'

Harry pointed to the door of The Wreckers. 'In there you weren't exactly wearing sackcloth and ashes.'

'What do you want, blood?'

'Unfortunate choice of phrase in the circumstances.'

'Yeah, well. Anyway, old man Stirrup's got nothing to feel holier than thou about. He didn't understand Claire, couldn't give her what she wanted most. Couldn't even keep his old lady happy, come to that, could he? Never mind a fifteen-year-old kid who thought there was more to life than doing up a musty old dump of a house that should have been condemned long ago.'

'So what did Claire want most?'

The sneer returned. 'You wouldn't understand either.'

'Try me.'

'Okay.' The student gave a triumphant look. 'She wanted to take risks. She wanted to be rich. And most of all she wanted to make an impact.'

'She wasn't exactly destitute,' said Harry. 'And what sort of impact did she have in mind?'

'To capture people's attention,' he said slowly. 'To dare to be different. It's easy to be one more face in the crowd. We wanted to make people sit up and think.'

'And how did you plan to do that?'

Kuiper shrugged. Harry had spent most of his professional and married lives being lied to; he recognised the gesture as a prelude to evasion.

'She's managed it now, hasn't she? She's a household name. The girl The Beast murdered.'

'How do you know she was killed by The Beast?'

'I read the papers.'

'Don't give me that. How do you know?'

'I don't.' Kuiper looked at the ground. 'Honestly. But what other explanation can there be?'

'Were you with her last Friday night?'

'No. She was seeing another girl she knew from school, I think. I don't know who.'

'When were you last in touch with her?'

'That evening. She rang me at my flat, around half-five. She used to do that, before her father got home. He was mean about the phone bill.'

'What did she say?'

'She'd met some old prat her father had hired to find her step-mother. Claire reckoned he was so decrepit he'd be lucky to find his way back to Liverpool. That didn't bother her, she was glad to see the back of Alison.'

'And her manner?'

Kuiper considered. 'Fine. Giggly, even. Said something about giving me a surprise when I came round on Saturday afternoon. She was a bit of a pain, to be honest. Teasing. Said she liked to dangle men on a string, make them do as she wished.'

'Men? Did she have any other boyfriends?'

Kuiper was cocksure. 'No way. I promise you that. She just liked to pretend she was irresistible.'

'Anything else?'

'That's all I can tell you.'

'I don't believe you.'

Kuiper stared at him insolently. His bravado was returning.

'Really? Well, to be frank, Mr Devlin, I don't give a fuck. Now if you don't mind I'll be on my way.'

He had chosen his moment well. As he turned away, a group of young men emerged from The Wreckers, shouting

113

drunkenly. A pair of massive bouncers looked out from the doorway, following the gang's progress. Harry hesitated, realising that if he tried to detain Kuiper, the odds were on a free-for-all as the prospect of a fight attracted young men with fire as well as booze in their bellies.

Kuiper sat astride the saddle of his bike. He had donned helmet and gauntlets and as Harry began to move towards him he gave an ironic wave of the hand before revving loudly and disappearing into the night.

Where was he going? Only one way to find out. Harry broke into a run, heading for his car. One of the gang members jeered after him, yelling some unintelligible obscenity, before the emergence from The Wreckers of two girls in mini skirts diverted the yob's attention. Harry took no notice. Within seconds he had reversed out of the car park and was racing down the road in pursuit of the vanished motor-bike.

Dusk was beginning to fall. Away from the Wreckers, the New Brighton streets were quiet. Harry had no idea of Kuiper's destination and when turns and junctions came up, he chose his route as randomly as if competing in a fairground game. For once in his life he won the lucky dip: on taking the long, straight road out of the town he caught sight of a dark figure on a speeding motor-bike perhaps two hundred yards ahead. Peter Kuiper.

The gathering gloom gave the drive down Leasowe Road an eerie quality. To the left were houses, roads and street-lights, all the signs of suburban life. To the right was empti-ness: market gardens, golf links and common land stretching towards the sand dunes by the shore of the Irish Sea. Harry kept his distance from the motor-cyclist, following him past the lights and turrets of the old Mockbeggar Hall, curving inland with the road away from the ruin of Leasowe's land-locked lighthouse.

At the roundabout Kuiper took the road to the west of the peninsula. His course was unwavering; it was plain that he had a specific destination in mind. Afraid to lose his quarry, Harry closed in on him a little. They passed fields, shops, houses. Moreton, Meols, Hoylake. And, as he climbed the bridge over the railway which had its terminus at West Kirby, Harry realised where they were going.

Kuiper was returning to Prospect House. As soon as the thought occurred to him, Harry became unshakably convinced that he knew where the journey would end. There was something about the house on the hill which lured the boy, even though he would never see Claire there again. That was why he had turned up on Saturday afternoon. His claim that he had come to see her had sounded like an excuse, although at the time it had seemed the only explanation for his arrival. What had he wanted, what did he intend to do now? Surely a bruising encounter with Jack Stirrup was even less attractive than an evening in the company of the Merseyside Police?

First the motor-bike, then the M.G. went by the library which Claire had been supposed to visit on her last day alive. Could there be an unsuspected connection between Kuiper and his girlfriend's father? Or was that idea absurd?

Harry dropped back. There was no sign that Kuiper knew he had been pursued thus far; to blow the chase now would be folly. The motor-bike sped ahead and out of sight. Taking his time as he climbed the hill that led to Prospect House, Harry concentrated on finding a discreet place in which to park.

Fifty yards from Stirrup's driveway, a path led off the road into a small copse. Harry crawled past and saw the motor-bike. It had been dragged off the main road, but with no special effort at concealment. By now it was dark. Harry thought he saw a figure disappearing into the drive. He pulled over on to the grassy verge, locked the car and hurried in pursuit.

At the gateway to Stirrup's house he hesitated. That was a mistake. Everything was still and silent. No lights shone at any of the windows. The undergrowth of the garden remained thick and forbidding. The place was like a cemetery. What dead secrets might it be hiding? Suddenly Harry felt as cold as if he had stepped under a shower of icy water. He was on his own and didn't know what he was about to encounter.

For a moment he contemplated retreat. No shame in it. He could contact the police from the town. Leave to them the investigation of whatever was happening in this isolated spot. That would be the cautious, lawyerly thing to do.

Ahead of him something moved. Harry crouched under the spreading branches of an oak. He could sense, rather than see, that someone was making his way stealthily towards the house. It must be Kuiper. Harry inched forward, peering through the night in a vain attempt to sight the student.

Every twig cracking beneath his tread sounded to him like the 1812 Overture. Yet it was better to skirt the drive than risk crunching over the gravel: Kuiper would certainly hear that and choose flight – or, perhaps, violent confrontation. Harry had never considered himself brave. And he did not know if the student had a weapon.

At the bend in the drive, he looked through the trees and at last saw Kuiper's outline distinctly. The young man was picking his way round the side of the house. The care with which he was moving suggested that he too was absorbed in keeping as quiet as possible: there was no hint that he was conscious of Harry's presence.

Emboldened, Harry crept after him. The dark silhouette of the stable block loomed up in front of them both. A dozen yards away from it, Kuiper stooped down. He remained bent over something for half a minute. Finally, Harry realised that he was struggling to shift something heavy without making any noise. In a moment of empathy, Harry understood that Peter Kuiper's tension matched his own.

A low grunt reached Harry's ears across the night air with remarkable clarity. A grunt partly of satisfaction, mostly of relief. Kuiper straightened for a second or two before bending down again. This time he disappeared from view.

Harry waited for a minute to see what would happen next. Nothing. He approached the place where Kuiper had been. It was on the edge of the clearing in which the stable block stood. Harry remembered the scene in daylight from his previous visit. Even in the dark, he knew at once that something was very different.

A large rock which had looked immovable had been pushed aside. Below there was an opening into blackness. Scarcely daring to breathe, Harry drew nearer. He looked down. So far as he could make out, there were a few rough-hewn steps which led to some subterranean chamber.

Kuiper was beginning to climb back up the steps. He was carrying something in his arms. As his head was just about to reach ground level, Harry coughed. There was a clatter as the student dropped whatever he had been carrying. A white face turned up to look at him.

'Devlin?'

'Evening, Peter. Do you come here often?'

In the moonlight he could see panic spreading over the student's face and that was answer enough. For a few seconds Kuiper hesitated. The tip of his tongue appeared between lips no longer sneeringly curved. Harry heard the drawing-in of breath before the student lowered his head, and he was ready for the bull-like upward charge.

Blundering up the stone steps, eyes on the ground rather than on his intended victim, Kuiper never had a chance of catching Harry off-balance, of butting him in the chest and knocking him to the floor. With all the time in the world Harry took a step to one side, then brought both hands down together in a single blow. Kuiper staggered backwards down the steps, hitting his head against the back wall of the passage. As he fell awkwardly to the floor, Harry heard a loud crack as bone splintered.

Harry reached into the hole in the ground and, putting his hands under the boy's arms, began to yank him back to the surface. Kuiper moaned in protest as Harry dragged the rest of his inert body back up to ground level.

'That hurts.'

'Pity'.

Harry shoved the boy to one side and peered down the hole. In the light cast by the moon he could see the oddments which Kuiper had dropped lying on the ground at the bottom. Items so everyday that the effect was surreal. A tin of baked beans. A small tub of biscuits. A boil-in-the-bag packet meal. Rations for a hermit? For a wild moment he thought he had uncovered a hiding place where Alison Stirrup might at last be found. Had she been the victim of some bizarre kidnap plot, imprisoned beneath the grounds of her own matrimonial home? Even as his mind played with the possibility, he caught sight of the retailer's labels on the bits and pieces which Kuiper had let fall. They all bore the name and logo of the Saviour Money supermarket chain. At last the truth dawned.

Peter Kuiper had led him to a poisoner's den.

Chapter Seventeen

One glance at Kuiper convinced Harry that the student would not be leaving in a hurry. The boy's face was buried in the dirt. He was making a strange noise, the muffled weeping of pain and rage and defeat.

Panting after his exertion, Harry trudged towards the main building. He did not relish explaining to Jack Stirrup that his daughter's boyfriend had used the grounds of Prospect House as an operational base in an attempt to hold Bharat Kaiwar's business empire to ransom. Nor would words of persuasion alone convince Jack that the lad had not also killed Claire. If not checked, Stirrup's interrogative techniques would leave Peter Kuiper yearning for a little genteel police brutality. As Harry pressed the doorbell, he steeled himself for his third physical confrontation of the evening and wondered why Liverpool Poly's careers adviser hadn't warned him that success in the law was marked by the award of a Lonsdale Belt.

No lights snapped on in response to his ring. After a minute he tried a second time. Again no answer.

Harry walked round the side of the building. No sign of life. Just the flickering red light of a burglar alarm box high up on the side wall. No window or door had been left conveniently open to allow him access to a telephone in the deserted house. Harry swore. Feeling hungry as well as tired, he was beginning to regret his failure to finish the microwaved pizza. To get the police here fast and leave them to sort everything out was all he wanted right now.

He picked up a half-brick left by the builders and hurled it through the kitchen window. The lack of finesse would have appalled the least sophisticated of his criminal clients, but he was past caring. He pushed in what was left of the shattered pane and opened the window. No casement lock: Stirrup should have consulted his neighbourhood crime prevention officer rather than frittering money on electronic gimmickry. An alarm siren started wailing, but there was no-one to hear it except the crippled young man who lay prostrate fifty yards away. It was the work of a moment for Harry to heave himself up and inside. He found the phone and dialled a number he knew by heart; it belonged to Quentin Pike.

'Got a client for you,' he said and described in half a dozen sentences what had happened.

'Good God! Blackmail, you say? And you're not able to act?'

'Conflict of interests. The kid doesn't know you exist yet. But he'll need a good brief.'

'Incidentally, what's that bloody awful racket in the background?'

'The sound of a wasted investment.' Harry had already been in the house longer than it would take a seasoned burglar to strip everything of value. So much for home security.

He rang off and after trial and error in opening cupboard doors, discovered the control box inside a walk-in pantry and switched the siren off. It seemed easier than it ought to be. He put on an outside light, then rang 999 to summon the police and medical help. Next he found a couple of tumblers and filled them from a bottle of brandy he found in the dining room. He took them outside to where Kuiper was now lying on his back.

The boy's face was a white blot on the blackness of the night, looking up at the starless sky. His tears had dried and he had tucked his bad leg awkwardly to one side.

'Get this down you.' Harry bent and held the glass to Kuiper's lips.

The young man slurped a little as he drank. 'My ankle's broken, you bastard,' he said indistinctly.

'Think yourself lucky. If Jack Stirrup had been home, you'd be a candidate for intensive care. As it is, the police and the medics can argue over who's going to have the privilege of looking after you tonight. They'll be here any minute.'

120

Kuiper closed his eyes. His expression was stripped of hatred, fear and anger. All that remained was exhaustion and a grimace of pain.

'So, it's all over.'

'For you and Claire, in different ways. Whose idea was it to blackmail Saviour Money?'

'Mine, of course.' The old cockiness had not quite drained away. With a flash of understanding Harry guessed that the boy wanted to explain what he had done. Now Claire was dead, he needed to look elsewhere for an audience.

'Tell me.'

'Claire was talking one day about the catering course she wanted to do. She rabbited on about hygiene in the kitchen. Food poisoning, all that stuff. About the junk people eat and how you never know if what you're eating is full of bugs. I said something about those scare stories you read in papers, about people threatening to poison food shops if they're not bought off. It set me thinking.'

Kuiper shifted his position on the ground, flinching with the effort. 'Shit! That hurts.'

'Carry on.'

'Poisoning fascinates me. It's a subtle crime. Guns and blunt instruments are for mindless thugs. Murderers who use poison think their crimes out in advance. They're usually intelligent.'

'You think so?'

'Yes. Yes, I do.' The whites of Kuiper's eyes gleamed in the darkness. 'And even the fools carried it off with more style than your average gangland hood. You've heard of Major Armstrong?'

'How could I forget? The only solicitor ever hanged for murder.'

'Right. I often think about him, handing out his arsenic-laden scones for tea. So prissy. So English. He learned the law in Liverpool, you know.'

'Somehow that doesn't surprise me.'

Kuiper contrived a hoarse chuckle. 'Don't say you wouldn't like to get rid of one or two of your professional rivals the same way. Or what about Armstrong's other victim, his wife?'

Harry said, 'My wife was murdered. Stabbed to death in the street. Eighteen months ago.'

There was a long silence. Then, in a tone humbler than Harry had ever heard from him, Kuiper said, 'No answer to that, is there? Sorry.'

'Okay. But you see the point, don't you? Crime's not fun, it's squalid and belongs in the sewer. Like your silly prank with the supermarket.'

'I only tampered with a handful of things. And I gave them fair warning.'

'So that makes it all right? Anyway, why pick on Saviour Money?'

Kuiper made a faint movement with the upper half of his body, a painful attempt at a shrug. 'Why not? But there was a reason, actually. Bryan Grealish was on their board.'

'So?'

'It was Claire's idea to go for him. Grealish was at odds with her father, she said. I never knew the details. Some business dispute . . . you'll know better than me. Stirrup hated the guy, so Claire did too. She was still a daddy's girl at heart. More than he deserved, the fat old prat. So she wanted to teach Grealish a lesson.'

Something occurred to Harry. 'And the Majestic? The glass in the greens the other week? Another of your little japes?'

'You've got it.' Hurt Kuiper might be, but he couldn't keep a faint note of satisfaction out of his voice. 'Our first attempt at – contamination.'

Harry stared hard at the boy. Even in the dark he didn't like the look that had stolen over Kuiper's face. It was an ageless look, an end-justifies-the-means look, a look a Nazi scientist might have worn when discussing his ideas for improving the human race.

'Call it a trial run. We didn't ask for money, never contacted Grealish once. We simply wanted to prove we could bring it off, that's all. That was the spur. Once we'd done the Majestic, we knew we could try something bigger. And make real money.'

'Claire didn't need cash. The only daughter of a rich man.'

'You don't get it, do you? What's the point of inherited wealth? There's no challenge. We both agreed on that. The ransom was to make people sit up and take notice. They might not know who we were. But we'd have them dancing to our tune.'

Harry indicated the hole in the ground. 'Who decided to run the campaign from here?'

'She showed me the place. She'd noticed there was something here one day when she was mooching round, but she hadn't the strength to lug that boulder to one side. I opened it up. Nobody had gone down there for years, that was obvious. It's an old ice-house, I think, left in ruins and overgrown. The perfect spot to keep the cans and stuff. Tell you what though, when I heard the police had come sniffing round looking for Stirrup's bloody wife, I pissed myself. Needn't have. Good old PC Plod, can't see the nose in front of his face.'

'And Jack never knew the ice-house existed?'

'No way. Though it's plenty big enough down there. Room for two. Till the ransom thing took over, we had another use for it.'

'She was only fifteen.'

'Yeah.' Another throaty chuckle. 'But all woman.'

'All you could cope with, isn't that nearer the mark?'

'Jealous? She wasn't a . . . shit, they're here!'

The wailing of the police sirens pierced the night air. Two cars came screaming along the drive, pulling up close to where Harry and Peter Kuiper were waiting. Harry got to his feet.

'I forgot to tell you – you'll need a good lawyer. I've called a man called Pike. He'll be looking for you at the police station. He's all right. His advice will be simple: say nothing. Okay?'

He walked towards the detectives, not interested in any words of thanks. None of the wary faces of the men who had climbed out of the cars were familiar to him. In charge was a tall inspector, sandy-haired and supercilious.

'Mr. Devlin? The name's Swarbrook. Detective Inspector. I understand you think you may have apprehended someone who has been demanding money with menaces from a local business?'

With such a talent for circumlocution Swarbrook ought to be a lawyer, Harry thought. But he simply said, 'He's over there.'

'I see. We'll need a full statement from you, of course. The necessary . . .'

The noise of another car engine interrupted him. Someone else was coming up the drive, headlights tracing a path through the trees. It wasn't a panda car this time. Brakes squealed as the driver found his path blocked by the police cars parked near the front of the house. A door banged. Harry peered through the gloom and saw two figures getting out of a Jaguar. Jack Stirrup had come home.

'What the bloody hell is going on here?'

Harry moved to meet his client, a couple of paces ahead of DI Swarbrook.

'Jack, it's me. Been having fun and games in your absence. It's . . .'

But his voice trailed away as he looked beyond the red face of his client to the person who had been a passenger in the Jaguar. A lithe, long-legged woman with a mass of frizzy brown hair. The nervous way she was biting her lip contrasted oddly with the confident provocation of her tight black dress. Harry didn't know who she was. One thing he did know: this wasn't Alison Stirrup. Nor, by the look of her, someone Jack had invited back simply for a quiet evening's game of snooker.

Chapter Eighteen

'Why did Peter do it?' asked Valerie.

They were together on the sofa in her Crosby flat. A candle's unsteady light cast strange shadows across the room. After a Mexican meal washed down with plenty of wine, Harry's mood was mellow. He hoped for once in his life he might end the night feeling more like Warren Beatty than Woody Allen.

He found it hard to believe that only twenty four hours had passed since the bizarre events at Prospect House. The discovery of Kuiper's cache of contaminated foodstuffs and of the other woman whose existence Jack Stirrup had kept so quiet. Explanations seemed to Harry to have lasted half the night before Swarbrook was willing to let him crawl home to bed. And even then, much had been left unexplained.

How much better it was to be here with Valerie. She was curled up beside him, her pale green frock revealing much more than it concealed, her Giorgio fragrance deepening the intoxication of the moment. All evening they had talked of things other than Peter Kuiper's arrest and Jack Stirrup's embarrassment. The conversation had ranged from sixties music and *Entertaining Mr Sloane* to Jim Thompson's books and Chandler's screenplay for *Double Indemnity*, while sixties love songs played in the background. Now Harry was relaxed and ready to tell her about the previous evening, for the only taboo tonight was talk of going home.

'He had at least a hundred thousand reasons. You can do a lot with the kind of ransom he was after. All the same, I don't believe the money was everything to Peter.'

'What else, then? The lure of living dangerously?'

'If you like. He wanted to put himself beyond the law. Above it. Remember *Rope*?'

She nodded. Her love of Hitchcock movies exceeded even his. He slipped an arm round her bare shoulder.

'Or its true life equivalent, the Leopold and Loeb case? Peter reminds me a little of what's his name, Nathan Leopold. The clever student who felt superior to the outside world and turned to crime to prove it.'

'Nietzsche has a lot to answer for.'

'Doesn't he play in goal for Bayern Munich? Anyway, Peter had the perfect help-mate in Claire Stirrup. A young girl, intelligent enough but naive, adoring and eager to share in whatever scheme her boyfriend-who-could-do-no-wrong might dream up. An experiment in blackmail which promised a small fortune as well as the thrill of teenage rebellion was simply too much to resist.'

Valerie moved her face close to his. '*Folie à deux*. Where two people share the same delusion.'

'Folly is right,' he said.

He looked into her eyes, trying to read what was in her mind. His fingers traced an invisible pattern on the smooth skin of her shoulder. He had never possessed the gift granted to so many other men of being able to slip at will into slickly seductive chat whenever a woman gave the slightest encouragement. The sexy lines refused to spring to his lips.

She shifted her position, sitting more upright. He left his hand where it was, just resting on her, not venturing further. The memory came to him of back-row fumblings in the Odeon years of his youth. Mistakes he would not repeat again.

'Have you spoken to Quentin Pike today?' she asked.

'Called him this afternoon. Swarbrook's given Peter a hard time. Serve the young bugger right. Anyway, the top and bottom of it is that no-one can pin Claire's killing on him. He's adamant he didn't see her on Friday and no-one can prove otherwise. He reckons she seemed excited on the phone, but he put that down to his news that Saviour Money had agreed to cough up the ransom demand.'

'Daddy tells me that Friday was when he finally bowed to the blackmail threat.'

'So I gather. I don't know how they communicated with Peter. He kept phoning from different call boxes, I suppose. Your father probably told you, the company put a downpayment in a building society account which the lad had opened in a false name.'

Harry refilled their glasses. 'Peter's idea was to make random withdrawals from hole-in-the-wall cash dispensers. The police couldn't mount a round-the-clock surveillance of every single one. Or so he assumed. Anyway, he made the first three withdrawals on Saturday. First in Freshfield, then St Helens, finally at Ellesmere Port. Quite a distance apart, even for a biker who sees a speed limit as a challenge to his virility.'

'So he didn't have an opportunity to meet Claire on Saturday morning?'

'On the basis of the timings, Quentin's sure Peter couldn't have abducted her before he turned up at Prospect House. And after Jack and I told him his girlfriend had vanished, he says he panicked. Dumped the cash in a night safe then skulked out of sight hoping to hear from Claire. Convincing the police is another matter, but there isn't a shred of forensic to link him to the murder.'

Valerie placed a honey-coloured hand on his and began to stroke.

'He must have been petrified that if detectives started sniffing round they'd uncover the blackmail plan. Even if they found Claire alive and well but simply put her under pressure with their questions.'

'It's the criminal's nightmare,' said Harry, content to keep the conversation going, at least for the moment. 'To become caught up in someone else's crime.'

'So the plot thickens. If Claire intended to meet someone on Saturday morning, and that someone wasn't Peter Kuiper, who was too busy collecting his ill-gotten gains -- what was she up to?'

'No idea. Of course the library books may be a red herring. Suppose she simply forgot them? Realised what she'd done and decided to walk back home. It was a sunny day, she may

127

have fancied the exercise. Suppose she caught the eye of The Beast . . .'

'You think that's what happened?'

'No-one's come up with a better idea yet. Of course Jack's still howling for Peter Kuiper to be charged with her death.'

'And when he pauses for breath, how does he explain bringing a new lady friend home the night after his daughter was murdered?'

'Not so new, I suspect. Jack and I had a long conversation this morning. Plenty of bluster, as you might expect. The woman's name is Rita Buxton and she manages his branch at Heswall. Divorced, mid-thirties. According to Jack, she's been a comfort since Alison disappeared.'

'Oh, yeah?' said Valerie satirically.

'Trouble is, my memory's better than Jack gives me credit for. Rita Buxton's name came up at the time Trevor Morgan was sacked. He had a brief fling with her a couple of years ago, as I recall. Sounds like a lady who believes in keeping the management satisfied, never mind the customers.'

'So Stirrup has known for some time she was available?'

'Cynic. But yes, you're right. He's adamant they haven't been sleeping together, before or after Alison disappeared. I'd find it as easy to believe Trevor Morgan had gone teetotal. Jack says he needed to be with someone after he learned about Claire. Fair enough, but . . .'

'Not the behaviour of a worried husband?'

'Exactly. So much has happened lately, it's easy to forget Alison is still missing. You can bet Doreen Capstick will be telling Bolus I-told-you-so as soon as she gets to hear that Jack really does have a bit on the side.'

'Together with a motive for losing his wife?'

'Two and two occasionally make four,' Harry admitted. 'I pressed him again today. Jack insists he doesn't know what has happened to Alison.'

'And you accept that?'

'What choice do I have? I'm sure he's not telling me the whole truth, but there's still no evidence to suggest he's done Alison any harm. Maybe she found out about Rita and did a runner. Jack may be as baffled as the rest of us.'

Valerie's nails glided along the back of his hand. His whole body began to tingle with anticipation.

'I don't like much of what I've heard about your client, but I can't help sympathising with him. For Peter Kuiper to use his house as HQ for major crime as well as seducing his daughter was adding insult to injury. And on top of that, the girl's been savagely killed.'

'Claire's death still hasn't sunk in properly yet. Perhaps it never will. Peter may have been right when he said she was devoted to him, but Jack couldn't have loved her any more. If he never finds out for sure that Peter was screwing the girl, so much the better.'

'So you think it's healthier to live a lie than to face up to the truth?'

Her manner was pensive. The question seemed to have a special, unfathomable meaning for her.

He put his cheek against hers. 'No, I don't. It's less painful, though.'

'You couldn't do it yourself, Harry. Kid yourself forever, believe in an illusion. You're not made that way, you're too inquisitive, not prepared to take things at face value. On trust.'

You didn't know me when I was married to Liz, he felt like saying.

'One thing I don't kid myself about – that what is right for me is right for my clients, for everyone else.'

'Don't get me wrong. It's important to trust those we care about, to have faith in them, come what may. Perhaps it's the most important thing of all.'

She paused, then opened her mouth as if to add something else. He had the impression for a second that she was going to impart a confidence. But the moment passed and she folded her lips together again in a sad smile of mingled affection and regret. He wished he knew what she thought about him.

Squeezing her shoulder gently he said, 'Would you like to go to bed?'

He had meant to hide how nervous he felt but the croakiness of his voice was a giveaway. The question seemed to wash over her like the tide. He held his breath as he waited for her answer. She seemed to choose it with care.

'I don't believe in getting too serious too soon, Harry.'

'Are you saying no?'

'I'm saying yes. I simply wanted you to know how I feel.'

He kissed her on the lips. 'You bet I want to know how you feel.'

And then he took her by the hand and led her to the narrow bed in the room next door.

Chapter Nineteen

'To the detective instincts of the English lawyer,' said Bharat
Kaiwar, raising his glass. 'Mr Devlin, I congratulate you again
on your persistence.'

Harry shared a look of amused complicity with Valerie. It
was late in the afternoon and they were the last customers left
in the Ensenada after a long and lavish lunch. Two empty
bottles of Veuve Clicquot peeped out of the ice bucket in
front of them. Harry privately regarded their meal more as a
celebration of the previous night than as a thank you for his
unintended apprehension of the Saviour Money blackmailer,
but it was hardly diplomatic to say as much in earshot of
Valerie's courteous, old-fashioned father. After a few token
disclaimers he had been content to grin amiably whenever
Kaiwar reiterated his gratitude and re-filled their glasses.

'Stop it, Daddy,' said Valerie. 'He's inquisitive enough,
without your encouragement.'

'How can you say that?' said her father. 'You, who have
always been so interested in people. And the truth. Why else
did you take up a career in the law? Not for the financial
rewards, I'm sure, not after telling me for many years that one
should work for a cause in which one believes, rather than for
money alone.'

Harry glanced at the girl. She was looking at her father with
that mixture of impatience and affection which so many
children feel for their parents. Bharat Kaiwar was a grey-
haired, softly spoken man with a gentle dignity of manner
more common amongst clergymen than tycoons. Only the cut
of his suit and the finger-snapping authority with which he had

131

ordered the food hinted that he was accustomed to the power that riches bring. Yet beneath his quiet exterior ran, Harry did not doubt, that streak of single-mindedness which divides those who do from those who dream. That sense of purpose which his daughter had inherited.

'One thing I've learned already,' she said, 'is that the law is not concerned with the search for truth.'

'Justice, then?'

'Occasionally. Though each day in court I see injustices done.'

Harry felt like a spectator at a game which Valerie and Bharat Kaiwar had played many times before. For all the bond between father and daughter, the generation gap would always be a chasm between them.

When Valerie had departed to the loo twenty minutes earlier, Kaiwar had told Harry of his pride in her and of his anxiety that she was sometimes headstrong and too easily hurt. Harry sensed that he was himself being assessed for suitability as a boyfriend of a millionaire's only child. Most of the easily measured things – age, status, income – were against him. He was even in the wrong branch of the legal profession. At least the Kuiper episode meant he would be spared paternal disapproval. Yet it occurred to him that Valerie would expect Bharat Kaiwar to frown on the men in her life, would be ready to go her own way and make her own choices. Earning her father's favour had in itself done nothing to cement his relationship with her. It was somehow typical that she approved more of the small steps he had taken to fix Kuiper up with a capable lawyer. Her sympathy would always be with the underdog.

Charge card in hand, Kaiwar ambled over to the cashier. Harry felt Valerie's hand creeping along his leg, sending a *frisson* of excitement down his spine. He moved his head so that he felt her hair against his cheek. Last night they had been hot with passion. After making love they had lain naked on the bed together, warmed by each other as well as by the heat of the high summer evening. They hadn't said much, had been content with the touching of their bodies.

'Don't stop,' he said.

'Happy?'

'Mmmm.'

He brushed a finger against her cheek. The skin was cool.

'And you?' he asked after a pause.

'I enjoyed last night, Harry. Of course. And I'm glad to see Daddy relaxing today. He aged ten years while the scare was on.'

It wasn't the answer he'd been hoping for, but this was not the time to argue about it.

'I'm glad it's over for him.'

'Here he comes.' Valerie withdrew her hand from Harry's leg as Bharat Kaiwar returned.

'Well, Valerie, Mr Devlin. I'm grateful for you taking the time out from your busy days to let me organise this little celebration.'

'Harry. Please call me Harry.'

'Harry, thank you again.'

'Look, I already said it was a pure chance. I'd no idea what Kuiper was up to.'

'Nevertheless. It was my company's good fortune that you acted as you did,' said Kaiwar as they walked to the door with thanks and smiles from Pino. 'My colleague on the board, Bryan Grealish – I spoke to him this morning. He is delighted also. The problem at the Majestic with the glass worried him. Of course he never dreamed there was any connection between that matter and the trouble at the supermarkets.'

'You know we've been invited to a sixties party at the Majestic, Harry?' asked Valerie. 'This evening. It's Bryan's birthday. He's planning to mark the occasion in style. Want to come?'

Harry could have thought of better ways in which they could pass the time, but he responded to the mood of the moment and said, 'Love to. When?'

'Would you like to pick me up about eight?'

'I'll see you then.'

Outside they said goodbye. 'Don't pretend you're going to work after all that champagne,' said Valerie as her father searched for a taxi.

'Best time. The law seems to make more sense when I've had a few.'

She laughed. 'Till tonight, then.'

133

The sun was beating down as he headed for the Law Courts. Passers-by in the street looked relaxed, but as usual the heat wave was throwing the country into a panic. Farmers moaning about a drought, environmentalists warning of the greenhouse effect. You can't ever win, thought Harry. Even he was worrying now that Valerie might be cooling towards him, repenting of her ardour the previous night. Telling himself to relax, not to conjure up unnecessary fears, was logical but didn't do any good. Why can't we, he wondered, learn to trust our luck when fortune grants rare favours?

In the court library he checked on the law of attempts – on behalf of a client so inept that he'd been caught picking the empty pocket of an off-duty policeman – and on his way out spotted a familiar stoop-shouldered figure emerging from a doorway at the other end of the landing. What had Jonah Deegan been doing in the Probate Registry?

Harry frowned. He had been trying to phone the detective without success. Naturally Jonah did not have any truck with an answering machine and this morning a quick visit to Albert Dock on the off-chance had failed to yield results. A progress report on the search for Alison would be welcome.

He quickened his pace only to be distracted by the sound of someone calling his name.

'Harry. What news?'

He turned to confront another acquaintance in immaculate three-piece suit and bow tie.

'Just finished my case,' said Julian Hamer, mopping his brow. His face was grey; perhaps the after-effects of gruelling advocacy. The man's elegance, Harry had begun to realise, was all on the surface. 'A landlord and tenant dispute, about as fascinating as watching traffic lights change, but plenty of money at stake. What I wanted to know is, any response from Mrs Capstick yet?'

Helpless, Harry watched his quarry disappear downstairs. He would have to catch up with the old man some other time.

'Nothing constructive. Sounds as if she wants her day in court.'

Julian tutted. 'At all events, her foolish letter fades into insignificance compared with what has happened since. I was sorry to hear about your client's daughter, Harry. Please convey my sympathy to him.'

'Thanks, I will.' Hamer's words were right, he thought, but uttered so mechanically as to divest them of meaning. He studied the barrister. At close quarters, the man looked ill.

'Are you all right, Julian?'

'Fine, fine.' Hamer made a dismissive gesture with a handful of court papers. 'More importantly, what about you? Rumour has it you're no longer content with defending villains. You're even chasing and capturing them now.'

'Anything I can do to make more work for the profession.'

'Valerie told me that her father was going to host a celebratory lunch today.'

'I'm just staggering back to the office.'

Harry wished he could shake off the prickly reaction he experienced whenever Julian Hamer uttered Valerie's name. Surely after last night he had no need to fear competition? But the barrister's next words did nothing to cheer him.

'She's a remarkable girl, Harry. Even you don't know the half of it about her.'

As Hamer spoke, his haggard expression softened. Harry wondered if he was being teased intentionally.

'Yeah, well.'

'Anyway, I mustn't keep you. As I say, I'm sorry to hear about Stirrup. Troubles never come singly, do they?'

With a nod Hamer strolled away to the cafeteria. Harry wasn't sorry to see him go. The liveliness which the first couple of glasses of champagne had sparked in him had gone. All at once he felt dry-mouthed and melancholic. His achievements of the past two days seemed to have diminished.

All right, so he and Valerie had become lovers. But from what she had said before parting, he sensed that last night meant less to her than to him. And with Hamer lurking in the background, evidently on the cosiest of terms with her, Harry still felt insecure.

And all right, so he had contributed by accident to the uncovering of a crime, but the mystery of Stirrup's double loss remained. Curiosity kept nagging at him like a disgruntled wife. Until he understood the fate of Alison Stirrup and her step-daughter, there would be no rest for Harry Devlin.

Chapter Twenty

A tiny blonde girl pretending to be Mandy Rice-Davies kept simpering, 'Well, he would, wouldn't he?' whenever a pause occurred in the conversation. She had a naive smile and, for all that her leather skirt was slit to the thigh, lacked both the wit and the cheap allure that Harry associated with Stephen Ward's playmate. The arm round her shoulder belonged to a leering middle-aged man whose disconcerting facial resemblance to Tony Hancock was not matched by his Geordie accent and habit of guffawing at his own unfunny jokes. Harry understood that from nine to five the couple played the parts of Bryan Grealish's insurance broker and his secretary. He hoped those roles suited them better.

The party was in full swing and the Gracie Fields Room in the Majestic was packed to capacity. The walls were adorned with life-size cardboard cut-outs of the heads and shoulders of sixties heroes like John F. Kennedy and Bob Dylan. Over the hum of conversation, Gene Pitney wailed about his abortive journey back to Tulsa and complained that he could never, never, never go home again.

Talk had turned to the permissive society and the abolition of capital punishment. Slipping out of character, the insurance man tapped a pipe-smoking Harold Wilson on the shoulder and said, 'What about deterrence, then? Take this bugger The Beast for instance. Now tell me this . . .'

Harry decided it was time to move on. At least that was in keeping with his chosen character. Richard Kimble, the TV fugitive who never had much luck catching up with the one-armed man seen running away from the scene of a crime.

Distantly Harry could recall from his youth the occasional graffito saying KIMBLE IS INNOCENT. But he couldn't recall whether in the end justice had been done.

In the corner of the room Valerie, dressed as Diana Ross in her Supremes hey-day, was being chatted up by a hairy-chested Fred Flintstone. She seemed to be enjoying herself. Harry picked up another glass of wine from a tray carried by a girl made up to look like a youthful Mary Quant.

'Having fun?'

He turned to face a mask of mascara topped with a mass of platinum blonde hair. It took him a moment to penetrate the disguise and identify Grealish's girlfriend. What was her name? Stephanie, yes.

'*I Just Don't Know What To Do With Myself.*'

'What?'

'You're Dusty Springfield, right?' He sighed. 'That was the best of her songs.'

'Yeah?' The girl wasn't into pop history. She studied him with a frown. 'You haven't bothered to dress up. I think you're the only one here in a suit.'

'Do you mind?' Harry tried to explain about Kimble, the man suspected of a crime he did not commit, but Stephanie had not even seen the repeats on Channel 4 and he soon gave up.

'So where's Bryan – or should I say Elvis?' Grealish made a good Presley; he had the King's lip curl off to perfection. 'I haven't seen him for a while. Last time I spotted him he was deep in conversation with one of the coppers from Z-Cars.'

'His accountant, would you believe?' Stephanie yawned. 'They went off in a huddle. I got told to circulate.'

'The perfect hostess?'

'Do me a favour, I'm bored stiff. And as for bloody Bryan, he's so wrapped up in talking about his money and his deals, he wouldn't notice if I stripped off and lay down in the middle of the floor.'

'Try it. The Gracie Fields Room would never be the same again.'

'You must be joking. And who was Gracie Fields anyway?'

Harry thought about explaining that all the public rooms here were named after stars of yesteryear who had appeared at long-gone New Brighton landmarks like the Tivoli or Winter Gardens, but decided against it. To Stephanie, even the sixties were a bygone age.

'Men!' she snorted. He had the feeling she liked to have an audience, even if only of one mere male. 'No consideration. Bryan's a typical feller. No different really from Claire's old man.'

'You've met Jack Stirrup?'

'There was a parents' day at school. Claire introduced us. He thought the sun shone out of her backside.'

'Yes.'

'Sorry. I didn't mean to sound, like, callous.' She shivered and Harry didn't think she was being theatrical. 'The sooner they catch him, the better.'

'The Beast?'

'Right. The crazy bastard. It's frightening. That's two girls I know he's attacked. Makes you feel he's getting closer all the time. And then there's the blonde hair thing. I haven't gone out on my own since the papers wrote about that.'

'Claire wasn't blonde.'

'No. You'd have thought she was safe. Shows you, doesn't it? No one's safe.'

'You said you knew someone else, another of The Beast's victims.'

'Right. Gina. Gina Jean-Jacques. She goes to the same school – Hilbre Hall.'

Harry stared at her. 'Jean-Jacques, you say?'

'Right. Why?'

'The name reminds me of someone, that's all. Anyway, what happened to her?'

Stephanie Elwiss looked at the floor. All of a sudden Harry remembered he was speaking to a young girl whose sophistication was as easy to wipe away as Dusty's make-up.

'She was raped. One day when she was walking along the Wirral Way at Caldy. It's a public place, you'd never believe anything could happen to you there in broad daylight. But it did.'

'Do you know Gina well?'

'We were friends for a while. Not so much now. She's young for her age. And terribly shy, more interested in her ponies than boys. Different from me. When I got mixed up with Bryan, I reckon she decided I was a bit of a slut.'

'How is she now?'

'How would you be? I went to see her once, we all did. It was like meeting a different person, Claire said the same. Gina always used to be going on about her bloody horses. When I went to see her, she didn't mention them once. As if she'd grown up overnight and hated it.'

'You talked about her to Claire? I didn't realise you two saw each other out of school.'

'We didn't, as a rule. No, she came round to the house last Thursday. Bryan was busy, so I was spending the evening at home with Mum.'

'So this was out of the ordinary? A visit from Claire on the off chance that you were in for once?'

'What are you getting at?'

'No idea. I'm interested, though. Jack Stirrup's a good client of mine. Anything I can do to cast a little light on what happened to Claire will help.'

Stephanie shrugged. 'Not much I can say.'

'Don't be so sure. What did she want to see you about?'

'All she said was, her conscience had been nagging her to go round again and see how well Gina was recovering. She'd gone with Pam McDougall soon after it happened. That was the only time.'

'Did this talk about conscience surprise you?'

'Well.' Stephanie pondered. 'Suppose it did.'

'Why?'

'I wouldn't have expected it from Claire. Some people, yes, but not her. Never speak ill of the dead and all that, but she wasn't exactly Florence Nightingale, you know? The way she went on after she got that yellow belt in karate! Mind you, she probably needed self-defence with that creepy boyfriend of hers . . . But I wouldn't have thought she'd want to waste any more time with Gina. They were never pally.'

'What did you talk about?'

'Claire kept going on about how nightmarish it was. You know, to be raped by a man who wore a mask. So that you could pass him in the street a week later when he was ordinarily dressed and you wouldn't even give him a second glance. Nothing to recognise, you see.'

'Anything else?'

'She said she was going to visit Gina again the next day. Last Friday.'

Harry felt a finger stroking the back of his neck. He knew that touch.

'Escaped from your prehistoric friend?' he asked without turning round.

'Jealous?' Valerie put her arm round his neck and pulled his face towards hers. Her smile was as provocative as the way her hips swung beneath the mini dress.

'I'd better be going,' said Stephanie. Without another word she melted into the crowd.

'Fancy her?' asked Valerie.

'Who's jealous now?'

'We don't own each other. Not even after last night. I don't mind if you want to chat up pretty girls.'

'As Dusty used to sing: "I Only Want To Be With You".'

She leaned against him, using his strength for support. 'Bet you say that to all the lady barristers.'

Something impelled him to say, 'I mean it, Val. You're the only one.'

The small dark-skinned girl smiled. There was a woozy flirtatiousness about everything she said and did tonight. Harry guessed that at lunch and this evening she had drunk far more than she was accustomed to.

'I'm flattered. Really I am. Only . . .' Her face clouded for a moment.

'Yes?'

'Don't get possessive, will you?'

'Why not?' he asked softly.

''Cause I'm not ready for it, that's why not. Life's short. Why make chains for yourself before it's time?'

'Meaning?'

'Nothing in particular.' She stood upright with an effort at dignity which merely emphasised her lack of sobriety.

'Come on, what are you saying?' Harry knew he was making a mistake, but he too had been drinking and he felt the need to press the point, to ignore the voice in his mind which urged discretion.

'Oh well, if you must know. I don't want to get tied down too soon. Do you understand?'

The message behind the question made Harry bite his lip in dismay. It was as if a ghost had started tapping on his shoulder. When Valerie was so unlike Liz, in looks and background and personality, when everything about their relationship was so different, why did she suddenly remind him of his former wife? Uninvited, the answer crept into his head. Because you need her more than she needs you, that's why.

'I think so.'

'Oh Christ. Don't sound so defensive. Perhaps it's time for me to go.'

'Okay. I'm ready.'

'No need for you to come too, Harry. We don't have to spend every night together.'

'I'd like to spend tonight with you.'

Valerie wrinkled her brow. 'Look, let's slow down a little, shall we? I already said, I don't want to drift into something heavy just yet. We both have our own lives to lead.'

A sickening sense of frustration engulfed him. For a moment he was seized by the urge to strike out blindly, heedless of the consequences.

'And you have your own private interests to pursue, I suppose?' He didn't try to keep the bitterness out of his voice.

'What the hell do you mean by that?'

'Come on, Val. Julian Hamer's hovering in the background still, isn't he?'

She stared at him, her face reddening with either embarrassment or anger. Or both.

'For God's sake! What's Julian got to do with it?'

He should have stopped there, while an escape route remained open, but drink and disappointment had hold of him and he plunged on recklessly.

'Quite a lot, hasn't he? The two of you seem very close.'

'Harry, I never thought you'd be so puerile. We're adults, I'm entitled to do as I want. Julian's a very dear friend, let me tell you. He helped me when I was starting out in the law, persuaded David Base to pass me the briefs he had to turn down because of pressure of work. I owe him a lot. He's been going through a rough time lately and I've told him, anything I can do to help, I will. Your behaving like a jealous child won't make me change my mind.'

142

The real Elvis was crooning from the speakers now. He sang that he was caught in a trap, protested that they couldn't go on together with suspicious minds.

Harry said, 'Have it your own way. Do you want a lift home or shall I call a taxi?'

She could match him for stubbornness. 'No need. I can call a cab myself. Good night.'

As she stalked off through the crowd, he realised too late how badly he had behaved and called after her despairingly, 'Valerie, I'll give you a ring. Okay?'

But she didn't give any sign that she had heard and he stood with bowed head long after she had disappeared from sight.

Chapter Twenty-One

The sun was high over the River Dee as Harry drove slowly along the promenade at West Kirby, checking the numbers of the houses to his left. Hearty businessmen who had slipped away from work early to take advantage of the glorious afternoon were filling the air with plummy-voiced camaraderie as they tinkered with boats on the marina. The atmosphere was so genteel that it was hard to believe that on the peninsula's other coast, no more than seven miles away, were the scruffy novelty shops and litter-strewn burger bars of New Brighton.

Harry identified a smartly painted three-storey maisonette as the place he was seeking. As he rang the doorbell, he became aware of an unexpected nervousness, a weak feeling in the pit of his stomach.

Sally Jean-Jacques answered at once. She was as attractive as he had remembered. He knew her to be forty but her shoulder-length ash-blonde hair was as fine as that of any teenager and her sky blue jump suit displayed a figure still slender and tempting.

'Harry, how good to see you again.'

When they had spoken earlier on the phone, he had recalled how her gentle way of speaking had always appealed to him. There was nothing strident about her. She was one of those people who, even after a gap in time, can pick up a friendship or acquaintance as if it had continued without interruption for half a lifetime.

'Thanks for being willing to talk, Sally.'

She didn't offer to shake hands; she wasn't someone to whom formality appealed. Instead she smiled and said,

'Come in. You'll have to take us as you find us, I'm afraid. I haven't bothered to dust or anything since you called.'

'Are you well?' He didn't ask out of mere politeness. He hoped she was fine; she deserved to be.

'Speaking for myself, seldom been better,' she said, leading him into a large living room with a vast Indian rug draped over the floor and oriental hangings suspended from the picture frame. 'Take a seat. Would you like some tea?'

'No thanks, I won't take up too much of your time.'

'No hurry.' They sat down facing each other and she smiled at him. 'Hughie works long hours. He isn't due until half-seven. We won't be eating till after then.'

'Hughie?'

'The new man in my life,' she said with a laugh. 'Hughie Wakefield. He runs a business which digs holes in the ground and then fills them in again at a large profit. I always knew business works in a mysterious way, but I never realised how mysterious till I met Hughie.'

'Wakefield Waste?' Harry nodded. 'I know them. Big company.' Unexpectedly, he felt a sense of disappointment at her news which was as irrational as it was unfair. Sally had known hard times. Why should he begrudge her a little pleasure?

As if she could read his thoughts, she said, 'It took a while for me to get over Clive. Now I'm simply spreading my wings again.'

'I'm glad,' he said. And, after his momentary pang of envy, he meant it.

Three years earlier he had acted for Sally Jean-Jacques in her divorce. She had been widowed at thirty and left a tidy sum by her first husband, a dentist twenty years her senior who had died of cancer. Too quickly Sally had re-married, to a marketing consultant from Bermuda whom she had met while taking a hard earned holiday after months of nursing a dying man. Clive Jean-Jacques had been fun when times were good between them, violent when they were not. After he had fractured her jaw in a fit of drunken temper she had decided that enough was enough and had walked out with Gina and returned to her roots in Merseyside.

Harry's professional shoulder had been there for her to cry on and she seemed to value that as much as his advice on the matrimonial proceedings. When the case was over and the file closed he had once or twice wondered what would have happened if he'd taken her to bed instead of confining himself to a chaste farewell kiss on the cheek. It never could have worked out, he told himself, for two vulnerable people there would have soon have been an end in tears. Whether he really believed himself was another story.

'You sounded very mysterious on the phone,' she said.

'Sorry. It was – quite strange talking to you again after all this time.'

'I was glad to hear from you. As you ought to have guessed. But what is all this about Gina? How can she help you?'

'As I said, Claire Stirrup's father is a client of mine. I gather she went to the same school as Gina and a girl called Stephanie Elwiss. I was speaking to Stephanie last night. She told me that Gina had been attacked by The Beast.'

Sally's eyes clouded. 'That's right. Four weeks ago and a night hasn't passed since without her waking in the night, crying out for me to help her.'

'Christ, Sally, it must be hell to live through something like that.'

'And yet, what else can you do but live through it? You can't simply give up the ghost. Life goes on. We all ought to count our blessings. And all the other clichés I've heard a thousand times. You know what I mean.'

'She's lucky to have you to lean on.'

'You think so? I feel very inadequate sometimes.'

He looked at her, his face grave. 'Not you, Sally.'

'Well . . . you're still kind, still good for my morale. Anyway – what can we do for you?'

'Claire came to visit Gina last Friday night, I believe.'

'Yes, she did. The police asked about it. Apparently they saw all the girls poor Claire knew at school, but Gina came in for special questioning simply because she was one of the last people to see Claire alive. I doubt she could tell them much they didn't already know, but obviously they think the man who raped her may also have murdered Claire.'

'Were you surprised when Claire came to visit on Friday?'

'To tell the truth, I was. This sounds dreadful after what happened to her, but I'd always thought of her as a self-

147

centred girl. She and Gina were never close. Not that Gina has many good friends, poor girl. At least not of the two-legged variety. You'll remember she's crazy about horses? Or was, before . . .'

'Sally, would you mind if I talked to Gina about that evening? I'm trying to piece together what Claire was up to just before she was killed.'

'Why, Harry?'

'Because I think it may help me to understand why she was murdered.'

'Surely the police . . .'

'Don't ask me to explain yet, Sal. I'm not sure I could if I tried. My mind's a jumble at the moment. All the same, I think Gina could help me clear things up, if you and she were willing.'

'It's all right by me. I know you'll be sympathetic when you talk to her.'

'Sit in with us if you like. There's no reason why you shouldn't.'

'No. I spoke to her after you called. She liked you. That time she came with me to your office, she remembers it to this day. Take her for a walk along the front, it's a beautiful afternoon. I want her to start trusting men again, to be willing to be alone with them. Within reason, of course. She's got to learn that you're not all brutes.'

'Sometimes I wonder about that myself.'

'Nonsense. There are good men and there are bad men. We all have to make our judgements about which are which. No-one can go through life expecting the worst of everyone they meet. I'll call her down now. If you want me later, I'll be in the kitchen.'

She left the room and he heard her calling her daughter's name. There was the soft sound of footsteps coming down the carpeted steps, then the creak of the door as someone came in behind him.

He got to his feet, 'Gina, how are you?'

The girl's fair hair had been as long as her mother's when last he had seen her; now it was cropped short. All the colour seemed to have been washed out of her cheeks and she was painfully thin. Immediately he suspected anorexia and wished he hadn't asked the conventional question.

148

To his surprise, she answered in a level tone. 'Okay, could be worse, could be better.'

'I was sorry when I heard . . .'

It was another sentence which he regretted as soon as he started to utter it. Gina was not the first rape victim he had met. He had acted for clients who had been attacked, as well as several who were attackers. Why he felt so awkward with this girl, he wasn't sure. Was it the sense of intruding on misery, the awareness that to satisfy his own curiosity he must force this child to recall the worst moments of her short life?

She shrugged away the brief embarrassment. 'I'm getting over it. You may not think so to look at me. But I am.'

'Good.' He was uncertain how to continue.

Again she rescued him. 'Mum told me you work for Claire's father. She didn't know what you want from me, but she said you wouldn't ask to see me if you didn't have a good reason.'

'So is it okay with you that we talk?'

When she nodded he went on, 'Your mother suggested we stroll along the promenade. How does that sound to you?'

'Selfish.' Gina managed a smile. 'It means she can listen to her Barry Manilow records in peace for a few minutes. Shall we go?'

Once outside they crossed the road and leaned on the railings, looking across the estuary towards the three small islands, Hilbre, Middle Hilbre and Little Eye, each of them so near and yet somehow so remote. The sanctuary where monks had once lived a life of penance and prayer had long ago crumbled. Now the islands were home to terns and wading birds rather than men of God. All that remained was the air of peace; you could sense it even from the mainland.

For a few minutes neither of them spoke. Harry guessed the girl was summoning up her courage to talk about her ordeal, trying to draw strength from the tranquility of the scene.

At last he heard her take a deep breath before turning to face him and saying, 'Are you buying the ice creams, then?'

He grinned and went to buy a couple of 99s from the kiosk down the road. Munching the chocolate flake, they ambled along the promenade.

'I gather Claire came to see you a couple of times.'

'Yes. After it happened – well, word soon got round somehow. Even though my name's never been in the papers. There's a law against that, isn't there? Anyway, she popped in with some of the girls from school. A nice thought, I suppose, looking back on it, but I simply wasn't in the mood at the time. And anyway, she and I had never been all that close. Plus the fact she spent most of the time going on about her boyfriend.'

She concentrated on the cornet for a moment, deep in thought, and then said, 'Of course, I shouldn't say those nasty things. She's dead now.'

'I want to know the truth, Gina. Not what you think you ought to say. You didn't have much in common with Claire. So were you surprised when she paid a second visit on her own?'

'Yes. I'd started making an effort to get back to normal. Not that I'm there yet, even now, though Mum's been terrific. And when I heard Claire had been killed – I felt sick. As well as a bit guilty. Because I soon got fed up with her when she was here last week.'

'Why?'

'Oh, she was so ghoulish. If the idea was to cheer me up and take my mind off things, she went about it in a funny way. Every time the conversation veered off you-know-what, she made this big effort to drag it up again.'

'In what way?'

Gina gazed towards the hills of Wales. Harry waited for her to continue.

Not looking at him, she finally said, 'She wanted to know what he was like.'

'The man who attacked you?'

'Yes. The Beast. Beast is too good a word, though.'

'And?'

'I didn't want to talk about it. I know I can't simply forget everything, I've got to come to terms with it and I think I'm starting to do that now. But I couldn't understand what she was after. She seemed fascinated by what had happened to me, like some real sicko. She even wanted to know if he'd kissed me . . . oh God, I'm sorry.'

Her voice broke and tears welled in her eyes. Harry put his arm round her shoulders, an unthinking gesture of support. Feeling her body stiffen with anxiety, he cursed his instinctive reaction. She wasn't yet ready for physical contact with any man after her ordeal.

What had Claire been after? There must be a link between her call on Gina and her own fate. Whether she knew it or not, Gina might hold the key. Yet he could not find it within himself to cross-examine her further. One last question, he said to himself, and then leave her alone.

'Would you recognise his voice again?'

'The police asked me that. I can't be sure. He was very cold, but he spoke quietly, barely above a whisper.' Gina hesitated. 'You know, this has never crossed my mind before, but perhaps he was almost as frightened as me.'

They had reached the end of the promenade now. For a few minutes they watched the little boats bobbing on the water, then Gina added, 'I was glad when Claire went home. Of course I never dreamed that twenty four hours later . . .'

'No one could have foreseen that.'

'It's such an incredible coincidence, that within such a short space of time the same man should have murdered her. It sounds horrible to say so, but I feel almost grateful, that perhaps I got off lightly after all.'

Harry studied the skin-and-bone young girl with her pale cheeks and fearful eyes. Maybe she was learning to cope with the assault on her, but it would be a long time before she would ever be able wholly to trust a man again. Maybe suspicion would always lurk at the back of her mind.

'I don't think you got off lightly,' he said.

And though he did not say so, he did not believe that the murder of Claire Stirrup was such an incredible coincidence, either.

Chapter Twenty-Two

Atlantic waves were crashing against the sea wall at Miranda Beach. Through the night air drifted the sound of a band playing *That Old Feeling*. Ned Racine had that old feeling, too. He flirted with the blonde in the white dress who had caught his eye as she walked out of the concert.

'You're not too smart, are you?' she asked.

Harry was spending the evening at his flat with a bottle of Johnnie Walker for company. For the twentieth time he was running his old tape of *Body Heat*, although he knew the dialogue so well he hardly needed to glance at the images on the screen. Racine, the gullible small town lawyer and second rate Romeo. Sometimes Harry worried that he might have more in common with Ned than he would like to admit.

He wasn't being too smart about Valerie, that was clear. She hadn't been in touch all day and he didn't think that ringing her was the right thing to do. Was he being childish, letting pride elbow aside his need to be with her? To press too much now might destroy their relationship. And yet, while he stayed here she might be spending her time with Julian Hamer, drawing nearer to him, forgetting that she didn't yet want to be imprisoned by commitment.

Come to think of it, he'd not been too smart over Brenda Rixton or Sally Jean-Jacques either. Two older women, with either of whom he might still be involved had he played his cards differently. Now they were fixed up elsewhere. As the evening wore on and the whisky warmed him and blurred his memory of the past, he recalled Brenda's soft flesh and the interest he had once seen in Sally's eyes and he realised that he had no idea what he wanted from women, or of whether he would ever find it.

At least Racine knew. Racine, who had sniggered when Matty Walker said, 'I'm a married woman,' not realising how easy it was to walk into a snare. Racine, who suspected nothing until it was too late. Easy to identify with him.

The pictures moved. Now Oscar, the black detective, was sitting in the snack bar, hat tipped on the back of his balding head.

'When it gets hot, people start to kill each other,' he was telling Racine.

Violence. There was no escaping it. It had found Gina, had killed Claire. And possibly Alison too. Might her body, like that of her step-daughter, be lying undiscovered somewhere beneath the ground? She must be dead, surely. The victim, if not of her husband, or of the man who had murdered Claire, of another sex killer who had seized and violated her. What else could explain her sudden disappearance, her failure to make any contact with either her husband or her mother?

In the film, things were starting to fall apart for Racine. His lover's husband was dead, the money seemed to be there for the taking. But there was that funny business over the will and his friends, the policeman and the prosecutor, could tell that he was heading for disaster.

'She's trouble, Ned. Big time, major league trouble.'

Might Alison have been trouble, as well? The notion swam around in Harry's mind like a solitary fish in a pool. If she had contrived her disappearance, what could be the reason? To set her husband up – for what? If she was alive, it seemed extraordinary that she had claimed nothing from Stirrup when up to fifty per cent was hers for the taking. And she could claim nothing unless she re-emerged from the shadows.

If she was alive, he was overlooking something, making a false assumption somewhere. He toyed with possibilities. They all seemed ludicrous. Might Alison and Doreen Capstick, for instance, be conspiring to keep a deadly secret? A secret connected with Claire, perhaps? Doreen had no love for either her son-in-law or his daughter from his first marriage. She wouldn't scruple to tell the lie direct. Yet Harry could not credit that she was so good an actress. And it was

154

impossible to see how Alison could gain from such an elaborate charade. She was in no position to cash in on the police
interest in Jack which Doreen had inspired. No, he was letting
his imagination run riot.

Ned Racine had been equally slow on the uptake. Even as
the evidence mounted, still he was unwilling to accept that
he'd been betrayed. Bitterness edged his voice as he confronted the woman who had contrived his downfall.

'Experience shows I can be convinced of anything.'

Ned's just like me, thought Harry wearily. It's so easy to
believe what you want to believe. How to strike the right
balance between trust and naiveté? As for the mess with
Stirrup and his missing wife, a clue must exist to help make
sense of all that had happened. Earlier, driving back after
talking to Sally, he had felt on the edge of something that
would lead him to the truth, but then he had arrived home,
poured himself one drink, then another, and the answers to
his questions had slipped further out of reach.

'It was so – perfect,' said Racine at last.

And for a moment Harry thought he caught a glimpse in his
mind's eye of what had happened. But he was on the point of
sleeping and soon he was absorbed in a dream about Liz. She
was alive again and had come home for good.

He woke late the next morning, still lying cramped on the
sofa. His back ached and he felt dirty and dishevelled. The
red light on the video recorder blinked at him as if in
reproach. In his dream he had talked to his wife, they had put
things right with their marriage. He had stroked her black
hair and felt her tongue on his lips, her teeth rubbing against
his neck. To be awake and alone seemed much less like real
life.

A cold shower couldn't wash away the anti-climax of
returning to the quiet morning world of the Empire Dock. At
least the sun was glinting down on the water's surface and he
recalled his father's favourite cliché as he walked the short
distance to Fenwick Court.

'Every day's a bonus,' the old man had liked to say. 'Every
day's a bonus.' Poor old bugger, he hadn't earned enough
bonus days.

Harry's first client, an angry young man accused of kerb
crawling in Falkner Square who claimed merely to have been

155

practising for his advanced driving test (but for forty minutes round the same block?), had just been dispatched when Suzanne put Jack Stirrup through.

'I'm getting out,' he said without preamble.

'Out of what?'

'Of everything. The house. Merseyside. The business.'

'You can't be serious.'

'Never more so.'

'Jack, I don't think this is a good time to be making hasty decisions.'

'Name me a better time. My oldest mate's suing me for sacking him. My wife's pissed off God knows where and the police think I've done her in. My daughter's been butchered by a fucking nutcase and her bloody boyfriend's been using my cellars as a terrorist base. No thanks, Harry boy, I've had enough. There's nothing down for me round here. You can tell that slob Morgan I'll pay him a year's money in full and final settlement, by the way. Though he'll drink it away in no time if I'm any judge.'

To reason with Stirrup in this mood was, Harry knew, like trying to halt a damburst with a sieve. All the same, he had to try.

'Jack, things couldn't have been tougher for you lately. No-one knows that better than me. If you only . . .'

'Listen. I thought you'd have understood. I can't take any more. Got that? I've bloody had it up to here. But if you're not the man I thought you were and pounds, shillings and pence are all that count where you're concerned, the sums add up, don't you worry. Grealish has come up with an extra five hundred grand for my shares in the company. No strings.'

If the news hadn't taken his breath away, Harry would have whistled. Half a million more, unconditionally. The price they had put on Stirrup Wines as a try-on, an opening shot in those abortive negotiations earlier in the year. Grealish had rubbished the offer then, claiming neither his accountants nor the bank would support an acquisition at such an over-value. So, at last he had yielded.

'It's a good price,' Harry said reluctantly.

'It's what the business is worth. Anyway, I've said yes. Grealish is telling his lawyer to draw up the agreement. I've told him you'd probably get Crusoe to handle my side of it. All right?'

'Sure.'

Advising on takeover arguments was more in Jim's line than Harry's. The big man could argue over the whereases and the hereinbefores, check wordy warranties and blue-pencil indemnity clauses with the best of them. It would be the biggest deal Crusoe and Devlin had ever handled. And the most lucrative. The fees would pay for a new computer system and fax machine. The whole technological shooting match. Harry knew he ought to be punching the air with a footballer's roar of delight, but instead he felt like a non-swimmer on the shore, watching someone about to drown.

'Selling up doesn't mean you have to pack your bags and leave the area. What would you do?'

'I'll think of something. With that much money, I won't be short of places to go. Or people to help me spend it.'

'And Rita Buxton? Is she part of your plans?'

A snort of disgust came down the line. 'Might have known you'd drag her into it. No smoke without fire, is that what's going through your mind? Well, it's like I told you the other day. Rita and me only got together since Ali disappeared. When my wife was around, I never looked at another woman. Maybe that was my mistake. Should have made her jealous, want to fight to keep me.'

'You realise how the police will react?'

'So bloody what? They can't pin anything on me. I'd have more time for them if they concentrated on lifting whoever killed my little girl instead of twittering about why ever a woman who should have known better could walk out on the good life like Ali did.'

'And Doreen Capstick?'

Stirrup's scorn sounded in his laugh. 'Do me a favour. That old hag's the least of my problems. Listen, I'm still in my prime. I want to live a little before I get too old. What are you worried about? Crusoe can sell that house while he's at it. It's never been the home I wanted it to be. You two will be quids in.'

'Why not wait a while before you make any moves? Take a holiday, a long break. It'll do you good. When you get back, you'll be more relaxed. Then decide what to do next.'

'Look, I'm not calling to ask your opinion, simply to tell you what I'm going to do. Right? My mind's made up. There's nothing more to discuss. I'll be in touch.'

Stirrup hung up without pausing to hear a reply. Harry replaced the receiver slowly, shaking his head.

Did this sudden turn of events signify anything more than a release of pent-up frustration? Was Stirrup running away not only from the sequence of disasters that had befallen him but also from the guilt of having killed his wife?

Even Jim Crusoe, when told the news, allowed himself the rare luxury of speculation.

'He's settling with Trevor, did you say? Generous pay-off by the sound of it. Too generous, do you think?'

'What do you mean?'

'Hush money? Does Trev know something Jack would rather keep quiet? Another reason why he might want to make himself scarce, perhaps?'

Harry remembered the drunken words Morgan had uttered the other night. *Bloody murderer. Bloody murderer.*

'It might make sense,' he admitted. 'Let's say Trevor had some inkling about what happened to Alison. Even if he's bought off, Jack was right. Odds are, the money would be in the brewers' pockets before long. And then Trevor might come asking for more. Not so easy if Jack is overseas.'

They looked at each other, toying with the idea that they were acting for a wife killer.

The phone trilled. Jim picked up the receiver and listened for a short while.

'For you.'

'I'll call back.'

'Not so fast. It's Jonah Deegan. Let's hope he's not ringing to tell us he's found Alison Stirrup buried under the floor at Prospect House.'

Harry winced. 'Put him through.'

Jonah's voice sounded different from usual. It took Harry a few moments to identify the change. The habitual note of complaint was gone. The old detective sounded smug.

'What is it, Jonah?'

'No need to be sharp, Harry. This call box is costing me money.'

'Put it on your bill and spit out what you have to say.'

'We need to meet. There's plenty to tell you and I hate the bloody phone anyway. Not in your office, it'll be like a furnace on a day like today. Somewhere out of doors, get a breath of air.'

'I'm due in court in ten minutes. I should be free by twelve. I'll see you in the garden at the back of the Bluecoat if you like. And Jonah, the last I saw of you, you were coming out of the Probate Registry, for God's sake. What's your news?'

'Well, it's a long story.'

Watching his partner's frustration grow with Jonah's every prevarication, Jim winked. He was enjoying the build-up as much as the old man.

Harry controlled himself with an effort. 'Jonah, you're obviously dying to tell me something. If you want me to rush out to the Bluecoat, you'd better give me some idea of why.'

'It's about Mrs Alison Stirrup, you see.'

Harry felt his stomach muscles tighten.

'Yes, yes, what about her?'

At the other end of the line Jonah Deegan paused like an old ham actor before speaking again.

'She's alive and well and living in sin with a Mrs Catherine Morgan.'

Chapter Twenty-Three

Today, as always, the calm of the courtyard garden at the Bluecoat was as welcome as it was unexpected. This was a sanctuary for refugees from urban life. Less than one hundred yards away people swarmed through the city's shopping centre but here you could forget for a while the noise and ugliness of the world outside.

Harry walked through the back door of the art gallery building into the open air. Jonah was sitting on a wooden seat in the midst of trees and troughs of flowers. The old man was rolling a cigarette, careless of the tobacco he spilled on the ground.

'Jonah, you'd pollute the Garden of Eden.'

'Stop mithering and take the weight off your feet. I've earned this. Want one?'

'No thanks.' Harry was briefly nonplussed by the uncharacteristic generosity until he remembered that Jonah knew he had given up the weed.

Jonah finished his act of creation, lit up and then puffed reflectively, testing Harry's patience to the limit.

'All right, this place, isn't it? Peaceful.'

Aware that he was being teased, Harry spoke in a mild tone. 'You dragged me over here,' he said. 'What's your news?'

'All in good time, Harry.' Jonah exhaled and a smile began to scale his rocky features. 'Surprised you, did it?'

Harry could still scarcely believe what the detective had said on the phone, but he'd turned the idea of a relationship between Alison and Cathy over in his mind. And the more he considered the new picture, the more he began to understand.

'You're absolutely certain?'

Jonah tugged at one of the hairs growing from his nostrils. 'Is the Pope a Catholic? I tell you, those women are holed up together, close and cosy as peas in a pod.'

'Go on.'

'Sure you wouldn't like a smoke?'

Jonah had the true story-teller's knack of building suspense, Harry thought to himself. He was in the wrong job.

'Give me a break, Jonah. I know you're dying to get it off your chest.'

'All right then.' Jonah cleared his throat in ceremonial fashion, like a scruffy Poirot, about to reveal all to hapless Hastings.

'See, the problem I've had all along is the lack of leads. No-one had any idea what this Alison Stirrup was up to. I had to assume she was alive until the opposite was proved. Trouble was, I had nowhere special to look.'

He paused, as if expecting sympathy. Harry waited for him to continue.

'So I started by trying to think of what she might be up to if she'd deliberately decided to cut herself off. Maybe with some bloke Stirrup knew nothing about. Yet no one so much as hinted at a boyfriend in the background.'

'Doreen Capstick was adamant there was no one when I spoke to her. Said the same to you, I imagine.'

Jonah winced at the memory. 'Mutton dressed as lamb, that one. No way would her little girl play fast and loose. How often have I heard that from parents in my time? Not that I thought she was lying. Mrs. Capstick hates Stirrup, she'd have been glad for Alison to give him the elbow. She just hadn't been let into the secret.

'Any road, I dug around a bit, didn't turn up anything new. You could count her friends on the fingers of one hand and she didn't seem on the same wavelength as her mother. Made me wonder if she hadn't been trying to escape the Capstick woman as well as Stirrup.'

Jonah's voice had lost its histrionic edge. He was talking to himself now and Harry felt he was catching a glimpse of the shrewd policeman Jonah had once been.

'I was trying to work out what Alison was like. I talked to her neighbours in those posh houses in Caldy, but the size of the bloody gardens gives people no choice but to keep to themselves. They agreed on a few things. She was a loner. Hard to get to know, not any kind of a flirt. Didn't sound to me like a happy woman, though with a husband like Stirrup and a step-daughter who could be a real little cow, who could blame her?'

He finished his cigarette and had ground it with his heel into the path before Harry could utter an environmentally-conscious word of reproach.

'She read a lot, people said, long boring novels. And made patchwork quilts – that was the closest she came to a passion. They take an age to design and stitch together, apparently. Lonely business, by the sound of it. Nobody could tell me anything else. When you'd said that, you'd summed her up.'

A rare cloud masked the sun. It was as hot as ever in this endless summer, but Harry shivered. Although he had known Alison Stirrup for years, he could not add to Deegan's thumbnail sketch of her. How little we really know of the people we meet in daily life, he thought, how seldom we guess what lies behind the camouflage of social conversation.

'One thing bothered me. She had a friend I couldn't get to see. The wife of Trevor Morgan. Stirrup told me the two of them were pally, but it turned out Cathy Morgan had done a flit a few weeks before Alison disappeared. That got me interested. I decided to find out a little more about Mrs Morgan. And, curiouser and curiouser, there were several similarities between her case and Alison's. A sudden departure, tracks well covered. No known boyfriends lurking in the background. One big difference, though. Cathy Morgan was loaded.'

Harry stared. 'Loaded?'

'Her father was Paul Newman. The builder, not the film star. You'll have heard of Newman's Estates, more than likely. They threw up several of those barrack estates over the water. Mostly on the edge of Birkenhead. Newman died in the early seventies before Cathy got married. He and his wife only had the one kid. They'd had Cathy late in life and before long the old girl went senile. She had to go into a home and bloody Cathy never bothered much with her. And though the mother died six months ago, Trevor Morgan told me he thought she was still alive.'

'Didn't he realise there was money in the family?'

Deegan shook his head. 'Nor did I till I checked up. The day you saw me coming out of the Probate Registry, in fact.'

The fog in Harry's mind was starting to thin. 'And?'

'Newman died before the seventies property bubble burst. He left his old lady all the loot and she barely touched a penny. So it's been quietly picking up interest all these years. Cathy must have had a shock herself when Ma died and she finally realised what the old lady was worth. Far as I can tell, she inherited the thick end of six hundred thousand.'

Harry whistled. 'No wonder she wasn't chasing Trevor Morgan for alimony.'

'There you are. Isn't that women all over?'

The cloud had passed by and the courtyard was bathed again in sunlight. A young couple walked by, their arms entwined. The boy was talking softly to his girlfriend; she laughed musically at something he said. As they disappeared within the craft centre, Harry felt a pang of loss and of jealousy.

'Any idea what Cathy did with the money?'

Jonah's attempt to look modest yet efficient collapsed into self-congratulation.

'You're talking to an ex-CID man here, Harry. Finding out is second nature. There was the name of a solicitors' firm on the probate papers. Maher and Malcolm.'

Harry groaned. 'My old firm.'

'Is that right? Well, I happen to know the senior partner there. Geoffrey Willatt.'

A fellow Freemason, thought Harry. The old pals' act.

'And?'

'I managed to have a word with Geoffrey. He's the soul of discretion and couldn't break a client's confidence, naturally.'

'Naturally.'

'But from what he said I managed to piece the story together.'

Surprise, surprise. 'Which was?'

'They'd acted for Newman for years. Wrote his will and his widow's. It's a good firm, no reason why the daughter shouldn't use their services. And Geoffrey did let one thing slip. They'd acted for her in buying a place out in Cheshire. A house with small shop attached. Together with someone she described as a business partner.'

'Alison Stirrup?'

'Correct. The deal went through two months ago, before Alison buggered off, but he didn't know the background, or anything about Alison. The instructions came from Cathy and one of his assistants did the donkey work.'

Geoffrey Willatt hasn't changed, thought Harry. 'And the shop was where?'

'Town called Knutsford. Just off the main street.'

The soul of discretion had obviously been in expansive mood on this occasion.

'And you traced Cathy? Found Alison with her?'

Jonah frowned. He didn't want to be rushed, to have his narrative flow disturbed.

'I went over there. I'd spun Geoffrey a bit of a yarn about the Newmans being old friends and he got his runner to phone me with the address. Funnily enough, when I turned up for a recce I thought I'd made a mistake.'

Again the significant pause. Harry obliged this time by asking obediently. 'And what was that, Jonah?'

'New signboard over the window. Currer and Acton Bell. Trading as Patches.'

Something stirred in Harry's memory. He put his hand through his hair, trying to visualise the old market town. Years had passed since his last visit, yet he could remember it well. He and Liz had read something in the paper about the May Day procession and had driven over to take a look.

'I know Knutsford,' he said. 'Mrs Gaskell, the nineteenth-century novelist, didn't she come from there? Of course. She wrote about it in *Cranford*.'

'So?' Jonah looked irked.

'She also wrote a biography of Charlotte Brontë, one of those sisters tucked away in their Yorkshire parsonage, pouring all their imagination into novels in the days when writing was a man's game. They used pen-names. Charlotte was Currer Bell. Anne was Acton Bell.'

'Bloody fanciful if you ask me.'

'Not so fanciful for two women with a liking for Victorian literature who decided to run off together where no one knew them and set up a little cottage industry, flogging pricey patchwork quilts to the gin and tonic set south of Manchester.'

His thunder half-stolen, Jonah said grumpily, 'Any road, I sat myself outside the shop and waited. The women were easy enough to recognise. I'd got a good description of Mrs Morgan from her husband and Stirrup gave me a photograph of Alison. They seemed very lovey-dovey when they weren't attending to customers.'

'Jesus.'

Jonah regained some of his original complacency. 'Not a bad job of work, though I say so myself.'

Harry grinned and patted the old man on the shoulder. 'Bloody well done. Have you told Stirrup yet?'

'No. Thought I'd have a word with you first.'

'Appreciate it.' Harry reflected for a few moments. 'Okay, I can see why they wouldn't move out and set up home together in a blaze of publicity. But why do you think Alison has kept quiet, even though she must have read about Claire's disappearance and the discovery of her body?'

'I've asked myself that one. Of course she didn't have much time for her step-daughter, but even so . . .'

'I need to talk to her,' said Harry.

'Thought you'd want to. But don't get any ideas about doing the decent thing and not letting on to your client if his wife begs you to keep her secret safe. I want my fee paid.'

'Don't we all? But let's take it step by step. If Jack finds out Alison has deserted him for another woman and left him to persuade the police that he didn't bury her in the garden, he just might decide to make up for lost time and drive over there and do her in with his bare hands.'

'And how can you stop him?'

'Your guess,' admitted Harry, 'is as good as mine.'

Chapter Twenty-Four

No matter how hard he tried, Harry could not get Liz out of his mind. Going back to Knutsford re-awakened memories which had long been slumbering.

Driving past the heath, he recalled the carnival atmosphere which had greeted the two of them on their May Day visit here years ago. This was where the procession had finally wound up, led by Jack-in-the-Green past side streets decorated with coloured sand. The procession, with its morris men and its dancing troupes and its decorated floats and its children's bands. Liz had loved all of it and Liverpool's dirt and smells might have been part of a different world.

As they might again today. For Knutsford was basking in the afternoon sun, scarcely less indifferent to the world beyond its boundaries than in the age of Elizabeth Gaskell. As Harry locked his car – even here you couldn't be too careful, invaders from Merseyside might be skulking out of sight – he heard the well-modulated tones of women in designer leisure wear discussing difficult decisions about whether a jacuzzi added more to the value of a five-bedroomed detached than UPVC double glazing throughout. Elegant economy might be a thing of the past, but Cranford was still possessed by the Amazons.

He walked along King Street, past the Gaskell memorial tower which an amateur architect with a taste for Italian style and money to burn had erected in the centre of town. Every other building housed a prettified tea room or an expensive gift shop. An American tourist tapped him on the shoulder and asked the way to the heritage centre. The outside world had to beat a path to Knutsford, not the other way round.

Fifty yards ahead he could see woodland and a sign marking an entrance to Tatton Park. Harry turned into Swan Lane, to be confronted with another example of weirdly imaginative Italian architecture, a turreted fantasy which housed a firm of solicitors. He found it difficult to imagine an environment more different from Fenwick Court. Next door stood a smaller building, like a cottage with a shop front. Above the door was the sign in Gothic lettering Jonah had described.

Samples of patchwork hung in the window. Smaller pieces were laid out on a trestle table outside. Harry stopped to look at them. All shapes and sizes were there, in every design and colour he could think of. Cushions, framed work, quilts and wall hangings.

The shop was open. Inside two women were talking. One voice, that of a customer, he didn't recognise. The other he did. It belonged to Alison Stirrup.

So it was true. He had not doubted Jonah's account, yet he never found it easy to take things on trust. He preferred the evidence of his own eyes and ears.

Through the window he could see Alison, engrossed in conversation about a commission she was undertaking for the other woman. Her fair hair was shorter even than in the past; she seemed a little more relaxed than during her married life. Otherwise he could see no change; she might be using a false name, but she hadn't been so crass as to resort to disguise. Her good looks were quiet, very English. He could recall once thinking Stirrup was a lucky man: how long ago was that?

The customer said something about calling in next week.

'I'll have it ready then,' he heard Alison promise.

'Super, thanks so much.'

Harry waited for the woman to pass him and disappear in the direction of the main street before entering the shop. Alison was behind the counter, busying herself with invoices. She glanced up in welcome.

Her smile died the moment that she recognised him. Her heart-shaped face had more colour than in the old Caldy days, but all that drained away at the sight of his rumpled figure in the doorway. Incredulity spread over her face, as if she were seeing someone risen from the grave.

'Hello, Alison. Or should I call you Acton?'

'Harry.'

Her voice was barely audible. The way she clasped and unclasped her hands confirmed his first impression. This was a frightened woman.

'You remembered,' he said. 'Not that I've changed my name lately. Unlike you.'

'Has Jack sent you?'

'Not directly. Of course I'm acting for him, but he doesn't know I've traced you here. Not yet, that is.'

'How did you find me?'

'It's a long story. Though not as long as the one I think you ought to be telling me. About how and why you set up here with Catherine Morgan.'

'So you know about Cathy too?'

'That the pair of you have a home and business here, yes. There's plenty I don't know or understand. I've come here in the hope you can fill in the gaps for me.'

'Why should I? You're Jack's solicitor, why should I confide in you?'

'Alison, you can't hide forever. Okay, so you've chosen a different way of life. If you're happier now, that's fine. I can guess it wasn't easy living with Jack. Specially if you found out you weren't suited to a conventional marriage.'

'Under-statement of the decade,' she interrupted bitterly. 'You've no idea.'

'Give me an idea, Alison. I'm not threatening you. Talk to me. Let's see where we go from here.'

She considered him for a moment. He stood in silence, waiting for her to make up her mind, hoping his journey would not prove to have been wasted.

She passed a hand across her face for a moment, as if composing herself, then spoke more steadily than before.

'Cathy's out. Looking at silks in Macclesfield. She won't be back for another hour. We can't talk in the shop. I'll close early and we can go to the cottage. Behave yourself and I might even make you a cup of tea.'

'You're on.'

He helped her lug the table inside, then stood back as she locked up and stuck a sign in the window apologising for the

169

early closure. When it was done, she led him through a door at the rear of the shop and along a short corridor into the domestic part of the building, picking a way through mounds of brightly coloured fabric on the floor.

After she had directed him into the low-ceilinged sitting room and disappeared into the kitchen, he took stock of his surroundings. This was a warm place, expertly decorated in creams and golds. Patchwork quilts adorned every inch of wall space; they were yet more intricate than those for sale next door. The furniture, antique pine, suited the age of the property. Opposite him stood a six-foot tall bookcase. Fat volumes on interior design, art, patchwork and gardening set side by side with Penguin and Oxford classics from the Victorian age. Alison Stirrup hadn't been slow to replenish her collection of the books she loved.

She came into the room again bearing a tray with tea things and biscuits.

'Very civilised,' said Harry. 'I can tell I'm in Knutsford.'

'You gave me a shock when you walked through the door, obviously. But on a personal level, it's nice to see you again. Considering you were so close to Jack, you always struck me as a reasonable human being. Funny, I sometimes wondered if you disliked him. Not because you sneered or fawned or gossiped about him behind his back. Quite the opposite. And thank God you never tried to chat me up or pat me on the backside when he wasn't looking. Unlike some. Loathsome Trevor Morgan, for instance.'

'Jack's my client. I don't have to like him.'

'What I'm saying is, I'm willing to talk to you. No preconditions. You'll do whatever you have to, I realise that. And perhaps you're right. It may be better to speak to someone who knew us when we were together, you may find it easier to understand.'

He sipped the tea. Lapsang Souchong, smokily distinctive. Now he would keep quiet till she felt ready to unburden herself.

'Where do I start?'

She was, he felt, posing the question as much to herself as to him. For all he knew, this might be the very first time she had confronted the drastic changes she had wrought in her life. Better not to hurry her. Everything would come out, given time and patience.

'You know my mother, don't you? She and I could hardly be more different. I've always been a disappointment to her. Not a temptress, not a voluptuous blonde. I took after my father. You never met him, he died when I was young. A heart attack. Only forty eight. The kindest man you could wish to find. I blamed her. I still do in my heart, I suppose. She was always on at him for one reason or another. He had no peace. And after he was gone, she poured all her energies into me, wanted to recreate herself, re-live her youth through me. I rebelled, but not enough. I always kept things bottled up inside. I got involved with a sweet boy, he played guitar in a band. He died too. A sailing accident. It devastated me. I met Jack soon afterwards. He was fun, took my mind off things.'

She sighed. 'And so eventually I did something right in mother's eyes by marrying a wealthy man. Only problem was, she took an instant dislike to him and to Claire. It wasn't long before the gloves came off. If anything, that drew me closer to Jack, but soon it was clear we had nothing in common. Not age, not interests. Not even bed. Tell you the truth, I'd never been wild about that side of things, not even with Graeme – he was the guitarist I mentioned a moment ago. And with Jack it soon became a real turn-off. He used me for his pleasure, there was nothing more.'

While she paused for breath Harry finished his drink.

'Would you like another cup? There. Well, as I was saying, I had little enough to share with Jack. And nothing at all with Claire. I wasn't a good step-mother, I suppose. I'm not child-crazy. Jack fancied having another kid at one time, but I put my foot down. Claire was quite enough to handle. She never cared for me and the feeling was mutual. Probably the greater responsibility rested on me, but she was such a – a surly bitch. Oh, I know she's dead now and I'm sorry about that. No one deserves such a fate. But I won't be hypocritical, I won't pretend it was sweetness and light between the two of us.'

Alison gazed at him for half a minute before continuing in a tone stripped bare of any semblance of emotion.

'So there I was. Unhappily married to a hot-tempered Philistine with a sullen lump of a daughter in tow. Tied to the home – after all, I'd never trained for anything worthwhile, when I left school I messed about for years, temping – and totally frustrated. And then one evening Cathy gave me a ring. We knew each other quite well, the men were bosom buddies. The four of us would have dinner together, occasionally go for outings when Jack wasn't too busy making money. Cathy strikes people as a tough cookie. She gave Trevor a hard time, although he deserved it. We got on socially, but that was really about all. Then she called me and suggested we go to see a play together at The Empire. One of the later Ayckbourns. I said yes, we fixed for an evening when Jack and Trevor were away on business. And the rest, as they say, is history.'

'You fell in love?'

'I like to leave that kind of talk to teenage magazines. Let's say, we discovered each other. There's much more to Cathy than meets the eye. She's sensitive and generous, but she liked to shelter behind the image of the domineering wife. We went to the Chester Gateway the next time. Started planning other things together. One night, late on, we'd both had a bit to drink. The men were away again, the two of us were over at the Morgans' place. She put her arms round me. It seemed natural and right. We spent the night together.'

There was a faraway look on her face when she spoke. Do I have a similar expression, thought Harry, whenever I think back to the early days with Liz?

'Have you ever come across the book by Frances Hodgson Burnett, *The Secret Garden*? For me, becoming Cathy's lover was like discovering my own secret garden. The ordinary world might be as drab as ever, but when I was with her it suddenly became wonderful. She'd had some experience with another girl years ago. It didn't work out, she'd thought it was an adolescent phase. I'd never dreamed of getting involved in a lesbian relationship. Sex never appealed to me so much. Now I had someone who would care for me as a person, someone I could care for too. It was a new feeling. And indescribably good.'

'When did you first decide to live together?'

'At first we didn't know what to do or how to do it. Coming out and making the break was – such a final thing. We're both

172

quite conventional people, whatever you may think. And then Cathy came into money. A great deal of money.'

'Her father's estate.'

'Oh, you know that as well. It gave us a chance to set up Patches, to build something worthwhile together without any contribution from the men. I'd known Knutsford since I was a child. I once had an aunt who lived down Ladies' Mile. And I'd always meant to take my patchwork more seriously. Jack was only interested if I could make money out of it. Cathy's attitude was different. If it will make you happy, let's do it, she said. She's always fancied running a little cottage industry anyway. So – here we are.'

'I can understand why you wanted to put the past behind you,' said Harry slowly. 'Which of us hasn't longed to do that? And yet, there is one thing I don't follow. I can see that planning your getaway would have been exciting. But why did it have to be so secret? Surely you didn't have to steal away in such a fashion, so that not even your own mother knew where you were, or whether you were alive or dead. Why the big mystery?'

'I tried to explain before. My relationship with my mother, however she might like to glamourise it, was as empty as a saucepan on a rack. The same was true of my marriage. Neither Jack nor my mother were losing anything they had not already lost years earlier.'

Harry shook his head.

'Alison, I hear what you're saying, but it doesn't add up. For God's sake, Doreen has accused Jack of murdering you. You're safe and sound, but neither of them know that and the police certainly don't know it either. You didn't even get in touch when Claire went missing or after her body was found. As you say, no-one deserves to finish up the way she did. Especially not at fifteen. You're not a brutal woman and I'm sure you're not a coward either. However bad life was between Jack and yourself, surely you owe him a little consideration. He's not an ogre. Won't you contact him yourself?'

She coloured as he spoke. He could see traces of guilt on her face, red spots high on her cheek bones. She closed her eyes and said, 'Harry, that's impossible. I'm happy here. I want things to stay as they are. And I'm not just being selfish. There's a very good reason why Jack mustn't find out I'm alive.'

'You're the one who's asking the impossible.'

She said softly, 'As I said, there's a good reason why you shouldn't tell Jack where I am. Are you listening? I'm terrified that if you do, he'll come out here and kill me.'

'Christ, Alison, that's ridiculous! We all know he's got a temper, but . . .'

'Some of us know more than others,' she broke in.

'What do you mean?'

'If he finds me, he will murder me.'

One of the oldest lawyers' rules is never to ask a question to which you don't already know the answer. Harry had disobeyed the old saw often enough this afternoon. An obscure instinct urged belated caution. But he could not help himself.

'Why in God's name do you say that?'

She gazed at him levelly, pausing for a moment before her reply.

'Because I know he's committed murder before.'

Chapter Twenty-Five

As darkness fell Harry drove back towards Liverpool, wondering once again whether Jack Stirrup was a murderer.

After leaving Patches he had eaten in a Knutsford pub with low beams, an inglenook and a real fire. The locals were preparing for a quiz night, tossing trivial questions and obscure answers back and forth like Wimbledon stars knocking-up before a Centre Court final. Who wrote the music for *Psycho*? Where did Crown Prince Rudolf of Austria die? What was discovered by the brigantine *Dei Gratia* in 1872? The home team's captain, a bespectacled youth who consumed bitter over mild as if there would be no tomorrow, never seemed at a loss. Harry had half a mind to seek from him a second opinion on Alison's story.

There was not a shadow of doubt that she was telling the truth. Yet that did not necessarily make Stirrup a killer. Hence his dilemma. There was no master of ceremonies with the answer already written down in a book, he would be unable to groan it-was-on-the-tip-of-my-tongue when the truth came out. If it ever did.

Alison's account of her last weeks as a wife had been candid. She did not absolve herself of blame for the collapse of the marriage: it had been a union of two incompatible people. After deciding that her future lay with Catherine Morgan she had scarcely bothered to conceal her contempt for either Jack Stirrup or his daughter. Rows between the three of them became ever more frequent and bitter.

For her part, Cathy vowed not to tell Trevor, out of work and hitting the bottle, about her impending departure until a

175

suitable opportunity arose for Alison to break the news to Stirrup. The two women were arranging to start up Patches in secret in the meantime. Alison's fear of her husband's tempers were rooted in experience. He had struck her once in a rage, a year or so earlier, and she was afraid that if he found out she was leaving him for another woman he would lose all control. So it was vital to pick the right moment; yet the right moment never seemed to come.

As things turned out, it never did. A quarrel about Claire's rudeness escalated one night. The girl had gone to her room, weeping and saying she hated Alison. Stirrup, tense at a time of sticky negotiations with Grealish for the sale of his business, had bellowed with anger until he was hoarse.

'Do you want me to go?' Alison had asked. Perhaps the time had come, perhaps it was worth risking his fury. This endless fighting couldn't continue.

'What do you mean?' Stirrup had spoken with a sudden softness. She recognised it as a danger sign, like the intensity of his stare.

'You're not happy with me. And I'm not happy with you. It makes sense for me to move out.'

'Listen!'

He'd grabbed her wrist, hurting her, making her afraid that he was about to break it.

'You're moving nowhere. No one walks out on me, do you understand? No one. I'd sooner kill you.'

She had squirmed in his grip, trying in vain to escape. It only made him tighten his hold and hurt her more.

'Don't be stupid. I don't belong to you. Marriages do go stale. Ours has. What else can I do?'

'You're my wife, got that? My wife! And you don't move out. You stay here and toe the line. I meant what I said.'

She'd summoned up her courage or maybe her folly and spat at him. As if he'd had an electric shock, he let go of her, but within a moment lifted his right arm and smashed it against the side of her head, sending her spinning to the floor. Luckily he'd aimed high and wide and her hair had taken some of the sting out of the blow. Two inches lower and a little straighter and he'd have broken her cheekbone for sure.

Standing over her, he spoke harshly.

'I'd sooner kill you. Do you believe me? You ought to.'

Looking up at him through pain-misted eyes, she'd said, 'What are you talking about?'

'Margaret . . . your bloody predecessor! You thought her car simply went out of control, didn't you? That it was an accident?'

'What are you saying?'

'The brakes, Alison. I fixed them. Quite a coincidence, she was about to leave me. She'd gone head over heels for some other fool, so I made sure he'd never have her again. She should've realised I'm not a man to mess around. The truth was, she couldn't care less about Claire or me. I tried to reason with her at first. Then I warned her. No good, her mind was made up. I'd told her I'd never let her humiliate me, but she took no notice. She brought it on herself.'

So that was it. Jack Stirrup's confession to murder. Listening to Alison describe the scene, Harry could visualise his client, breathing hard, speaking with a furious passion. Easy to imagine Alison full of horror as she heard her husband condemning her either to a life sentence of misery or to death. No wonder she'd chosen a clandestine escape route.

She and Cathy resolved that nobody must guess their plans. At least Stirrup and Morgan were no longer in touch; they were unlikely to put their heads together, but even so it was important that the disappearances of their respective wives should seem unconnected. Cathy left Trevor at once; it was easier for her, she'd been dealing with the business arrangements and the cottage purchase in Knutsford. She put a curt note of farewell on the kitchen table so as to eliminate any suspicion that she'd been abducted or killed.

They agreed that Alison should somehow hang on with Stirrup for a little longer and pretend to make an effort to heal the rift. The activities of The Beast gave her an idea. She was a blonde, a potential victim. He might be thought responsible when she vanished. The thought that Stirrup might be suspected of her murder had occurred to Alison; the idea held an ironic appeal, but since no one had ever suggested he was responsible for the death of Margaret, it seemed more like wishful thinking. She'd never anticipated that Doreen Capstick would point an accusing finger at her own son-in-law.

Abandoning Doreen herself had been no hardship. On the contrary, she said, it ranked as a bonus.

'I read about Claire, of course. It did cross my mind to get in touch. But what good would it have done? He would only have kept looking for me. The fact you're here now shows how determined he is to track me down. I didn't even realise I could have cleared him of suspicion of killing me. Though I must be honest, Harry. When I think of the misery I suffered when we were together, I can't pretend I'm sorry he's been through the mill lately. Jack's used people all his life. It's time he understood how it feels.'

'I think he does.'

'A sadder and wiser man? I'll believe it when I see it. Only I don't want to see it.'

'You're wrong, Alison. He wouldn't follow you to ends of the earth to wreak revenge.'

'Really? Then what are you doing here?'

'Blame my insatiable curiosity.'

As he explained the sequence of events since her disappearance – Bolus's inquisition, Stirrup's idea that tracing her might silence Doreen Capstick and put him in the clear. Jonah Deegan's sleuthing – he juggled facts and impressions for his own benefit too. Facing the issue he'd dodged for so long. Trying to decide whether Stirrup's behaviour smacked of guilt or innocence.

And now, as he reached the end of the M62 and headed down Edge Lane towards the centre of Liverpool, certainty continued to elude him. The Stirrup he knew was capable of claiming in the heat of the moment to have committed a crime which had only taken place in his imagination. Harry had not known Stirrup in the days of Margaret; his knowledge of that marriage was confined to odd snippets of conversation over the years, filed away in his memory. Yet the man had spoken of his first wife with affection, not unmixed with grief at her death. She was, after all, the mother of his beloved Claire.

Alison, however, was in no doubt.

'I realise you're bound to tell him I'm alive. I can't expect you to do anything else. And of course the police must know. Can't have them wasting any more time over me. But Harry, will you do one thing for me? For God's sake, don't say where

I am. Lie to him, say I've gone abroad. Anything. But if you don't want to have a crime on your conscience, I'm begging you not to give him any hint that Cathy and I are here.'

Harry didn't have to say a word. He and Alison had never been close. He owed her nothing. She was a fellow human being, though, and one look at the uncharacteristic, imploring expression on her face was enough to make up his mind.

'All right, Alison. I promise.'

As the words had left his mouth, he heard the rattle of a key in a lock. Catherine Morgan was back. Alison jumped to her feet and ran out into the hall to explain in frantic whispers about their visitor.

'So,' said Cathy Morgan as she walked into the sitting room, 'a face from the past.'

Her own face was as grim as Harry remembered. It seemed to be composed entirely of straight lines. No curves, no compromises, no nonsense. Harry hadn't expected her to be overjoyed to see him – their brief acquaintance had been polite, no more than that – but he would have preferred not to be examined with the kind of distaste most people reserve for the appearance of dogshit in the middle of their previously immaculate lawn.

Nor did she disguise her distrust for his links with Jack Stirrup. Harry's tentative suggestion that Stirrup might have made up the story about killing his first wife met with scorn.

'You're fooling yourself,' Cathy Morgan had said. She might have been chastising a child who claimed to have seen a ghost. 'You wouldn't waste your time with any such idea if you'd seen the state this poor girl was in even twenty four hours after that bloody man made his threat.'

This poor girl was now sharing the sofa with her lover, curled up in the crook of a comforting arm. She seemed to have shrunk the moment Cathy walked through the door. Harry had no trouble in guessing who wore the trousers in this particular household. Was it too cynical to think that Alison had merely exchanged one form of tyranny for another?

No scope existed for further debate. Harry said thanks for the tea and it was time he was going and Alison did not try to persuade him to stay. Cathy followed him out into the narrow hallway.

'Look,' she said as she opened the front door, 'Alison means everything to me, do you hear? Everything. I won't have her harmed. You may think you mean well, but your finding us is the most dangerous thing to have happened since we came out. How can we trust you to be discreet?'

'I hate to sound pompous, Cathy, but I'm a man of my word.'

'You're a man. Full stop.'

'Part of the dreaded freemasonry, is that what you mean? Shity, deceitful, not to be depended on?'

'Something like that.'

Harry had sympathised with Alison, understood her motives and fears. Yet Doreen Capstick and Jack Stirrup, whatever their faults, had suffered through not knowing her fate. He suspected Cathy of stiffening Alison's resolve not to get in touch and felt a surge of dislike for this large, powerful woman, with her cynical green eyes and her manipulative ways.

'Then you'll just have to wait in suspense wondering when my weak knees will finally give way.'

With that, he had shambled down the street towards the nearest pub. Now in the dark warmth of the M.G. he asked himself for the first time whether he would indeed cave in when Jack Stirrup pressed, as he surely would, to be told where his wife was hiding?

Speeding through a traffic light as amber turned to red, he decided that attack must be the best form of defence. Rather than fret about Stirrup's demands for information, he must seize the initiative. A road sign loomed up: straight on for the Mersey Tunnel. He put his foot down. No time like the present. He would go to Prospect House tonight and find out for himself whether Jack Stirrup was a killer or simply a crude hoaxer.

Chapter Twenty-Six

'I asked you last week if you thought I'd done away with Alison.' Jack Stirrup didn't want to be overheard by the woman in the adjoining room, but his voice was husky with suppressed anger. 'On the way to the Majestic. Remember?'

'I remember,' said Harry. So long ago it seemed, a time when Claire was alive and he'd thought that Alison was dead.

'You dodged the issue. Typical bloody lawyer. You weren't willing to take my word. Will you take it now? Once again: I-did-not-murder-Margaret.'

He drilled home each word as if addressing a halfwit, then sat back in his armchair with folded arms, challenging Harry to disbelief.

The clock chimed eleven. They were in the drawing room of Prospect House. Outside the builders' skip had gone. Stirrup had abandoned the renovations as soon as he'd decided to put the place on the market. With no Alison and now no Claire already it resembled a museum rather than somewhere people might live. Big wooden crates of belongings stood in the hall.

Harry had come to confront Stirrup, to break the news that the guilty secret was out. To his dismay Rita Buxton answered the door. She had kindly offered to help with the packing, according to Stirrup, but the buttons undone on her creased mauve blouse told a different story. Now she sat on the sofa next door, watching a Burt Reynolds movie, waiting for Harry to leave.

When he'd announced Alison was alive, Stirrup's involuntary flinch betrayed dismay, not delight. His recovery had been swift, but not swift enough to dispel the memory of that first reaction of alarm. All the same, the instinct of self-preservation was strong. He interrupted with a fierce denial before Harry came to the end of Alison's explanation for disappearing without trace.

'Never. No way. I loved Margaret. Our marriage was all right. Okay, we had our ups and downs but so do all couples. You know that as well as anyone, after all.'

Passing his tongue over dry lips, he'd continued talking, almost as if to convince himself.

'It was an accident, what happened to her, a terrible accident. Nothing to do with me. The brakes were gone. I always blamed the garage, but nothing could be proved. Margaret took a bend too fast, it was over in a second. No one ever hinted at anything sinister. The police were satisfied – for once.'

Listening, Harry drummed his fingers on the table at his side. Each time Stirrup opened his mouth, he gained in conviction. Even assuming he was guilty, he'd had plenty of time to prepare a plausible defence. And he wasn't fool enough to deny that he had tried to frighten Alison when she threatened to walk out on him by claiming to have murdered Margaret.

'Okay, it was stupid of me. I was desperate, willing to clutch at anything. Wouldn't any man fight to keep the woman in his life?'

Harry thought back to the dreadful night when Liz had confessed her love for another man. He hadn't threatened or cajoled or begged. He'd simply stared at the floor and in the end surrendered to what seemed inevitable. If he had not – this was what tortured him whenever he was careless enough to let his mind stray towards what might have been – she might be alive today. Who could be sure of the right thing to do? Perhaps, despite its crudity and its ultimate failure, Stirrup's response had been the more courageous. Perhaps he rather than his client should have handled things differently.

Hard as he found it to accept that Alison would be terrified by a mere cock-and-bull story, his job was not to act as judge and jury. Guesswork and intuition fell far short of knowledge. In the absence of proof that Stirrup was lying, Harry knew he ought to accept what he was told.

'Okay, Jack. So it's all been a terrible misunderstanding. The fact remains, Alison doesn't see it like that.'

'Where is she?'

'Like I said, I can't tell you.'

'Now look, you're supposed to be my man, remember? What kind of lawyer are you?'

'A tired, confused and probably incompetent one. That's beside the point. I told her I had to let you know she was alive. Nothing more. As for Bolus, I'll call him tomorrow morning.'

Stirrup said through gritted teeth. 'She's my wife, Harry. Have you forgotten?'

'No. But the marriage is over. Clearest case of irretrievable breakdown I've ever seen. And now you have Rita.'

'I want to talk to Alison. Find out what the bloody hell she's been playing at.'

'Can't be done. At least, not until she changes her mind. And for that, I don't recommend you hold your breath.'

Stirrup swore, but Harry gazed at him without blinking. He hadn't mentioned anything about Cathy Morgan, had simply confirmed Alison's determination to carve out a new life under an assumed name and in a different town.

'And that's it?'

'That's it, Jack. Sorry. She's alive and well, that's all you need to know. End of the pressure from Bolus – Doreen too, come to that. Alison's no wish to see either you or her mother again. So the time's come to get on with the rest of your life. For your own sake as much as hers.'

'And that's your best professional advice?'

'For what it's worth.'

'Which is bugger all.' Stirrup lumbered to his feet. 'All right, Harry, piss off. You're not my solicitor as from this moment. Send me your bill for work up to date. I won't quibble about the sums. I'm not the untrustworthy bastard you think I am.'

Harry stood up. Far from coming as a surprise, the parting of their ways was unavoidable, had been from the moment he'd assured Alison he wouldn't reveal her whereabouts. He extended his hand.

'Okay, Jack. I'll be off. I'm sorry it's . . .'

'Save it.' Stirrup ignored the outstretched hand and jerked his head in the direction of the door. 'You know the way out.'

Once outside the house Harry allowed himself the indulgence of a self-reproaching groan. He had achieved the worst of all worlds. Crusoe and Devlin had waved goodbye to their biggest client and any chance of cutting a slice off their overdraft in the foreseeable future. And for what? A promise given to a woman whom he did not know any more. An unnecessary promise, if Stirrup was telling the truth now and his claim to have killed Margaret was a lie invented to keep Alison.

On the way home he wrestled with his dilemma. Had he been unfair to Stirrup? The man had lost his wife and daughter in quick succession. He might be to blame for the first misfortune; the second was quite outside his control.

As Harry drove and turned his thoughts to Claire, her behaviour before her death started to bother him again. He had meant to ask someone – was it Gina Jean-Jacques? – a question and had failed to do so. Now he'd let it slip his mind, the more he strained for recollection, the more elusive it became.

Back in Empire Dock, his flat seemed as barren of life as Prospect House. If only Valerie were waiting for him. What would she be doing now? If he had the guts to pick up the phone, he could ask her over. It was late, yet she might be willing to come.

He dialled the number which he'd committed to memory weeks before. The tone kept ringing, insistent and repetitive.

Come on, he muttered into the mouthpiece. Surely you're not out on the town tonight?

Finally he heard a click at the other end. A man spoke. Sounding weary, as though he'd just climbed out of bed.

'Hello?'

Harry froze, unable to utter a word.

'Hello? Hello?' A note of irritation crept in. 'Hello? Who's that?'

The man banged the receiver down in evident disgust. Harry maintained his grip on the handset for another minute before he slowly put it down.

Of course he had recognised the voice. It belonged to Julian Hamer.

Chapter Twenty-Seven

Through the keyhole he could see Valerie in her room at Balliol Chambers. The place was dark except for the glare of the desk lamp on her face. Her lips were open, as if she were trying to scream, but Harry couldn't hear a sound. Her eyes were following the movement towards her of something out of his line of vision; her pupils dilated in terror even as he watched. Harry grasped the door knob, squeezing it so hard that it began to crack in his hand, but she had locked him out. And locked someone else in with her. An unseen hand switched on the overhead light and Harry saw that Valerie was powerless to defend herself. Her arms and ankles were tied by thick cord to the chair on which she sat. Into view came the stooped back of a man in waistcoat, white shirt and pinstripe trousers. He approached her slowly, as if relishing her fear. In his hands was a black silk cravat, knotted into a ligature. Valerie shut her eyes and bowed her head, surrendering to her fate. The man bent over her and at last Harry found the strength to cry out.

'No!'

The man turned round and Harry saw at last the face of The Beast. A wolf's face, teeth bared in a savage grin. Then The Beast raised a gloved hand and peeled the rubber mask away. To leave Harry staring into the mocking eyes of Julian Hamer.

Suddenly he woke. He was naked and in his restlessness he had cast off the duvet, yet his skin was sticky with sweat. His bedroom was as dark as Valerie's chambers in his dream. A glance at the alarm clock told him it was ten to four. The sun had not yet risen. Even at this hour it was so hot that his limbs ached and the lack of air made it hard to breathe.

For a while he lay motionless, angry that he had let his envy of Hamer turn sleep into a torment. Of course he had lost Valerie: he was too experienced at missing out on the good things of life not to recognise the stomach-turning awareness that something worthwhile had slipped out of reach, like a child's beach ball borne away on the tide.

The clock's hands had crawled past the hour before he forced himself off the bed and into the living room. There he poured himself a generous measure of Johnnie Walker, downing it at a gulp. The sharp bite of the alcohol made him feel better and the flat somehow less empty. He poured another and settled down in an armchair. This time he did not drink so fast.

He closed his eyes but his mind roamed, trying to pick a path through the maze that had defeated him for so long. Now he realised that the search for Alison had led him to a dead end. And although Stirrup might have murdered his first wife, he could never be convicted if he maintained his categoric denial of guilt. Yet the killing of Claire continued to be a torment. Why had she suffered a fate that did not make sense even in the context of any of The Beast's previous crimes?

Harry concentrated on images of the dead girl. Claire at Caldy. Claire in Balliol Chambers. Claire's unexpected visit to Gina Jean-Jacques. Claire's mysterious trip to West Kirby. Somewhere amongst the childish deceptions of her young life lay, he felt sure, the clue to her death, the reason why The Beast had for the first time abandoned his preference for blondes.

For hours, it seemed, he struggled with the conundrum. Eventually sleep returned and this time he did not dream.

It was half nine before he awoke once more; neither the alarm nor the shafts of light falling through the narrow gaps in the curtains had stirred him. The day ahead would be long and busy and he was already late. Yet that did not seem to matter. He opened his eyes to the morning and stretched his arms to the heavens, as if freed from a slave's chains. He felt intensely alive and all-seeing. Now at last he knew the solution. And a solution, what was more, that gave him grim satisfaction.

He rang the office to say he wouldn't be in until noon at the earliest. Slinging his jacket over his shoulder he headed for the city centre. In Chavasse Park young girls lazed on the grass, soaking up the sun, but he didn't give them a second glance. Inside ten minutes he was climbing the stairs of Balliol Chambers.

Denise sat behind the desk in reception, her pale pink top revealing tanned flesh. As she caught sight of him she lifted her eyebrows and smiled.

'Oppressive, isn't it? This must be the hottest day we've had yet. They said on the weather forecast that a storm . . .'

'Where's Julian?'

She frowned at his brusqueness.

'It's Mr Hamer you'd like to see? I didn't realise a conference was booked.'

'I haven't an appointment. But I need to see him right now.'

Denise pursed her lips, put out by this breach of professional courtesy.

'Let me see, David Base is having a day off at home. Now where has he put the diary . . .?'

'If you don't mind, I'm going straight in.'

Before Denise could utter a protest Harry walked past her and down the corridor. At Julian's door he knocked briefly and went straight in.

The room was empty. Harry scanned it slowly, as if the barrister might be lurking under his desk or between bookshelves, then tried Valerie's room. No luck there either. She must be out at court. For an instant as he looked round, Harry recalled the nightmare which had woken him earlier that morning. The memory chilled him and he slammed the door on his way out.

'Mr Hamer's on a case,' said Denise in reproach. 'I could have told you if only you'd waited.'

'Sorry, love. I'm in a hurry. Where is he?'

'The Law Courts. A medical negligence claim.'

'And Valerie?'

'Miss Kaiwar's over there too. Road traffic.'

Harry raced down the stairs again. The thought that Valerie was in the same building as Hamer gave him a curious sense of unease. Yet nothing dangerous could happen in a court of law. Could it?

He was soon in the Law Courts, checking the typed daily sheets on the noticeboard to find his quarry. Court number three. He reached the room in half a minute and slipped in at the back.

The court was three-quarters full. A young girl in a wheel-chair sat at the front, surrounded by friends here to support her case against the doctor whose clumsiness, Harry presumed, had caused her to lose the use of her legs. Her expression was anxious. No, more than that, panic-stricken. And the people with her were also twitching with alarm.

Julian was on his feet. He was speaking slowly and slurring his words. Yes, there could be no mistake. Fumbling foolishly with his papers and slurring his words. Drunk in court? Harry could scarcely believe that this was the same smooth adversary who had stolen the affections of Valerie Kaiwar.

Suddenly a couple of sheets of paper slipped from Julian Hamer's hands.

'My Lord. Er – please excuse me.'

Julian bent down and scrabbled around on the floor, trying to gather together the bits and pieces he had let fall. In the row behind, a grey-haired woman solicitor had the look of a schoolmarm watching a blue movie. Her opposite number was whispering in the ear of his barrister. Chuckles were audible.

The judge was old Borrington, a kindly soul who liked to snooze in the afternoon. He peered down at Julian Hamer and in the fluting tone which Harry believed to be in itself a qualification for the Bench said, 'Mr Hamer, I wonder . . . the day is rather warm. And even in this fine building the air-conditioning is not quite as one would wish. Perhaps if we were to adjourn for ten minutes?'

'My – my Lord, I'm most grateful.'

The court rose as the ancient in ermine pottered out and the defendant's barrister exchanged a smirk with his instructing solicitor. Hamer stumbled to the door, leaving the grey-haired woman to talk in hushed, urgent tones to her client.

'Julian, can I have a word?'

'What are you doing here?'

'I need to talk to you.'

Hamer flushed. He ran a hand though the normally sleek fair hair.

'What about?'

'In private, if you don't mind.'

'Look, can we do this some other time? You can see I'm right in the middle of a big case. And f . . . frankly, it's not going particularly well so far.'

'So I see. But this can't wait.'

'What's got into you?'

'Come on.'

Harry grasped Hamer's arm and propelled him down the passageway towards the robing rooms. Finding the barrister's sanctum empty, Harry bundled his captive inside and onto a chair before releasing his grip.

'For God's sake, man. What's all this . . .'

'Claire Stirrup's dead.'

Hamer's face was a puzzled blank. Dark rings curved under his eyes. Someone else hasn't been sleeping, Harry thought.

'I know. We spoke about it.'

'Why did she have to die, Julian?'

'What do you mean? She was murdered by a maniac.'

'The Beast, yes. But her death troubled me. You know, the way The Beast usually chooses blonde-haired girls, whereas Claire was dark.'

'I don't follow you.'

'Here's another mystery. Claire laid a false trail on the Saturday when she died. Claimed she was going to the library, but she didn't take her books with her. So what was she up to? I wondered for a while if her father had lied about the library himself. Perhaps he might be implicated. He has guilty secrets of his own, I think. Yet I know he'd never harm his own daughter. He worshipped that girl. So Claire lied to him. Why?'

Wearily, Hamer said, 'God knows why you're asking me. The answer is obvious, isn't it? She was off to see some lad and Daddy wasn't to know.'

'Possibly. But the date wasn't with her regular boyfriend. I'm sure he's telling the truth on that score. And repellent though he is, I don't think she had eyes for anyone else.

Which led me to think that she must have been up to something different.'

'Look, I'm in the midst of a trial. I haven't the time to indulge in your guessing games. I'm sorry the client's child was killed, but it's nothing to do with me.'

Hamer made as if to get up and leave but Harry again put his arm out in restraint.

'Let me finish. Shortly before she died, Claire did one or two odd things. She visited a girl, not a close friend, who had been raped by The Beast a few weeks earlier. Yet Claire was no angel of compassion.'

'Where is all this leading?'

'To you,' Harry said softly.

'To me? I don't understand.'

'After she met you, she started behaving oddly. I've asked myself what could explain everything that happened to her.'

'And?'

'And I've come up with the answer. She recognised you.'

'What the hell do you mean?'

'She was on the Wirral Way the afternoon her schoolfriend was attacked. Waiting for her boyfriend. Suppose she saw a man hanging around? Thought nothing of it at the time, but later wondered if he might just have been The Beast. And what if when she attended the conference in chambers she realised you were that man?'

Hamer's cheeks were as white as mortuary sheets.

'This is monstrous speculation. Absolutely monstrous.'

'No wonder she was so preoccupied that day. Imagine coming face to face with The Beast. Jack Stirrup said something about her mooning over you at the conference. He misunderstood what she saw in you. So she spoke to the other girl, the one who was raped, though I doubt she learned much. Then she got in touch with you, tried a little blackmail. Her boyfriend had given her the taste for it. She may have asked for money, I don't know. But most of all she wanted power over another human being. So when she told you to meet her in West Kirby, she insisted you bring her a dozen red roses. A token of your submission to her will, I guess. She loved the thought of having you on a string. And as a bonus she could make her boyfriend jealous if she flourished the

190

roses under his nose later that afternoon, make him think she had a secret admirer.'

Harry swallowed hard. 'She was naive enough to think she could look after herself. For what it was worth, she'd learned self-defence, picked up a bit of karate. She didn't take any precautions. I suppose she thought of it all as a kind of game. A deadly game, though. You managed somehow to catch her by surprise. I suppose you had your car handy to take her body to New Brighton. Where you scattered the roses over her corpse and left it to rot in the cave.'

'You must be out of your mind.'

Not Hamer speaking, but a newcomer. Someone Harry recognised only too well. He saw in the doorway the figure of Valerie Kaiwar. A thick bundle of documents tied with pink ribbon was under her arm. Her face was burning, not with the heat of the day but with rage.

'Valerie!'

'Yes,' she said, mimicking the surprise in his tone. 'Valerie.'

'How much did you hear?'

'Enough to realise you've finally gone round the bloody bend.'

'You don't understand why . . .'

'Don't you tell me I don't understand! Compared to you I'm a genius of detection. How dare you stand there and calmly accuse Julian of rape and murder?'

'Valerie, the facts . . .'

'What do you know about facts? Look at Julian, look at him! How can you possibly have the nerve to say those terrible things?'

Hamer buried his head in his hands. He was beginning to shake. The pathetic spectacle reinforced Harry's conviction. The man was demoralised because he had been found out.

'Everything points to his guilt, Valerie.'

'Crap! You don't know the first thing about him.'

'I know enough.'

'Really?' Her manner was withering. 'Let's test that bold assertion, shall we? For instance – when do you think The Beast hid Claire Stirrup's body in the cave?'

'The police can't be sure. Even if she was killed around mid-day, they reckon her body was kept somewhere – a car boot, presumably – until darkness fell and he had the chance to lift it into the cave unobserved.'

'Right. Now we're getting somewhere.'

'Are we?'

'Yes, Sherlock, we are. You want to know why? Listen – all the time when you think he was over on Wirral burying that little girl, he was at home in Liverpool. And I can prove it. Shall I explain? Because I was there too. Yes, you can wipe that look off your face. It's true. I was with him all evening.'

Chapter Twenty-Eight

'You're lying,' said Harry. 'Lying to protect him.'

Valerie exclaimed in anger. Hamer still had his head in his hands. She glanced at him before beckoning grimly to Harry to follow her as she stepped backwards into the corridor.

As soon as they were outside the robing room she banged the door shut and hissed in his ear.

'You utter bastard! How could you do that to him? How could you? And how could you accuse me of – of – God, you're an idiot! How is it I've only just realised?'

Her storm of anger had shipwrecked him.

'Valerie, we need to talk.'

'Too right. Come with me.'

She led him past a couple of doors before pausing outside the entrance to the library.

'We may as well try this place, God knows, there's seldom anyone here.'

They went inside, squinting along the tall stacks of books. No-one was mugging up on the last minute point of law. Valerie walked past the shelf marked CRIME and sat on one of two high stools next to BLASPHEMY AND OBSCENITY. She motioned him to do likewise.

Quietly, as if the books might eavesdrop, she said. 'You've made a complete and utter fool of yourself.'

'If you're right,' said Harry, 'it wouldn't be the first time.'

'Nor the last, I expect.' She sighed, pushing a small hand through the thicket of her hair. 'Why did you have to do it? To Julian, of all people?'

'Everything fits, Valerie.'

'Nothing fits. For a start, Julian would never terrorise a woman. I'm not guessing. I know him well.'

'So it seems.'

'You can cut out the sarky comments for a start.'

'What would you say if you were me? You've already given him your alibi. And I rang your flat last night. Very late. He answered the phone.'

She stared at him. 'You're serious, aren't you? You actually think Julian and I are lovers?'

'Do you deny it?'

'For Christ's sake!' Her anger had returned and with it, her voice rose. 'You don't know what you're saying.'

'What do you expect me to say?'

Wincing, she said, 'I can see I'm going to have to satisfy your bloody curiosity, even though it does mean breaking a promise.'

'Maybe you owe me an explanation.'

'Don't be stuffy, Harry, it doesn't suit you. And remember this – I don't owe you anything.'

'Okay, okay, okay. Are you going to tell me or not?'

A warning light shone in her eyes, making him feel like an ant about to be crushed by a sledgehammer.

'Julian has MS.'

'What?'

'Multiple sclerosis, you know?'

Now it was Harry's turn to stare.

'He's had the symptoms for months, but he's said nothing to anyone until recently. Things got worse, he eventually went to see the doctor and the diagnosis was confirmed.'

'Christ.'

'Before I came in and heard you haranguing him I was having a word with the solicitor in the case Julian's handling today. I gather things went badly. People thought he was pissed.'

'That's right. At least – I did.'

'After a night of lust with me, I suppose you thought?'

'Something like that,' he muttered.

'Harry, you prick.' Her voice trembled with contempt. 'Certainly he was with me. As he has been on several occasions when you've wanted me to spend time with you.'

194

'I see.'

'I doubt it. He swore me to secrecy. I'm still the only person he's confided in apart from the doctors. He daren't tell anyone. Not everyone with MS continues to degenerate. He's been praying that the symptoms are only transient. I try to persuade him he'll be one of the lucky ones, but he doesn't believe it and frankly neither do I. All I can do is offer him my time, company, whatever comfort I can. Not sex, if that's what you're bothered about, but friendship. We talk long into the night. Why do you think I've fobbed you off so many times when you wanted us to spend an evening together? He needs support more than any man I know. More than you, for a start. At least you have your life to lead, your business. But Julian knows this bloody disease will destroy his career. What solicitor is going to brief a mouthpiece who can't even guarantee to get the words out straight?'

She folded her arms and looked at him. It was a mannerism she had picked up in the courts, a let's-see-what-you-make-of-that look, more effective than any advocate's rhetoric.

Harry kept quiet for a long time, thinking of small clues he had misunderstood. Like the way Julian had dropped his tea cup that afternoon in Balliol Chambers when he first met Claire. A sign not of guilty recognition, but of the bit-by-bit deterioration of his body.

Hoarse with self-reproach, he said, 'You're right. I have made a fool of myself. What can I say?'

'Not a lot. What's done can't be easily undone. All I'll say is -- you're not the man I thought you were. And now, if you'll excuse me, I must get back and see Julian.'

She turned on her heel and left Harry to his thoughts. He took a step forward and knocked his head, not gently, several times against the shelf labelled CONTRACTS AND OBLIGATIONS. Out of the corner of his eye the title of an old, calfskin-bound tome caught his eye.

MISTAKE OF FACT.

'Shit!' he said. 'Shit, shit, shit!'

As he spoke a young woman, dressed so severely and looking so thirsty for legal knowledge that she could only be an articled clerk working for Maher and Malcolm, walked into the room. She took one look at him, crimsoned and then disappeared out of sight again.

Time to go, Harry said to himself. You've done enough damage in the last twenty-four hours to last a professional lifetime.

He loosened his tie, put his jacket over his shoulder and shambled out of the library, down the stairs and into the sweltering heat of Derby Square. There, he spotted a familiar figure limping towards him. Jonah Deegan. Uncertainty flitted across the old detective's face and he cleared his throat noisily before addressing Harry with less than his usual truculence.

'I was looking for you. Just been to your office. To have a word about Stirrup.'

'He's given me the sack.'

'He did say he'd had a barney with you.'

'About Alison. I refused to give him her address. Did he try to pump you?'

Jonah looked uncomfortable. 'As it happens, he did.'

Harry could already guess the answer to his question, but he asked it anyway.

'And?'

For the first time in their acquaintance, Jonah Deegan showed traces of embarrassment. His leathery cheeks went pink and he started fiddling irritably with the hairs that grew from his nostrils.

'He's a client. I owe him a duty. As a professional man, you know the score.'

'I know you'll be wanting your bill paid.'

'It's not a question of money. He hired me to find her. He had a right to know.'

'He told Alison he'd killed his first wife. That's why she hid herself away.'

'Doesn't make him a murderer.'

'Let's hope you're right. I'd best be off. I ought to phone Alison, put her on her guard.'

'I can save you the trouble. After Stirrup told me the background, I phoned her myself. Thought it best. She made a bit of a fuss. Seemed to blame you. Scared of some rough stuff, I reckon. I told her not to fret, that I'd heard more false confessions than fog warnings on the Mersey. Stirrup simply can't keep his mouth shut, that's all.'

Harry eyed the old man. Neither of them could be sure whether Stirrup had killed his first wife. Both of them knew he would never be punished.

'Stirrup's not the only one.'

A couple of minutes later he was back in the office. Clients weren't beating a path to the door. The reception area was deserted and Suzanne on switchboard was immersed in the problem page of a woman's magazine. As he headed for his own room, Jim Crusoe stepped out of the typists' room and hailed him.

'Hey, there's a stranger in town. All right?'

'All right? In the last twenty-four hours I've lost myself a girlfriend and the firm its biggest client. Give me a week and I'll have us both in Parkhurst.'

Jim Crusoe's solid features didn't flicker. 'Sorry to hear about Valerie. Want to talk about it?'

'No. Thanks.'

'Stirrup, then. Have the police pulled him in? Has he opted for Ruby Fingall's tender mercies?'

'No. Alison's alive and well.'

'What's the problem, then?'

Glad of the chance to unburden himself, Harry described Jonah's detective work and his own visits to Knutsford and Prospect House.

Jim rubbed his jaw thoughtfully. 'So you reckon he did kill whatshername – Margaret?'

'I could be wrong. I haven't been guessing well lately.'

'Think he'll try to harm Alison?'

'Maybe not. At least Deegan's tip-off should give her time to clear out. But in any case, Claire's murder has hit him hard. And he must realise the marriage is dead. The main reason he wanted to know where she lives was wounded pride, I suppose. But the police will lose interest now and with Rita Buxton to offer home comforts, maybe Jack will lose interest in any sort of confrontation with Alison. Looking back on last night, perhaps I should have given him the address. Then we'd still have him as a client.'

Jim shrugged. 'Win a few, lose a few. You did the right thing.'

It wasn't as simple or as obvious as that, and both of them knew it.

'Thanks.'

'And what about his daughter's murder? Have you heard anything?'

'From the police and from Stirrup, nothing. As you'd expect, that hasn't stopped my imagination working overtime. With the result that I've done my best to get us blacklisted by Balliol Chambers.'

Harry found himself describing the contretemps in the Law Courts that morning. His partner listened as if to nothing more melodramatic than a discourse on the law of registered title.

'It all seemed to make sense,' said Harry, reflecting on the logical steps he had taken on the road to his conclusion about Julian Hamer's guilt. 'The way the girl behaved at the con. Her interrogation of Gina Jean-Jacques. The secret rendevouz last Saturday – presumably with the man who killed her.'

'It might still make sense.' Jim was trying to let him down lightly. 'Stand back for a moment. Your clues may have more than one meaning. Remember that old case about the interpretation of a will? The man who left his estate 'all to mother'? It wasn't the gift it seemed. 'Mother' was his name for his wife.'

Harry nodded. In his mind, suspicions began to reform like patterns in the fireside blaze.

Tolerantly, Jim said, 'The look on your face tells me I've started you off again. Just try not to pin anything on the Bishop of Liverpool this afternoon, old son. We can use all the divine assistance we can get just now.'

Harry glanced heavenwards. 'This time, I'll be glad to be wrong.'

He hurried to his own room and dialled a Wirral number. At last he'd remembered the question he had meant to put to Gina Jean-Jacques.

'Gina, is that you? This is Harry Devlin. No, it doesn't matter that your mother's out. I wanted to ask you one more question. When Claire asked you what it was like being kissed by The Beast . . . what did you tell her?'

Chapter Twenty-Nine

'I never knew a boy so quiet,' said Mrs Warner. 'He was never any trouble to either Hubert or me.'

She sat back in her floral-patterned armchair and sipped her tea contentedly. A large, comfortable widow with white hair, varicose veins and nothing to be ashamed of. Harry was sure she had done her best for her nephew after his mother's death a dozen years ago and that she had not the slightest inkling of the dark thoughts that must lurk deep within his brain.

When she learned that the quiet boy had become The Beast she had read and gossiped about, her life would disintegrate like an old dock warehouse attacked by a demolition gang.

Harry finished his tea, uttering a silent prayer that his suspicion should prove as unjust and absurd as in the case of Julian Hamer. He cringed when he thought of the accusation he had levelled at a sick man – was it only four hours earlier? Valerie was right to feel disgust.

Yet now he dreaded the prospect of another mistake far less than the possibility that for once he might be right. It seemed like an act of cruelty to sit in this well-kept room, engaging Elsie Warner in friendly conversation, letting her believe his cock-and-bull story. He had said this was no more than a casual call on a professional acquaintance's home, whilst passing through New Brighton, on the off-chance that her nephew might be around. Guileless, she had invited him in. In truth he was seeking corroboration for the theory he had reconstructed about the identity of Claire Stirrup's murderer.

Gina Jean-Jacques' puzzled answer to his intrusive question had confirmed Jim's point. The fatal sequence of events became clear when you stood back and looked at it afresh. But he knew that this piece of guesswork, like the last, could bring nothing but misery. If only it were untrue. And yet everything Mrs Warner willingly told him about her nephew helped to paint a picture that she herself could never recognise. A portrait of a murderer.

According to Mrs Warner, her nephew had always been a lonely young man with very few friends. His parents' marriage had broken down when he was still in short trousers. The father had been violent, a drunkard and a womaniser whose wife had been prepared to tolerate his blows and infidelities for the sake of the child. But when, in a final beery rage, the man had thrashed the boy, she could take no more. She walked out with her son and they had lived in a scruffy council flat until one day the boy had come home from school and found his mother lying on the bedroom floor in her underclothes, dead after a massive stroke.

'We took him in, of course, Hubert and me,' Mrs Warner reminisced. 'We never had children of our own. I was already turned fifty, but there was no one else to look after him. Of course, there was a what-you-call-it – a generation gap. But we did our best.'

Harry wondered what it is that turns a man sour against women, against life. Of all the inadequates he had defended, he'd never found one common factor to unite them all, to mark them as men whom society should spot and lock away before they could do harm. There had been no lack of love in this household. Perhaps in the boy's life it had simply come too late.

A gilt-framed photograph on the scrupulously dusted sideboard caught his eye. A head and shoulders shot of a small-featured woman with curly blonde hair, smiling shyly at the camera. A picture Harry had seen before.

Mrs Warner followed his glance.

'That's poor Emma, of course.'

Harry looked inquiring and the story soon came out. Emma had been a girlfriend, the one and only so far as Mrs Warner knew. A pleasant girl from Liscard Village. The couple had got engaged on her twenty-first birthday: a wedding had been planned for the following June. A month later she was dead. She had suffered from anorexia nervosa since her early teens: the doctors reckoned it put the strain on her heart which had killed her.

'A tragedy, it was. Such a bolt from the blue. No one could believe it. And of course, he would never talk about it afterwards. Just bottled it all up inside. It's not the best way, Mr Devlin, it's not the best way.'

'No.'

'I keep hoping he'll find someone else. He's not a bad-looking young chap, though I say so myself as shouldn't. But he seems somehow to have lost all interest in girls.'

If only he had, thought Harry.

'Ah, well. It's a pity you missed him,' said Mrs Warner, not for the first time.

'You said he'd gone out for a walk,' prompted Harry.

'Yes, he often goes out on his own like that. Says he likes to be alone with his thoughts. I'm not sure it's a good thing, but what can you say? He's upgrown now, it's none of my business how he spends his time. Probably he's just set off for a stroll on the front. Though it's so muggy I wouldn't be surprised if we were in for a storm.'

'Might stretch my legs myself before it pours. Any idea where I'd most likely bump into him?'

'You could try the prom.'

'I will.' He stood up and cast another glance at the photograph of the dead girl. 'Thank you for the tea. It was kind of you.'

'Think nothing of it, Mr . . . Devlin, was it? Nice to meet one of his business friends and have a chat, it makes a change for me. Might see you again some day if you care to pop in. Though normally of course he's working on a weekday. He'll be sorry he was out when you called.'

Harry bit his lip. *Even sorrier when he finds out that I know the truth.*

'Goodbye,' he said and averted his gaze from the old woman's kind eyes.

Outside the heat had become oppressive, like a threat of war. Harry sensed a feverishness in the air, as if the passers-by

201

expected thunder and were scurrying madly, trying to make the most of the sunshine before the rain pelted down. When he came to the seafront he slackened his pace, looking for any sign of the man he was hunting.

Should he tell the police what he knew? In principle, yes – but what exactly did he know? He had no proof, no hard facts, nothing much other than surmise. Thank God he had said nothing about Julian Hamer; to have disgraced himself in front of Valerie was disaster enough. No, for the time being it made sense to keep his suspicions to himself. But what if he did catch up with his man? After the débâcle of the morning, Harry simply did not know what he would do.

He passed the Majestic and noticed a brand new Mercedes open top sports car with personalised number plates in the park. BG1. So Grealish had changed his motor. Perhaps he was celebrating the acquisition of Stirrup Wines. Harry wondered how long Stephanie would last before her lover tired of her lissom charms and traded her in for a new model too.

Hordes of kids shrieked around the paddling pool and formed a straggly queue outside the kiosk that sold ice cream. A little further on a shop was doing a roaring trade in Kiss-me-quick hats. A couple of young women were trying them on, giggling all the while.

Harry leaned over the sea wall, remembering the sickness he had felt at the news of Claire Stirrup's death. She ought to be here now, exchanging silly jokes with other girls of her own age. Her murder had been a waste of life and the senselessness of it appalled him, made him sad and angry both at the same time.

Watching the waves, he realised that he felt much the same about Claire's killer. The Beast, that figure enlarged into a nightmarish giant in the public imagination by lurid news stories, was in real life a man people would pass without a second glance. How else had he escaped the law's net for so long? In attacking blondes, did he think he was taking revenge on them for being alive when the girl he loved was dead? Did he gain pleasure from either the sex or the violence? Harry didn't try to answer himself. He didn't want to get inside the man's head, when all he was likely to find there was a tangled web of frustrations, jealousies and pain.

He kicked a pebble along the promenade. The sky had become overcast: one or two passers-by were looking up anxiously, making calculations about how long it would take to get back home.

The two giggling women had overtaken him. They were chattering together on the other side of the road. Both were leggy blondes; one had long hair, the other a tight perm. The girl with shoulder-length hair waved goodbye to her companion and sauntered off past the Floral Hall in the direction of The Wreckers. Standing with his back to the sea, Harry idly followed her progress. Her denim shorts were very short, her bare legs and arms richly tanned.

Suddenly a movement across the road caught his eye. A man coming out of an amusement arcade. A man in a pale grey tracksuit and trainers. A slightly built man with neat brown hair and a pleasant but anonymous face, a man easily overlooked in a seaside town.

Except that Harry recognised him as the man he had come to New Brighton for. The man he now believed to be The Beast.

'Could be anyone,' Bernard Gladwin had said of The Beast. But the killer had proved to be someone Harry had known for years. Someone Claire had indeed recognised when accompanying her father to Balliol Chambers.

David Base glanced to his right and began to quicken his pace. The blonde girl was fifty yards ahead of him. Harry realised that, like Gina Jean-Jacques, she bore a faint facial resemblance – something in the bone structure, perhaps – to Emma. Emma of the photograph at David's home and in Balliol Chambers.

Fear trickled down Harry's spine. There was only one reason for David to follow the girl. The hunger must have seized him again. Harry began to move briskly too. He must not let them get out of sight.

The girl swung her hips without a trace of self-consciousness. From behind she looked very good to Harry. He didn't know what ideas were flowing through David's mind. Did not want to know.

He felt something strange and unfamiliar touch his face. Yes, a drop of rain. People here and there were beginning to unfurl umbrellas. He felt another drop and another and another.

The girl strolled past The Wreckers. David Base was keeping the same distance between them. Feeling sick, Harry recognised that David was tracking his prey with an ease born of long practice.

As David walked, he took a peppermint from his trouser pocket and absent-mindedly tossed it from hand to hand before popping it into his mouth. That habit of his had been a giveaway. Claire must have noticed it when she spotted him close to Prospect House on the Wirral Way, minutes before he came upon Gina and raped her. No doubt she had seen him repeat the trick at Balliol Chambers before Harry arrived for the conference. Why else ask Gina about the taste of The Beast's kisses? Why else sound so excited when Gina said the man had not kissed her, but his breath had smelt of peppermint?

She hadn't been mooning over David, as her father thought. After the first shock of recognition, her moodiness had concealed the working of her mind as she devised a way to exploit her suspicion of his guilt. She wanted to savour having him in her power. Have him bring her roses. Presumably she'd phoned him and arranged a rendezvous in West Kirby. But she'd underestimated his desperation and had too much faith in her own skill at self-defence.

As the road came to an end and the riverside walkway began, Harry fell in directly behind the barristers' clerk. He was only thirty yards ahead. What if he turned round and saw Harry in pursuit? He did not have any idea what he should do or say.

The girl came to the gate marking the entrance to Vale Park. There she paused, as if uncertain what to do. David Base slowed at once. So did Harry. No need to worry. The clerk was intent on the object of his quest.

She turned into the park. David Base went after her. Harry reached the gate, then hesitated. Vale Park was as quiet as usual, a small oasis of trees, neatly tended flower beds and grass parched from the long drought. A place for relaxation and reflection, not for clandestine and cruel crime. Harry saw the rose garden was deserted. There wasn't even anyone exercising the dog.

The girl had taken refuge from the rain under the old bandstand with its domed roof and doric columns. She was nibbling at her fingernails. She glanced upwards and caught sight of Harry. Then she turned her head quickly away.

David Base was nowhere in sight. Where had he gone?

The girl looked round carefully. She seemed to be wondering whether to make a run for it and risk getting wet or wait until the worst was over.

She made up her mind and stepped out from underneath the shelter. But she did not hurry. Instead, she strolled, as if in slow motion. Almost inviting trouble. Harry was tempted to shout about the danger she faced. But instinct told him to wait until David showed himself again.

Numb with apprehension, he watched her follow the path towards the exit at the far end of the park. Suddenly she ducked and disappeared beneath a thick clump of bushes. Then he began to stride rapidly down the path. His heart was thudding. He was afraid of what David Base might be about to do. He cursed himself for waiting too long. Now he must get to her first.

What happened next was never entirely clear in his mind, no matter how many times he replayed the scene. Within seconds he was conscious of a girl's scream and a blur of action as she staggered back into his line of vision. She stumbled as her pursuer, wearing the mask of a snarling panther, leaped forward and caught hold of her. But then she cried out not in terror, it seemed to Harry, but in exultation. For all at once the park was full of people and a voice of command was bellowing: 'Police!'

Chapter Thirty

'Are you a Believer?'

The well-scrubbed young man sitting next to Harry had a face as pink as the carnation in his buttonhole. TRUST IN THE LORD exhorted the badge which adorned his other lapel. On top table Brenda Rixton – sorry, Redpath, Harry mentally corrected himself – and her new husband exchanged smiles, oblivious to the bit-part players at their reception.

''Fraid not.'

This was the first dry day since the storm which had signalled the end of the long hot spell. But Harry's stock of weather small talk was limited and he was glad when the toastmaster demanded silence for the best man's speech.

As the happy couple heard their virtues recited, Harry cast his mind back to that torrential downpour when it seemed the heavens were trying to cleanse the land following the capture of The Beast. But rain cannot wash away everything. No one could tell how long it would take for the community's scars of fear to fade.

With a shudder he remembered how near he had come to ruining the covert operation to entrap David Base. Scores of times he had asked himself what would have happened if he had caught up with and confronted David. A confession? Resistance? He was glad he would never find out.

When the police had arrested David in Vale Park, tucked into his tracksuit they found a ligature, a knotted strip of cord. Even Ruby Fingall would have been hard pressed to explain that and the mask away, let alone the one in ten million match between David's DNA and the traces found on Claire's corpse. The clerk hadn't given his defence the opportunity to test its powers of imagination. He'd been willing to talk straight away, according to the local legal grapevine. Almost as if glad that it was all over.

The scale of the undercover effort to catch The Beast had become public knowledge. Since Claire's murder, police had patrolled the peninsula's parks, its open spaces, with as much manpower as resources allowed. And womanpower. The leggy blonde and her companion whom Harry had first seen trying on Kiss-me-quick hats had both been policewomen. Even now Harry couldn't quite believe that their skimpy beachwear had concealed panic buttons and a two-way radio.

'And on that note,' said the best man, putting his memory cards face down on the table, 'it only remains for me to give you a toast: the bride and groom!'

Everyone stood and raised their glasses solemnly. As they resumed their seats Harry's neighbour whispered, 'Brenda really does look delightful.'

Bland as background music the young man might be, but he wasn't wrong. Today Brenda might have passed for ten years younger than forty-five. The blue chiffon two-piece suited her, as had the broad-brimmed hat she'd worn outside. As Colin Redpath stumbled through his speech, she gazed up at him, intent and loving. For an instant a memory surfaced in Harry's mind, a memory of a caring, anxious face and a soft, white, yielding body underneath his. He banished the image angrily and told himself to be glad she had found Colin and a new way of life.

The Redpaths were not alone in making a fresh start. Harry had rung Alison Stirrup a couple of times. A self-imposed sense of responsibility had made him fear for her safety. But she and Cathy were back in their Knutsford shop within days of moving out. Alison said her husband had never contacted her. In their conversations she had been uncommunicative, keen to get off the phone. When Harry referred to Stirrup's claim to have murdered his first wife, Alison was dismissive.

'You said it yourself, he made that story up to frighten me. I over-reacted. Surely you can understand why. The marriage breakdown. Coming out. It's been a strain. I got everything out of proportion. I simply needed to escape. From him, from my mother. That's all.'

208

'He told you he'd fixed the brakes on Margaret's car.'

'For God's sake don't repeat that. I don't want to be had up for slander.'

Jack Stirrup had had his fill of defamation law, reflected Harry grimly. And after cooling down he'd changed his mind about a showdown with Alison. He was no fool. He knew there was a limit to how many times you could get away with murder. Whilst she evidently intended to scrub the marriage from her mind as if it were no more than a dirty stain on her life.

According to a gossipy item in last night's local paper about the sale of his business, Jack was planning to emigrate to Bermuda. 'The last few weeks have been so traumatic, I've realised there's more to life than making money. It's time to put my feet up,' he was quoted as saying. A fuzzy photograph showed him overweight and cheerful, everyone's favourite uncle. He had his arm round Rita Buxton, who was described as his fiancée and was looking at him as tenderly as if he were a pension policy.

'And now pray silence for the cutting of the cake.'

The toastmaster exuded bonhomie, flashbulbs popped, the newlyweds laughed with embarrassed pleasure as they wielded the knife together.

'A day to remember,' enthused Harry's neighbour. 'And a jolly nice meal, too.'

Harry agreed. No worries about strychnine in the soup or mercury in the meringues here in the squeaky clean meeting place of the evangelical group to which Brenda and Colin belonged. Anyway, the poisoning career of Peter Kuiper was at an end. Quentin Pike reckoned the kid was planning to write a book about his experiences. One way of passing his time inside.

The rituals over, the Redpaths' guests began to disperse. Harry headed for the bar and over a glass of lager he recalled his conversation the previous evening with Trevor Morgan. They had bumped into each other at the Dock Brief, but the memory of the violent end to their last encounter seemed to have been wiped from the Welshman's mind.

After a couple of pints Harry had asked Trevor what he knew about the death of Margaret Stirrup. Her name seemed to have a sobering effect.

'What makes you ask?'

'You were in your cups last time we met. You called Jack a bloody murderer. At the time I assumed if you meant anything, you thought he'd killed Alison. Later I changed my mind.'

Trevor Morgan brushed flecks of beer foam from his mouth.

'Maybe Jack said a bit too much late one night over a jar.' He contrived the mischievous lopsided grin which had charmed so many women -- except for Catherine. 'We all shout how smart we are when we're pissed, it's human nature.'

'But is it true that he murdered Margaret?' Harry persisted. 'Cold-bloodedly, not in a fit of the famous temper?'

In a parody of bad acting, Trevor raised a finger to his lips.

'Mind your mouth, mate. Walls have ears, to say nothing of public bars. Best forget it.'

'Forget it?' Through the noise and the smoke and the smell of The Dock Brief, enlightenment dawned. 'I see. Jack's paid you off, so everything's okay now.'

Trevor grinned. 'Good lawyer, that bloke Fowler. The settlement cheque arrived yesterday.'

Hush money? Harry sighed. At least Trevor hadn't tried blackmail. But after all he had been through, Jack Stirrup wasn't going to risk a drunken ex-sidekick shooting his mouth off before the Bermuda flight was called.

Trevor smacked his lips. 'Twelve months' money, no tax. Not bad, eh? Have another. This one's on me.'

For once Harry had found it no hardship to decline.

'Your belly won't get any flatter if you keep drinking that stuff,' said a soft voice in his ear.

He twisted round, spilling some of his pint in the process.

'Brenda.' He considered her with care. 'You look so gorgeous I'll forgive you for trying to turn me against man's best friend. His booze, I mean. And the best of it is, you're happy.'

'Thank you.' She smiled. 'Yes, it's been a good day. And everyone's been so kind. They are nice people here, Harry, our friends from the Fellowship.'

'I'm sure they are. I won't pretend I've been converted. Seeing the error of your ways is one thing. Actually becoming a reformed character is quite another. But anything which has been so good for you must have something going for it.'

'Yes.' She leaned forward and straightened the flower in his buttonhole. 'That's better. Yes, I have something to believe in now. As well as someone. I can recommend it. But how about you? I'm sorry your girlfriend couldn't come.'

'Me too.'

Her blue eyes regarded him. 'Not a permanent rift, I hope?'

''Fraid so.'

'I'm sorry. She was a beautiful girl.

'Easy come, easy go.'

'You're a funny man, Harry. You always like to fear the worst. You ought to have faith, even if you think of yourself as an unbeliever. Things aren't always as bleak as they seem.' She paused, scanning his face for any trace of comprehension. 'Well, I hope you understand what I'm trying to say. I'm not much good with words, specially after so much champagne.'

'You're as good with words as you are to me. And that's saying something.'

She coloured faintly under the make-up and he realised she was thinking back to their affair. He hated himself for the clumsiness of his compliment. He hadn't meant to remind her of the past, not today of all days.

'I don't suppose we'll see each other much in the future,' she said. 'Now I've got a buyer for the flat and Colin has this job lined up in Manchester.'

'I'll be sorry to see you leave.'

She glanced over her shoulder. 'Oh dear. Colin's pointing to his watch. I have to change, put on my going-away outfit. We have a tight schedule if we're to catch the plane at Ringway.'

She proffered a hand, a gesture oddly formal and yet one which Harry found touching.

'Goodbye,' she said. 'Look after yourself. And – thank you for the time we had together.'

She hurried away without giving him a chance to say anything more. He watched her slim figure become swallowed up in the group of well-wishers around her husband.

'Same again,' he said to the barmaid.

As she served him she said chattily, 'Daft, isn't it? Weddings are such happy times. And yet they always make me want to cry.'

As he drank he thought about Valerie and how bitter and betrayed she had sounded on the one occasion when, made brave by an evening at the Dock Brief, he had telephoned her flat to make a stumbling apology for his behaviour towards Julian Hamer at the Law Courts.

'Someone told me he was giving up the Bar,' he had said.

'That's right. Now everyone knows about his state of health, he's not getting any more briefs. The fact his brain is as sharp as ever is neither here nor there to most of the gutless members of your profession. Thank God the University has more sense. They've offered him a teaching post to start next term. He'll be able to cope, even when he has to get around in a wheelchair.'

'It might not . . .'

'It might not come to that? Let's not kid ourselves any more, Harry. Let's be realistic.'

'And how are you?' he'd asked desperately, after a long pause.

'I was just getting ready for bed when you rang. I have a big trial tomorrow.'

'What sort of . . .'

'Look, I'm tired and I need sleep. I'm sorry, but I'm not in the mood for aimless chit-chat. I'll see you around some time, all right? Goodnight.'

Even now he could hear the click of the receiver as she'd hung up. He cursed his curiosity. When would the demon inside him which craved an answer for everything learn that sometimes the happiest of endings lay in mysteries lacking a solution? How comforting it would be to have the confidence to start taking things on trust. Looking around at the people who surrounded him, their eyes shining with their calm certainties, to his dismay he felt his stomach churn with jealousy.

He became aware of someone standing by his side.

'What can I get you?' asked the well-scrubbed young man who had sat next to him during the meal.

'An unsuspicious mind,' said Harry.

He didn't wait for a reply, but slipped off through the crowd towards the rear exit door that led to the car park, knowing that no one would notice him leave.

ALL THE LONELY PEOPLE
BY MARTIN EDWARDS

'Pungent Mersey whiff . . . A nice starter'
The Times

Harry Devlin, a Liverpool solicitor, is torn by conflicting
emotions. He has a passion for justice, but knows that for
most of his criminal clients conviction is an occupational
hazard. And he is still infatuated with his wife, Liz – even
though she has left him for another man.

When Liz shows up at his flat, obviously frightened, Harry is
only too pleased to offer shelter. But any hopes he has for
reconciliation are dashed when Liz fails to meet him as
planned the next day. And when her body is found in a lonely
alleyway, Harry's disciplined life is dramatically turned upside
down. He becomes the number one suspect.

Determined to prove his innocence, Harry's search for the
truth takes him into the city's sinister underbelly of shady
streets and sleazy clubs. To see justice done, he must confront
an obsessive killer – and have his illusions about Liz shattered
forever.

0 553 40485 7

A Bantam Paperback

BLOOD ROSE
BY WILLIAM HEFFERNAN

The body of a young woman is found in an open field, her mutilated corpse savaged by wild animals. Within days a second body is discovered, torn and defiled by human hands. Now a third victim bears mute witness to the terrifying presence of a depraved and relentless executioner.

For Paul Devlin, who fled his job as a New York City detective after a serial killer nearly claimed his life and his sanity, the nightmare has begun again. The safety he had sought in becoming chief of police in a small, Vermont town has vanished. Now there is another maniac on the loose and the clock is ticking. This time Devlin must capture a killer more elusive and more deadly than he has ever known. He must act before the woman he loves falls victim to the killer's knife – and time is running out . . .

0 553 40415 6

A Bantam Paperback

MUM'S THE WORD
BY DOROTHY CANNELL

For some women, motherhood can be murder . . .

Several pounds heavier – and gaining – blissful mother-to-be
Ellie Haskell knows her days as a thin woman are numbered.
Time to let out her clothes, put her feet up, and prepare to
enjoy the next nine months as a pampered wife. But the first
pangs of morning sickness have barely passed when Ellie's
handsome husband, Ben, is invited to compete for member-
ship in the world's most exclusive secret society of chefs, and
suddenly Ellie finds herself whisked off to America – to Mud
Creek, Illinois – and to a gothic mansion straight out of a
horror movie. Immortalized years ago in a Hollywood film
starring a sexy actress who happens to have the leading role in
this season's bestselling exposé, *Monster Mummy*, Melancholy
Mansion is no place for a woman in Ellie's delicate condition.
Within its shadowy confines, danger lurks behind every
chafing dish. And when murder is suddenly added to the
menu, it falls to amateur sleuth Ellie to serve up an unsavoury
killer with a taste for foul play.

0 553 40412 1

A Bantam Paperback

THE GOLDEN ORANGE
BY JOSEPH WAMBAUGH

Amidst the yachts, mansions and millionaires on the Gold Coast of Orange County, California, life promises no rich rewards for forty-year-old ex-cop Winnie Farlowe. Even his job as the Balboa island ferry captain ends in a wild night of drunken disaster at sea.

But notoriety may be his saving grace, for in Spoon's Landing, his favourite waterfront saloon, it brings him to the attention of the stunningly beautiful, sexually spirited Tess Binder. Tess could be Winnie's ticket to an exclusive world of clubs, ranches and the boat of his dreams. But she also carries with her the mystery of her father's death and the fear of her own fate. And soon, Winnie also becomes the target of an unknown assailant . . .

0 553 40255 2

A Bantam Paperback

A SELECTION OF CRIME AND MYSTERY TITLES AVAILABLE FROM BANTAM BOOKS

THE PRICES SHOWN BELOW WERE CORRECT AT THE TIME OF GOING TO PRESS. HOWEVER TRANSWORLD PUBLISHERS RESERVE THE RIGHT TO SHOW NEW RETAIL PRICES ON COVERS WHICH MAY DIFFER FROM THOSE PREVIOUSLY ADVERTISED IN THE TEXT OR ELSEWHERE.

☐	40059 2	**Down the Garden Path**	Dorothy Cannell	£3.50
☐	40058 4	**The Thin Woman**	Dorothy Cannell	£3.50
☐	40004 5	**The Widow's Club**	Dorothy Cannell	£3.50
☐	40412 1	**Mum's the Word**	Dorothy Cannell	£3.99
☐	40321 4	**An Inconvenient Woman**	Dominick Dunne	£4.99
☐	40485 7	**All the Lonely People**	Martin Edwards	£2.99
☐	17510 6	**A Great Deliverance**	Elizabeth George	£3.99
☐	17511 4	**Payment in Blood**	Elizabeth George	£3.99
☐	40167 X	**Well-Schooled in Murder**	Elizabeth George	£3.99
☐	40168 8	**A Suitable Vengeance**	Elizabeth George	£4.99
☐	40272 2	**The Assassini**	Thomas Gifford	£4.99
☐	40415 6	**Blood Rose**	William Heffernan	£4.99
☐	40070 3	**Ritual**	William Heffernan	£3.99
☐	17605 6	**One Was Not Enough (NF)**	Georgina Lloyd	£2.99
☐	17606 4	**Motive to Murder (NF)**	Georgina Lloyd	£2.99
☐	40074 6	**The Evil That Men Do (NF)**	Georgina Lloyd	£2.99
☐	40273 0	**With Malice Aforethought (NF)**	Georgina Lloyd	£2.99
☐	40422 9	**The Passion Killers (NF)**	Georgina Lloyd	£3.50
☐	17602 1	**Search the Shadows**	Barbara Michaels	£2.99
☐	17599 8	**Shattered Silk**	Barbara Michaels	£3.50
☐	17694 3	**Smoke and Mirrors**	Barbara Michaels	£3.99
☐	17204 2	**The Sicilian**	Mario Puzo	£4.99
☐	17524 6	**The Spy in Question**	Tim Sebastian	£3.99
☐	40055 X	**Spy Shadow**	Tim Sebastian	£3.99
☐	40056 3	**Saviour's Gate**	Tim Sebastian	£3.99
☐	17541 6	**Death in Tokyo**	Guy Stanley	£3.50
☐	40295 1	**Sniper's Moon**	Carsten Stroud	£4.99
☐	40255 2	**The Golden Orange**	Joseph Wambaugh	£3.99
☐	17697 8	**The Blooding (NF)**	Joseph Wambaugh	£3.99
☐	17555 6	**Echoes in the Darkness (NF)**	Joseph Wambaugh	£3.99
☐	40200 5	**The Harbinger Effect**	Sarah Wolf	£3.99

All Corgi/Bantam Books are available at your bookshop or newsagent, or can be ordered from the following address:

Corgi/Bantam Books,
Cash Sales Department,
P.O. Box 11, Falmouth, Cornwall TR10 9EN

UK and B.F.P.O. customers please send a cheque or postal order (no currency) and allow £1.00 for postage and packing for the first book plus 50p for the second book and 30p for each additional book to a maximum charge of £3.00 (7 books plus).

Overseas customers, including Eire, please allow £2.00 for postage and packing for the first book plus £1.00 for the second book and 50p for each subsequent title ordered.

NAME (Block Letters) ....

ADDRESS ....

....